*

To

PERIWINKLE

with love

*

DAVID UNWIN

The Governor's Wife

Michael Joseph
and the Book Society

THIS EDITION ISSUED ON
FIRST PUBLICATION BY
THE BOOK SOCIETY LTD
IN ASSOCIATION WITH
MICHAEL JOSEPH LTD
JULY/AUGUST 1954

*Set and printed in Great Britain by Unwin Brothers Ltd. at the Gresham
Press, Woking, in Baskerville type, eleven point, leaded, on paper
made by John Dickinson at Croxley and bound by Key & Whiting*

I

THE frontier post was a collection of untidy huts and hovels grouped about Government Office. There was a flagpole, a desiccated patch of lawn and small, sorry-looking flowerbeds bordered with smooth stones. Outside the verandah were parked, one behind the other, a shooting brake and an open truck loaded with camp equipment. The air danced above the wings, the radiators, for every metal surface was blisteringly hot under the four-o'clock sun.

The driver held open the door and Bulmers man-handled himself out of the car. I followed after. A young man, strikingly dapper and well-groomed, markedly respectful in his bearing, stepped down from the verandah to greet us.

'Good for you, Jimmy!' said Bulmers, limping across. 'So you've rustled up a wagon. I told Mr. Pole here he'd have to rough it in the truck.'

'Couldn't let you do that, sir. Come in and have a cup of tea.'

We drank our tea gratefully from thick, white mugs in a primitive and untidy office. Maps, calendars, official pronouncements, a tattered picture of the Royal Family, a photograph, curling in the heat, of a film star, were pinned haphazardly on the lime-washed walls. The desk behind which the District Officer had seated himself was completely covered with papers. As he rummaged around for a jar of sugar he disturbed the top layer and several papers tumbled to the floor.

5

'I do apologize,' he said. 'This is not such chaos as it looks, is it, Theo?'

The African clerk, hunched over a desk of his own in the corner, lifted his head. He pushed his spectacles on to his forehead and blinked rapidly.

'Too many safari, sah, too much trouble in the desert, not enough time in the office deal with letters, orders, regulations. Too many people send us papers, Colonel Bulmers. Sometimes we think we go crazy, that's right isn't it sah? Make whoopee, don't give a damn anymore!' And the little man, carried away by his own eloquence, thrust both hands into the mass of papers before him and with an upward scoop sent them flying into the air. Like a small and mischievous monkey, he sat in the snowstorm of his afternoon's labours, grinning happily.

Neither of the officials took the slightest notice.

'Theo's right,' said the District Officer. 'We're turning into an Aunt Sally for everyone to shy at. And to be frank, sir, we've had a spot of trouble. The D.C.'s gone up to investigate.'

'Trouble?' said Bulmers. 'What sort of trouble?'

'Murder, sir,' said the District Officer apologetically, running his hand over his neatly-parted, glossy hair.

There had been a fight, he explained, at a water hole. A feud of long standing had flared up. One of the askari patrols had brought in the body, speared through the neck.

'They don't often gore each other, which is perhaps just as well.' The D.O. pointed to the corner behind my chair.

The spear leaning against the wall was at least eight feet long. The blade took up more than half the total length, bevelled and narrow. A wooden handgrip joined the blade to a three foot, finely-tapered metal spike.

'Pick it up, sah!' encouraged Theo from his corner. 'The Wamai, they make the best spears of any tribe. You can *feel* a good spear, sah!'

6

The temptation was too much for the little clerk to resist. Next moment he had scrambled from behind his desk, scuttled across the room and grabbed the weapon for himself. Barely five feet high, stooping and bespectacled, wearing a crumpled and none too clean suit of white drill, a row of fountain pens and propelling pencils clipped to his outside breast pocket, he scowled fiercely as he tested the balance of the spear, handling it with the reflective intensity of a tennis player trying out a new racquet.

'They can throw, sah! Oh-ho!' His voice lifted; his eyes rolled up to the ceiling. 'They can throw!'

Suddenly he turned, crouching lower than before, and thrust the spike behind him, driving it into the packed earth of the office floor. The blade dipped, the point passing perilously close to my head.

'They face a lion—so! A Wamai warrior, sah, will take the shock of a charging lion, full on his spear!'

I was aware, by this time, that Bulmers and the District Officer had ceased to talk and were watching in silent amusement the clerk make a fool of himself. The young D.O. in particular wore the tolerant, pleased expression of a man whose pet animal has chosen to perform suitably before visitors.

Ten minutes later we all went out to inspect transport.

'I've checked the equipment personally, sir. Left nothing to chance. You'll find everything you need.'

'What's the road like, these days?'

'Much the same, sir—none too good. You may have some trouble getting through. One thing.' He dropped his voice confidentially. 'If they go ahead with this scheme of the Governor's, they'll have to spend money on communications.'

The sun blazed less fiercely and shadows, lengthening without wheeling, were creeping across the sand. A few solitary round hills had taken shape since we arrived, humping themselves over the horizon like great boulders, each hill still separated from the desert by the thin, vibrating white line of a mirage, so that they appeared to float like islands on a hazy sea.

'Something in that,' said Bulmers. 'Whistle up the boys, will you, Jimmy? Time we made a start.'

We had not been travelling for more than half an hour, seated together in the back of the shooting brake, when Bulmers began to grow restless. He kept shifting in his seat, banging around with his stiff leg, lighting his pipe and letting it go out again. At last he told the driver to stop and we waited, standing by the brake, for the truck to come up. The road we were following was a pair of tyre trails, no more, winding through the low scrub and the thorn trees.

'Can't stand being cooped up in this box,' he said. 'Don't see a damn thing.'

The truck groaned up the slight rise, sprouting over the roof of the cab a cluster of curious black heads. A wisp of steam floated above the radiator cap. Bulmers shouted instructions, there was a great deal of noise and excitement, arms waved, teeth flashed, and two of the boys leapt down from the back. Next moment he was seized and hoisted up the side, where willing hands hauled him aboard.

I put a foot on the top of the tyre and swung myself up. Bulmers had already had a hole made for his leg and was perched happily on a bedding roll. There was more shouting and the brake was turned into the scrub to let the truck pass.

We were close, now, to the nearest of the hills, a hummock of rock smooth as a crab and shining in the sunlight. Below us a herd of gazelles streamed like water through the bushes. Then a giraffe poked up a long, thin neck from behind a flat-topped thorn. The track began to climb, passing beneath the precipices of the hill that, from the frontier post, had looked no more than a deep blue knob. The truck panted and groaned, boiling steadily, and half-way up the slope gave up the struggle. The brake stopped behind and the two black drivers confabulated beneath the raised bonnet.

'She'll start when she's cooled down a bit,' said Bulmers, and in the end start she did. The sun, swollen and red, had dipped almost to the horizon when, with a lifting whine of the engine and a reassuring crash of gears, we topped the long rise and rolled forward into the plain beyond.

The scene was fantastic. The level, scrub-dotted land was littered, evenly, with squared chunks of blood-coloured lava. The floor of the desert appeared to glow crimson, to shimmer with an incandescence, as if the titanic explosion that had once spewed up these blocks of pumice and showered them in a rain of fire over the wilderness had taken place that very day. We looked out from the top of the truck across a horizon-wide and theatrical desolation.

Bulmers nodded, well satisfied.

'Wanted you to see that,' he said. 'Anxious moment when we stuck on the hill.'

Almost as he spoke, two hundred and fifty miles and more behind us, the palms of Banda swallowed up the sun. The crimson glow died, colour was instantly extinguished. The desert was seen to be scattered with lumps of lack-lustre rock, dull black. These blocks of lava looked like coffins in the half-light. A hundred thousand coffins littering untidily the level plain.

The truck jolted on, swaying like a boat across a land that was like the sea, immense, limitless, stretching away in every direction, empty of huts and houses, empty of tall trees, to the far edge of the sky. And the sky was huge. As the sunset faded behind us, the wing of the night (the earth's shadow drawn more clearly than I had ever seen it) lifted ahead and deepened as it came. I had never dreamed of a world as vast as this, a world of twilight colours, lilac, dove grey, bone and ivory. The sheer size of the plain affected me. I could not, at that moment, imagine that I should ever again

9

return to a London office. Only one thing mattered any more and that was to travel on through the warm twilight, travel across an empty land under a sky powdered with faint stars.

When we stopped for the night, an hour later, the first things to be unloaded were two canvas chairs. These were unfolded and placed side by side in the desert and upon them, gravely, Bulmers and I seated ourselves, the low moon to our left, behind us a rock-crowned hillock, over our heads the soapy trail of the Milky Way. A fire was soon crackling in a ring of stones, a pot of tea was set before us on a small table and while the cook prepared supper, the boys pitched camp.

Now and again I seemed to hear a dog bark in the distance. Jackals, Bulmers told me. The little animals sounded lonely out there in the middle of nowhere, for already the camp (that flimsy cluster of familiar and reassuring belongings; the circle of Africans, heads together, talking quietly; the dark bulk of the truck, the lesser shape of the shooting brake) had become a centre round which the emptiness lapped but did not penetrate. The desert was 'outside.' And 'out there,' after we had finished supper and the cooking fire had died to a red glow of ashes, I heard for the first time the eerie, lifting whoop of a hyaena.

I lay on my canvas bed that night and looked straight up at the stars. A warm wind came and went in fitful gusts, blowing round my neck. The hyaenas were noisy in the moonlight. I was dozing when another animal coughed resonantly, close to the camp, and the boys' quiet chatter was stilled. Branches were flung on the fire and flames shot up. Bulmers had propped himself on his arm and was listening. Without haste, calmly, I saw him stretch out a hand for the rifle.

The same cough again! The hairs on the nape of my neck prickled. I lay rigid, every muscle tensed. A minute crawled by, then another. After a while the boys began to whisper. The wind pried at the fold of blanket I had drawn up to my shoulders.

Bulmers put back the rifle and his bed creaked as he turned over and yawned. 'Wake me up,' he muttered sleepily, 'if you hear that lion again.'

I lay awake for perhaps an hour, listening to his husky breathing, the bark of jackals, listening always for the cough of a prowling lion. Wide awake, my mind active, I was drunk with travel. Close behind me, fog, frost, England. 'You're very pale,' Lady Mountclair had said almost as soon as I had met her, staring into my face. 'I can see the ghost of an English winter. You remind me that it's January.' (I had called at Government House; spoken briefly with Sir Christopher. A dinner had been arranged for my return.)

One of the boys, growing brave, laughed raucously. I looked along the length of the bed to the fire, saw the cropped, ball head thrown back, the squat nose, the dazzling teeth, and remembered the touch-down at Banda, the young African in a drill suit waiting my coming in the line of shadow by the door of the Customs shed. One hand clenched by his side, the other pulling at a coat button, anxiously he had studied each passenger in turn.

'Mr. Sebastian Pole, sir? From London?'

Gone, the tense and anxious air. With a brilliant smile he had lifted his topee with one hand, held out the other. Slim and smooth-skinned, his hand was softer and more womanly than I had expected.

'Welcome, sir, to Bandaland. Captain Gardener sends many apologies, not able to meet you in person. I am his deputy on these pleasant occasions. My name is Jonathan Bujobo and I am proud to make your acquaintance.'

My mind went cantering down the straight track. After

11

Mr. Bujobo, Gardener, the Public Relations Officer, unfolding telescopically behind his office desk. . . . He had thought it necessary to apologize for his rig. 'Playing polo.' Only then had I noticed that he was wearing jodhpurs. 'Sorry not to have met you myself at the airport.'

'Mr. Bujobo explained that you were busy.'

'Well, that is the excuse. But, between ourselves, we make the most of these little opportunities when they occur.' (The confiding smile; the row of even teeth.) 'Gives our African deputies something to do.'

Later, small-talk exhausted, the catechism.

'May I ask you a question, Pole? What first-hand experience have you had of Africa?'

'None whatever.'

'Exactly. You can have no inkling of our problems.' The long head had ducked forward, like a hound dropping to the scent. 'Done this sort of thing for long?'

'I joined the Trust after I was demobbed, nine years ago.'

'I ask because you look so young. We were expecting an older—perhaps I should say, a more experienced man.'

This had angered me. 'The Board,' I replied, 'considers me capable.'

'Quite so. No slight intended. Tell me now, what do you feel about the *magnum opus*?' Groping in the pocket of his linen coat, the P.R.O. had brought out a copy of Sir Christopher Mountclair's *Notes on the Nwambe Desert Irrigation Project*. 'The dam, you know, is very much the Governor's pigeon.'

I had been given no chance to reply.

'No doubt he's convinced you. Sir Christopher, you may be sure, has deliberately set himself out to convince. Incidentally, a fine piece of writing, as I'm sure you'll agree. His heart is in this scheme. Mine. . . .' Gardener had lowered his voice, 'is in the future of the country. The implications—' He had leaned across the desk and for the moment closely resembled an aristocratic and outraged horse. 'The implications disturb us all. I want you to be under no illusion about this. Politically, socially, nationally, the Project is dynamite!'

The impressive pause. The heaven-sent interruption. Uneven steps rapping along the verandah; the doorway blocked by a square and stocky figure. The weatherbeaten face. The jewel-blue eyes, the finely-wrinkled skin of a man who had lived his life in the open. Bulmers. The old-timer who knew the Desert Frontier District backwards. The authority on the Nwambe. Bulmers, who freshened the stuffy office with his presence, stumping forward, collapsing into a chair, his stiff leg thrust straight before him. Bulmers, the man of action, the celebrity.

'One of the few men to have engaged a lion in hand to hand combat and survived to tell the tale.'

The sheepish grin. The bashful hero. 'Come off it, Jack. Talk as if I'd challenged the brute to fight it out. Had no choice. Was lucky to get to my knife.'

The man snoring on the camp bed next to mine. . . .

Banda viewed from the club terrace that evening; the city glowing in a rose-mist under the hazy sky. The newcomer —presenting a pale and ravaged face, eyes sunk deep in his head—lowering himself into a chair at our table and sighing as he did so. One of the African waiters rustling up with a glass and a small bottle of tonic water. Bulmers glancing suspiciously at this bottle. . . .

'Not looking too well, Bob. Pole, this is Bob Glyn-Jones of the Co-operative. Notorious soak.'

The man had groaned quietly, and with his elbows on the table and his face in his hands had muttered something about a hangover.

'Mr. Pole works for the Halliday Trust. You've probably heard that he's out here to report on the Nwambe Project. We leave for the desert tomorrow.'

The hand reluctantly removed. The bloodshot eye, the

brief appraisal; the hand whipped back again, as if the light were painful to bear.

'Why choose to visit that poisonous place?' He had spoken petulantly through the gap between his wrists.

'Took Bob into the D.F.D. a couple of years back. He'll tell you he didn't appreciate the experience.'

The haggard, old-young face stared at me mournfully over the bottle of tonic water. If the man had not looked so ill, I might have found him more amusing.

'I'm in the Co-operative. Sell them blankets and—and beads and so on. I listened to Gerald's yarns about his race of pagan Gods. One should meet up with one's customers. Sound business practice. I'm a business man—not out here for fun. Trade follows the flag. Where was I?'

A guffaw from Bulmers. 'About to penetrate the unknown.'

'I wouldn't repeat that tour. Profits be hanged. The desert got me down and as for the Wamai, they're treacherous— and they stink.'

'The Wamai—' (Bulmers had fixed me firmly with his eye) '—are the most splendidly developed race in Africa.' His craggy face had softened; shone with enthusiasm. 'Straight as spears. Skins the colour of burnished copper. Why, they make the stumpy black Bandala look like figures of fun!'

'All the arrogance of a master race.' Glyn-Jones's voice was bitter. 'And faces covered with flies.'

Scuffling again. A sound from the half-light; from the waste of scrub and sand lying grey under the moon. Sleepers stirring and a shower of warm sparks, like fireflies, dancing up to blink and mingle with the blue-white stars. . . .

I saw the Wamai for myself at noon next day. We came upon them unexpectedly. A herd of camels nibbling at the

14

scrub by the road-side turned and scattered, kicking out comically with their back legs. Wooden bells clonked; pied goats rustled through the undergrowth. Ahead, clotted in dark rings, solid in the fragmentary, imperceptible shade of a cluster of umbrella thorns, sat the Wamai, still as stones in the breathless, intense heat. Women and men were grouped apart. Splinters of brilliant light flashed on metal bangles and shoulder-long ear-rings and quivered upon the thin, straight blades of spears. Not a head was turned. Not a man among them moved.

As soon as the brake stopped, Bulmers, as was his habit, thrust his twisted leg through the door, levering himself up from the seat, and his appearance drew the circle of warriors to their feet as if they were puppets attached to a master string. As one they rose, each with his spear, a strip of cured hide hanging from his right shoulder, copper skin glossy, shining with oil. 'Aah!' they said, broke rank and ran. A wall of near-naked bodies formed round the brake, imperious and unsmiling faces stared in through the windows, clouds of flies buzzed and settled upon eyelids and hovered over dung-daubed lumps of hair while a rank, sharp smell hung pungently upon the air.

Bulmers was a little while restoring order. In the end I found myself sitting beside him on the sandy ground beneath the largest of the thorn trees, facing the Wamai. Their sullen faces grew more sullen as he questioned them. They looked as wild and untameable as the giant cats they matched with their spears. They are not negroes and, as Bulmers had said, in no way resemble the Bandala. Their movements are fluid and buoyant. They are very tall. The breasts of the young women are pointed and shapely. But they disturbed me. Studying them, there did not seem to be any point of contact between men of my race and men of theirs. Even Bulmers I judged incapable of bridging the gap. Set beside them, Jonathan Bujobo, our driver Elias, the boys we had brought

15

with us, were all instantly, recognizably, fellow human beings whose features differed from our own, whose skins happened to be black. Such men laughed easily, could be hurt, embarrassed, grateful. But the Wamai, frozen in their pride, inscrutable, alien, might have been strangers from another planet.

Before we returned to the brake Bulmers walked across to the water hole that lay at a short distance from the group of trees. There were men down inside the rough-hewn cavity, one beneath the other, standing on ledges in the rock and perched on boughs wedged across the shaft (boughs worn smooth by the friction of many feet), lifting and swinging from hand to hand hide buckets, chanting in rhythm and keeping a chain going, the man at the top emptying the water into a long trough. A line of camels, bellowing raucously, were waiting their turn to drink.

'First well since the frontier post,' he said, 'and we've travelled ninety miles.'

Two hours later, hungry, hot, and dusty (we had not stopped for a midday meal) we reached the site of the dam.

We spent the afternoon dozing under the flysheet of the tent. The heat was flattening, lying over the scrub floor of the desert like an irresistible weight, a shimmering, prostrating load. Bulmers, who had come equipped with most things, including a pocket thermometer, observed at one point (not without quiet pride—the D.F.D. was living up to its reputation) that the shade temperature stood at 114°. 'Rarely tops ninety at Banda. Still, you have to allow for the humidity.' I was out for the count.

Life stirred again as the sun began to dip and a pot of tea was brought to us by the cookboy, who contrived to look fresh and tidy in a clean white shirt.

'These peoples, Bwana,' he said, 'are very dirty.' He spoke disapprovingly as he placed the tray on the floor between our beds. A Christian Bandala who washed himself each day with soap and water, he did not conceal his contempt for savages. He had no use for the Wamai. 'This bad country, Bwana. No food growing here.'

'If the Governor gets his way,' said Bulmers, stretching and rubbing his eyes, 'in two years' time corn will grow in the desert. Corn tall enough to hide a man.'

The cookboy was not so easily fooled.

'Bwana Government very big man. He can do many things. But even Bwana Government never make corn grow on *this* land.'

We climbed, an hour before sundown, the small range of hills below which we were camping. This range ran straight as a ruler across the plain, spanning the horizon, a wall of rocks, sand and scrub, shaling cliffs and spiky aloes, perhaps six hundred feet high. There was one narrow gap in the wall through which a river poured, a river of white sand snaking off across the plain. Dam the gap to half the height of the hills and when the rains came a lake ten miles wide and fifty long (so it was estimated) would form behind the barrier. A reservoir to feed the irrigation canals and channels that were to spread a net of life-giving water over hundreds of square miles of the desert.

The going was treacherous, a tough climb for Bulmers, but we reached the top of the ridge and saw the dry river bed below us in the trough of a shallow depression that, flooded, would form the lake. The same scrub and boulders spread monotonously on every side. A big herd of gazelle moved among the bushes on the far bank of the river, out of range. The land was golden in the evening sunshine but the horizon still trembled with the gathered heat of the afternoon. One big hill, a hazy, purplish mound, floated above the rim of the earth like a far-distant thundercloud.

'Dam the river, irrigate the desert, grow your crops,' I said, 'but you've still got to persuade your people to live in a furnace.'

'The point is,' said Bulmers, 'and I don't doubt the Governor's right, once start things growing and the climate will change of itself. Plant enough trees and they'll soon make clouds. This part of the Nwambe hasn't always been a wilderness. You've seen the crop samples? They prove the soil's fertile enough, provided it's watered. Twenty years and this place might very well become a paradise on earth —and that's his dream, of course. A paradise shared by the surplus populations of Equatoria and Bandaland. A food-producing area common to both countries. Believe me, I'm not exaggerating. *I've* no stake in the project. I'd be glad to hear the last of it. If this scheme succeeds, they'll start another and then another, if they can raise the capital. I'm frightened for the Wamai. My people need space. They must be left to wander. They're nomads. Fence them in and they'll die.'

'How many are the Wamai?'

'They've never been counted. Impossible to take a census. But, I should say, between sixty and seventy thousand.'

'And the African population of the Republic?'

'The Renduyu?' Bulmers groaned. 'I don't know.' He shrugged his shoulders helplessly. 'Several million. The country can no longer feed them, I know that. They're not lucky enough to enjoy the growing climate of Bandaland.'

'And how many Africans is it hoped finally to settle here?'

'Ask the Governor,' said Bulmers irritably. 'I'll not be fenced about by your infernal logic and statistics. All I know is that the Wamai are to be sacrificed. I'll fight it! I'm in the open now and I might as well say what I think. I'll fight the project. When the times comes, Pole, I'll fight for my people.' He thumped the ground with his fist, angrier than I had ever seen him.

'There's not space enough here for all?'

'Of course there's space,' he cried. 'Space enough for a leopard in a cage. We've pushed the Wamai around enough

18

as it is. When we herded them into this No Man's Land that nobody thought they wanted, we promised faithfully to leave them alone. We gave them our word that the Nwambe was theirs for eternity. Can we round on them forty years afterwards and say, "Sorry, you fellows, we want a slice of your territory after all"? And then, later on, perhaps another slice? Can we do it? Why, I'd be ashamed to face them. The Governor will have to appoint my successor,' said Bulmers savagely, 'if he chooses to break his pledge with the Wamai. I've done my best to keep off the subject till now—but there you are! And it's honest, at least, to let you know where I stand. I hate subterfuge. Hate politics. The matter's straightforward enough, in my eyes. We've given our word as Englishmen and we can't go back on that. If we do, we're damned. We might as well clear out of Africa.'

The Wamai passed by the camp that night, moving on their endless journey from well to waterhole, under the stars. They travel in the cool of the dark, driving their herds before them. I woke to the gentle sound of camel bells and saw, like a grey frieze, the procession pass; the men with guttural cries urging on their beasts; the goats rushing forward, pausing, rushing forward again with a ripple and scurry among the thorns. Long-legged, incredibly tall and slender in the light of the moon, straightbacked as willow wands, men, women and children strode by like figures out of a dream. For five minutes the procession passed, heading for the gap in the hills. Beyond the ridge lay fresh acres of scanty pasturage and, at the end of a long march, another oasis. The line dwindled, vanished; for a short while I heard them and then the sounds faded. The Nwambe had swallowed her people and lay bleached and empty again under the night.

Next morning we struck camp, and while the sun was still low in the sky began the return journey. We were riding on the truck again, perched above the cab roof, and I had already picked out, far ahead, the group of trees, a recognizable landmark in the level scrub. Rocking and bumping our slow way along the track, the white dust lifting behind us, we approached the waterhole. One moment the boys at the back were dozing peacefully among the crates and bundles; next, they were jammed in a tight bunch on the left side of the truck, shouting, gesticulating, pointing into the bush. I saw a line of red-ochre bodies, the size of dolls in the distance and all running at amazing speed. The long blades of their spears sparked in the sun like needles. A hunting party? There was no sign of a quarry. And strangely enough, the leader carried no spear.

Bulmers swore, twisted himself to his feet, grabbed the rail, leant over and shouted instructions through the cab window. Instantly the driver accelerated, we turned off the track and began to crash and jolt our way across country, bulldozing the bushes, bouncing into potholes. The men dwindled. Seizing his rifle, Bulmers pointed it above his head and fired. The sound of the shot was muffled by the surrounding emptiness. There was no reverberation. The men had vanished into the scrub.

We made a wide circle, returned to the track and drove at alarming speed to the waterhole. The Wamai were there in force. The ground under the trees seethed. Bulmers was helped down and limped in amongst them, barking like a sergeant-major. The men turned from him in open defiance. He had left his rifle behind and, as far as I knew, was unarmed. Our boys were frightened, hanging over the side of the truck, wide-eyed and silent.

The Wamai were angry. The women's voices bubbled up hysterically, the men muttered and growled, a threatening undertone across which Bulmers's words cracked like a whip.

As he spoke, he battered his clenched fist into the palm of his hand. The red-bronze warriors towered over him (he was like a stumpy pollard oak in a grove of poplars) and appeared to sway slightly as his words struck home. They were calmer. They were gathering to listen. The women had ceased their distracting chorus and were listening in silence. I stood by Bulmers. Slightly under six feet tall, I was dwarfed by these men. Sweat beaded my forehead and my mouth was dry.

There was talk on both sides. One of the warriors detached himself from the throng and strode off like a stork, moving his long legs delicately and placing his bare feet with precision upon the ground. We walked after him and he led us out from the brittle shadow of the thorns into the full glare of the sun. The reflected dazzle, the eddies of heat thrown up from the sand, hit our faces and hurt our eyes.

The man ahead picked his way with care. He was not strolling aimlessly, neither was he striding in a direct line towards some distant and known objective. After a while I realized that he was observing and following a line of tracks, small depressions, scuffles in the sand, the print of toes in the dry soil. We had left the waterhole far behind. We were walking through an absolute silence, a silence so intense that the ear caught and held every small rustle of our clothes. Suddenly the guide stopped and stood aside. Bulmers came up with him, stopped too, grunted, then took a pace forward. A black cloud of flies lifted deafeningly from the ground as he stooped.

The man was lying on his face, pinned to the earth like a butterfly on a board, transfixed by a spear. The shaft and tapering spike sloped from his naked back, half the length of the blade was buried. Implicit in the shape of the still, sprawled body, the slope of the spear, was the terrible force of the thrust that had killed him.

Bulmers tried to draw out the weapon but it resisted his

first efforts. He trod forward, putting his right foot in the small of the man's back. As the spear shifted, a little blood flowed again from the wound.

Far behind, other warriors approached, and behind again, bare-breasted women loitered curiously in small groups. Bulmers shouted, beckoned. Three of the Wamai, expressionless, silent, carried the corpse back to the waterhole. Bulmers carried the spear, which he tossed up on to the truck.

Our own gang of boys dug a trench a short way beyond the fringe of shadow and before the burial one of the women stepped forward and removed the carved ivory discs from the dead man's ear-lobes, the metal coils from around his neck and from his wrists the fine bracelets of wire and lion's hair. We watched while earth was shovelled over the body, stamped firm.

'Justice of a sort,' said Bulmers. 'He deserved what he got. But they've no *business*,' he cried, turning on me angrily, 'to take the law into their own hands.'

II

GLYN-JONES joined us on the club terrace, the evening of our return to Banda. He had recovered from his hangover and his mood was jocular. Apparently, he had heard about the killings. I observed the sardonic glint in his eye.

'What d'you expect from a tribe of savages who cake their hair in cow-dung and feed on blood?'

Bulmers grew huffy and retired behind his pipe. His silence was the aggrieved vacuum of the man misunderstood.

The sun was setting. Shouts from the tennis courts grew gradually less frequent; died away at last upon the muggy air. Three young women in white blouses and shorts, carrying racquets, crossed the terrace. Over-exercised, they had the same exhausted, boiled look, their skins fiery, their eyes glazed. I saw Jack Gardener in the distance, lanky, lugubrious, his head aureoled against the falling sun. He stopped to exchange a word with the tennis players; then came on towards our table, leading one of the women by the arm.

'I'd like you to meet Miss Jensen, Pole. She's over here representing the *Smithville Echo*. I've invited her to attend the Press Conference I'm arranging for you.'

The girl from Equatoria was small and slim with neat hands and feet and a neat, pointed face. She had smooth and very pale gold hair. She nodded towards me, greeted Bulmers, bounced her racquet on the top of Glyn-Jones's head and asked how he was feeling. Then she sat down and accepted a cigarette.

Almost at once she began to talk to Gardener. She was annoyed. One of the many African newspapers had apparently criticized the Republic and she demanded an immediate retraction; an apology.

'Everyone slangs my country,' she said. 'What a life! Sometimes I go to sleep and dream we're popular.' She blew out smoke, grimaced, and shook her head. 'You English are to blame for a great deal. You can't deny that your London Press does nicely at our expense.' She turned and for the first time fixed me with her big, slightly stony, light blue eyes. 'These are critical years. Whose side are you on?'

Glyn-Jones groaned; begged her to take an evening off. Bulmers, who had not recovered his temper, announced that he must be going and without more ado hoisted himself up and limped away. Pat Jensen looked after him thoughtfully. Then she pounced again.

'I read your papers. I listen to your broadcasts. I know what you people in England are thinking and feeling, and the ill-informed criticism from your country makes me see red! You're convinced you know better than we do, the people on the spot. Votes for the native! Down with the colour bar! You realize where this is all leading, don't you? You realize what you're doing?' Her voice was not quite steady. 'Driving the whites out of Africa.'

Now it was Glyn-Jones's turn to rise. He came round the table and stood behind us, supporting himself with a hand on each of our shoulders.

'Something wrong here,' he said. 'Charming young lady, blonde, good-looking, excellent dancer, unattached, pastimes—politics and race-relations. Leave you to sort the matter out.' He gave me a shake and drifted away.

The P.R.O., I noticed with alarm, was becoming increasingly restive. I looked round, wondering how to engineer my own escape.

'Let me remind you, Pole,' said Gardener, 'that you're

24

dining at Government House in approximately . . .' He peered closely at his wrist watch. 'One and a half hour's time.'

'Have you been invited to that dinner?' said Pat Jensen, opening her eyes very wide. 'Why, what a coincidence. So have I!'

We were suddenly alone. The evening air stirred sluggishly, moving round us like warm oil. The girl in her thin tennis clothes crossed her bare arms and shivered.

'Cold?' I said. 'You should try London.'

'London! Thank you! And have a black sit next to me in one of your buses?'

I told her not to worry. She could always take a taxi.

She put her elbows on the table and stared at me.

'You don't mind. I can see you don't mind. You English out from overseas are all the same. You meet so few natives. You can't understand.' She drew deeply at her cigarette. 'Are you married? No. Well, it doesn't matter. Let's say you were married and a hulking buck nigger sat down next to your wife. What then?' She appeared determined to probe to the root of the problem.

'I hardly think that would worry me.'

She shrugged, blew smoke into my face. 'Come and live here. You'll find out how wrong you are.'

'Miss Jensen . . .' I began, but she cut me short.

'Don't be so formal. Call me Pat.'

'Pat, then,' I said. 'I've noticed you talk about us as if we were foreigners.'

'Why not?' she said. 'I was born in Africa. In Smithville. My father was a Swede.'

We talked and the sky darkened. Banda became a jewelled web spangling the black hills. The light from the windows, growing stronger, strode out across the terrace and touched her smooth and glistening, lovely Nordic hair.

I had spent my first few days in Africa in the company of

men. Her views, I thought, might be odd, but she was delightful to look at. In the end, I suggested that we go into the club and find the bar.

We must have stayed too long at the club for by the time I had driven back, enjoyed a cold bath (or as near cold as I could make it) changed, and left the Guest House, it was twenty minutes past eight. I had offered to give Pat a lift, but she had refused, saying that she preferred to be independent. The Humber with the furled pennant on the radiator was waiting for me outside and Elias leapt from his seat and opened the door with a flourish.

'Government House,' I said, leaning back and parodying for my own amusement my awakening sense of self-importance. He slammed the door, saluted through the window, hopped round to the front. Pink-palmed hands spun the wheel, bare feet pressed home the pedals. He knew where to take me. He had had his instructions.

The car stopped. I climbed an imposing flight of stone steps. The Corinthian portico above me blazed under the moon, bone-white. The aide-de-camp in the entrance hall introduced himself as Major Wakefield, presented me with a chart of the dining table, indicated my position and then hustled me through open double-doors into the drawing-room. Fans whirled on the ends of long, thin shafts. African waiters in white uniforms and gold-embroidered skull caps were carrying round trays of glasses. My sense of self-importance deserted me. I had arrived late and the room was already filled with people.

'Sir Christopher Mountclair.' I shook hands with the Governor, the aide retired and I was led round the guests. The Air Vice-Marshal in the corner proffered his left hand and we fumbled and gripped awkwardly. Too late, I noticed his right sleeve pinned to his side. A cluster of ladies on the sofa unfurled for us like a flower. Their skirts rustled. Pat smiled up as we were formally introduced. I was sweating by this time. My double-breasted dinner jacket was stifling and I envied the other men their cool-looking, white linen coats. I felt conspicuous and uncomfortable and badly needed a drink.

We went into dinner almost at once and the atmosphere continued stiff and formal. The meal was a tedious affair. There were not enough ladies to go round and I sat next to a dark, aggressively-spoken man who at once, as if accustomed to the ritual, handed me his typed name card. *Mr. Douglas Cameron* I read, and handed him my own. With the fish, I learnt that he was a veterinary surgeon. With the chicken that he was the equivalent of a Harley Street specialist in the diseases of cattle. He had any amount of relevant information to impart, of which information I can remember extraordinarily little. On my other side was a quiet, elderly man whose name and occupation I never discovered and who was only with the greatest difficulty persuaded to talk at all.

We toasted the Queen, God bless her, and as soon as the ladies left we shifted our places, gathering at the end of the long table round Sir Christopher. This gave me an opportunity to watch the Governor. The Air Vice-Marshal had monopolized his attention. He was telling an involved anecdote and the small, old man was listening with an air of abstraction that was barely polite. His deeply-pouched eyes were fixed unblinkingly on one of the decanters, he held a cigar in his fingers, and now and again he allowed himself a smile so manifestly over-accentuated, of a charm so patently false, that it can only be described as an insult.

The Air Vice-Marshal's story rambled to a conclusion, and hard on the laugh that followed (in which, I noticed, Sir Christopher did not join) the Governor stood up. We stood with him and, one after the other, filed through into the drawing-room. At our appearance the ladies broke their circle and scattered to appropriate positions. I saw Pat a long way off, lost in a large armchair. We formed a group in the doorway while Sir Christopher directed us to seats in various parts of the room. He did this decisively, even a little peremptorily, and we hurried to obey. We might have been playing an absorbing and serious party game.

When my turn came the Governor let his hand rest for a moment on my shoulder. 'Now, Pole,' he said, 'you'd better sit by my wife.'

Lady Mountclair was already talking to the freckled official I had faced across the dinner table. She glanced up and smiled as I approached. I had, of course, spoken to her before, briefly, when I had learnt that this large, robust young person was, in fact, Sir Christopher's wife and not, as I had immediately assumed, his daughter. (The Governor had made a second marriage a few years before.)

I sat down and she broke off her conversation to ask about the desert. She said that I was looking better. Quite tanned.

'Colonel Bulmers insisted on riding on top of the truck.'

They both laughed, and Lady Mountclair informed me that her life's ambition was to penetrate the D.F.D.

'There's a clannish Men Only atmosphere about that corner of the Protectorate. . . . I regard the desert as a challenge. Any self-respecting woman would feel the same.'

The sandy official leant back and drooped his left eyelid. I interpreted the movement as a wink.

'You've driven through the country round Banda? Bananas. Nothing but bananas! I long for an empty landscape, a bare horizon. And then the climate here has such a depressing effect on people. What was it Major Wakefield said the other day? That the women become bores, the men boors. Not witty but uncomfortably close to the truth. Really,' she said, resting her arms on the small table between us and speaking in a confidential undertone. 'You've no

28

idea how oddly people can behave. Some of our old-timers are—are quite impossible.' She opened wide her fingers; shook her head. 'But you're new to it all, aren't you? And enjoying the experience.'

The official shifted restlessly in his chair, crossing his legs. I saw his foot twitch.

'My first satisfactory break from routine,' I said, 'since I left the army.'

'You know, you possess one great advantage. Hold on to it. You've arrived in Banda with an open mind.'

Her dark eyes fixed mine with the earnest entreaty of a woman, a good-looking woman, who demands to be taken seriously.

'You will find,' she said, 'the people in this country conservative and unenterprising. Blinkered. White or black, they hate change. Dislike anything new.'

She seemed about to say more; then altered her mind, sat back and pushed away from her face her thick black hair. The conversation became general and, half an hour later, as if at some pre-arranged signal, the company rose. The stilted proceedings came to a sudden end.

I did not immediately say goodbye, others claimed Lady Mountclair's attention, and I stood waiting a little apart, watching my opportunity. I saw my neighbour at table, the cow specialist, come up and take her hand. He bent towards her, said something in a low voice. She did not reply but looked steadily into his face. They were together for perhaps thirty seconds. At the time I was impressed not so much by the fact of their intimacy—it was instantly clear, of course, that they knew each other well—but by the extraordinary contrast this brief moment made with the rest of the evening. A clasp of a hand, a word, and a flash of genuine feeling sliced the soporific routine dullness like a sword.

My host, when I thanked him, took my elbow and guided me across the entrance hall to the far wall where hung full-length portraits of the men who, for the past fifty years, had governed Bandaland. Sir Tansley Deborough was there, one foot placed firmly upon the broad head of a lion, the butt of his rifle resting on the ground. Lord Melton, in a morning suit, had removed from his head and was handing to a curly-haired African child, who peeped shyly from behind his knees, a white pith helmet. Sir Christopher stopped and drew my attention to this portrait.

'In the light of what has come to pass,' he said, 'his gesture has interesting social significance. Sunstroke is no longer considered a menace and the topee has changed hands—for good. You will no doubt have noticed that the outmoded headgear has become the African's badge of office. He wears it with pride, not for protection but as an insignia of rank.'

We retraced our steps. By the doorway the old man stopped again, bowed slightly and wished me a courteous goodnight.

The preliminaries over, I settled down to work. I visited the Agricultural Department to talk to the chemists in charge of the soil tests. I went to the Treasury. I had a long interview with an engineer who showed me blue-prints and a scale model of the dam. But the days were sweltering and I grew to detest Banda's greenhouse fug. Always it was the same—a sky over the city like frosted glass, and the sun, rocketing to the zenith, burning with the diffused and headachy glare of an immensely powerful pearl bulb.

One sweaty morning, I was unexpectedly summoned to Government House. Lady Mountclair, I was told, wished to see me. I arrived on time; she kept me waiting seventeen minutes by my watch; then rushed in and overwhelmed me with apologies.

'I'm sweeping you off,' she said, 'to inspect a kindergarten. You must try to look bright and interested. You may have children of your own, one day. These, by the way, are black. I promised them this visit a long time ago, they'll be expecting me—you know what that means—and the Major was busy and there seemed nobody to go with. And then I had an inspiration and here you are!' I was given no chance to protest. She had already turned to lead the way out of the room. 'I knew,' she said, 'you wouldn't let me down.'

We drove south, in a small car, through the sprawling, thatched village-city of the Equator. The Bandala women everywhere were as bright as parrots. Short, purposeful, vivid in ankle-concealing, décolletée cotton gowns, their colours screamed in the sunlight—emerald, purple, orange, royal blue, jazzy stripes, blobs the size of dinner plates, tartans to make a Scotsman weep. The long skirts flattered their stumpy figures. They carried their shining black breasts before them like sails, their arms and shoulders glossy in the sun.

'The missionaries taught them to dress, sixty years ago,' said Lady Mountclair. 'Don't you adore the Victorian influence? I often wonder what would have happened to the Bandala if we'd arrived on the scenes a little later. In the 'twenties, shall we say. Would it be all flat chests and necklaces?' She shook with laughter.

We stopped outside a playground with an unexpectedly English assortment of slides and seesaws, climbing frames and sandpits. The sun and the clammy stifling air took us and without hurrying we walked up the path to the entrance. I could hear ahead a muted clamour. The low brick building was vibrating gently, like a bell.

A tall girl appeared, dressed in a sober grey uniform. Her hair was shaved and the tight curls clustered close to her head. She had the brown, wide-set eyes and thick lips of her race. She greeted us confidently, bending her knees in a half-curtsy with a silent clap of her palms. As she straightened her body, she took Lady Mountclair's hand in the conventional European manner.

'Martha, I've brought Mr. Pole along with me to see the kindergarten. He's from England and is interested in children. Miss Bifabishu is the teacher in charge. The daughter of a Chief,' she added in a low voice as we walked into the building, 'and the first girl in the country to gain her Montessori Diploma. We need more like her.'

Everything was quiet. The sounds that we had heard had ceased. We turned to the left and passed into a large, unfurnished, shady room, opening on to a verandah. The whole of the floor space, which was considerable, was covered with small black children and as we entered, like a nest of mice suddenly disturbed, the children scrambled to their feet, bobbed forward in the traditional curtsy and clapped together—not once but many times, excitedly—the palms of their hands. The sound was like a flutter of leaves in the wind. Bright eyes, a hundred, two hundred pairs of bright eyes, were fixed (or so it seemed) raptly upon my face. I put up my hand to straighten my tie and next moment ten firm black fingers struck a chord on a piano I had not noticed, tucked away in a far corner, and all over the room teeth, brighter than the whites of eyes, flashed on and off as the children burst, shrilly and jerkily, into God Save the Queen.

'Oh!' I heard Lady Mountclair exclaim beside me. 'How I wish they wouldn't!'

We stood awkwardly until, with an irrevocable crash of fingers upon the keys, the brilliant teeth snapped off for the last time and we were free to sit down upon the chairs hurriedly rushed up for us by two of the teachers.

Later, when we toured the classrooms, I found myself taken in charge by the efficient Miss Bifabishu. Gravely, she explained the equipment, demonstrating, praising.

'You see, Mr. Pole, this may look like play, but to the children it is work.'

I had come across the idea before.

'Manipulation, finger exercises are important for all children, but for our boys and girls doubly so. Many come from poor families and at home they lead simple lives. Often they wear no clothes. They have no toys. You have seen their houses for yourself—small boxes without doors or windows. Satisfactory in our climate but providing few useful exercises. Take an English child of about this age. Look what he is expected to do! His clothes are complicated and covered with buttons and he possesses shoes which tie with laces. In his home there are door knobs to turn and taps to twist. All the time he is learning to control his fingers, to become practised in mechanical movements. As a result he grows up adept and happy at handling tools. He is already halfway to a technician.'

'But is it so important,' I said, 'to breed a race of mechanics?'

'No, Mr. Pole. Now you're laughing and this is a serious matter. Believe me, it affects our people. We have to learn to handle the machinery, the equipment of this century. I chose to work here because I felt, in training the young, I could best serve the interests of Bandaland. I am patriotic, you see, but in my case this does not mean that I resent the English. I know that many do. My brother and his friends say stupid things, sometimes. But—perhaps because I am a woman—I am content to wait. Patience will bring its own reward.' She smiled and her solemn, heavy face was transfigured. 'We are fortunate in our Governor, and Lady Mountclair, too, has done much for us. We owe all this to her.' Her gesture embraced the school building. 'She has always understood us, and that I find is rare, even in those who are eager to help.'

By the time we came to leave a crowd had gathered

outside the building and the car was hidden behind the bright gowns of the women. They pressed round, friendly and fearless, a few carrying naked babies on their backs. Lady Mountclair talked to them in Landala, admired the infants, tossed remarks into the crowd, stirred them to smiles and laughter. Her display was faultless, professional and (I realized suddenly) genuine. We reached the car at last and I was thankful to escape the dazzle of misty sunlight, the press of bodies. Miss Bifabishu and her staff waved goodbye from the playground. The visit was over.

'I'm glad you were able to talk to Martha. She's my most successful protégée. I'm pleased, you know, Mr. Pole. I've achieved something. I had to make a thorough nuisance of myself for two years but in the end, to keep me quiet, they provided a kindergarten.'

'I put my foot in it badly,' I said. 'I was trying too hard. Conversation with an educated African is like walking a tightrope. One slip and you've had it. All the time a nasty little nagging voice inside my head was saying, "Behind me, Shakespeare, Wren, Newton. Behind this intelligent and charming young career woman, woven reed roofs and Witch Doctors." '

'There's no need to feel so gloomy. You did splendidly. Martha, I could see, was most impressed.'

'I gather she's anxious that I should meet her brother.'

'Samueli? Really? You can hardly expect me to feel happy about *that*.'

I asked her why. She told me he was an unreliable man. He had already been deported and had only recently been allowed back into the country.

'So I'm not to be trusted alone with an agitator?'

She laughed and told me not to be absurd. While there were so many worthwhile Africans to meet, why waste my time with a man like Martha's brother?

I lunched at Government House, in the small dining-room,

with Sir Christopher and Lady Mountclair, Major Wakefield and the Governor's secretary. I took coffee, afterwards, in the library with the Governor and his wife.

I had two more calls to make, that afternoon, and it was half-past five before I returned to the Guest House. I was hot and tired and not best pleased to be told that a memsaab was waiting for me in the garden. I glanced out cautiously between the fly-screens at the end of the lounge and was relieved to see a small blonde head over the back of one of the deck chairs. Patricia Jensen. I told the boy to bring drinks and went and joined her.

'Nice of you to come round.'

'I had a few questions to ask. Couldn't speak my mind yesterday, in front of the native editors. Frankly, whatever Captain Gardener may say, I consider these Press Conferences of his an utter waste of time.'

'Expecting me to talk sense? Not a hope, Pat. I feel like a wet rag. God forbid that I should ever have to earn my living in Banda.'

'That's how it gets us all. The place doesn't give you anything. I can tell you, coming here from the Republic wasn't funny. Now Smithville,' she said proudly, 'has the finest climate of any capital in the world.'

'I'm glad to hear it. Flying there tomorrow. Governor's instructions. Sprang it on me suddenly at lunch today.'

'What fun for you, Sebastian! Room for me in your luggage?'

'That's an idea. Why don't you come?'

'I've half a mind to. We could dance at the *Eyrie*. Our latest night club—at the top of a skyscraper.'

'Is this Africa? Sounds more like New York.'

'Smithville,' she said, 'is a modern city. You can *live* there. I'm sick and tired of stewing in this hole.'

35

The sun was on the point of setting and the shadows of the trees covered the grass. Their lace-work of leaf and blossom hung motionless against the sky. Crimson cannas, purple and pink bougainvilleas, blue plumbago, glowed softly from their setting of green lawns and red-earth beds. The air was absolutely still. Cicadas chirred. The soft green country beyond the garden rolled away to the subdued horizon.

We lay limply in our chairs. The softness of Bandaland is insidious; the air, like a cushion, invites the body to relax. We lay and relaxed, Pat and I, while houseboys padded softly across the verandah on their pink-soled feet, talked together softly, touched, picked up, moved things around with their incredibly soft fingers. There was a reassuring clink and a tray of drinks was placed between us. I held an ice-cold glass in my hand. Gin, fresh lime juice, soda. Somewhere behind the massed green leaves the sun set in a whorl of blood-coloured flame. A butterfly, turquoise spotted, still fluttered erratically from flower to flower. Wings creaked and a hornbill pitched into the tree over our heads, perching there, beak-heavy, off-balance. Looking up, I could see a bundle of black feathers and the curved yellow dagger of the bill. The bill opened and the bird uttered a harsh cry.

'What have you been doing with yourself today, Sebastian?'

'Trailing around with Lady Mountclair. Very interesting and all that, if I had nothing better to do. But it's not really my job to escort Governors' wives to kindergartens.'

We finished our drinks and I asked her to stay to dinner. She said she was sorry, she was already engaged.

'Have you met Terence Hatch?'

'No,' I said. 'I don't think so.'

'He's nobody important from your point of view. An English friend of mine. A Pest Control Officer.'

'Why did you think I might have met him?'

'Banda's a small place.'

'What about him, Pat?'

'Nothing. I'm going out with him, tonight.'

'Does he often take you out?'

'When he's around. He travels a lot.' She set her glass back on the tray. 'Sebastian, I'll have to be going quite soon.'

'Come for a stroll first. If I stay here much longer I'll be gummed to the chair.'

We walked slowly away from the lit windows of the house. The coarse mown grass was springy under our feet. At the far end of the garden we stopped and turned and she leant against the trunk of a tree. I could see her pale hair clearly, shining out of the dusk with a light of its own. It occurred to me, then, that she was waiting for me to kiss her. The air was warm under the leaves, a few faint stars pricked through the foliage, the breeze was scented. She looked up and I caught the gleam of her eyes, her smile. . . .

As we were walking back later to the Guest House, she said, 'Sebastian, if you have time in Smithville, would you visit my mother?'

'Your mother!'

'Could you bear it. I'm such a shocking correspondent—and she lives alone, which isn't much fun for her. She'd love to meet one of my friends. You could tell her how I'm getting along. You see,' she added, 'my father's not shown up since I was ten.'

'I'm sorry, Pat.'

'No need to be sorry for me, but mother feels it.'

She stopped and took a lighter from her handbag; flicked open the catch. I held the flame while she scribbled the address on her reporting pad, tore off the slip and handed it across. Then we walked round to the driveway and I put her into her car.

37

'Have a good trip,' she said. 'I'm very envious.'

'When I'm back we must have dinner together. I'll hold you to that!'

She started the engine. I slammed the door and waved her away into the night.

To my surprise, Gerald Bulmers was at the airport next morning. He limped across the concrete ramp to greet me as I came out of the Customs shed. He had heard that I was flying to Smithville.

'I gather you've had a talk with H.E.' His blue eyes under the craggy brows were anxious. 'Did you put in a word, old fellow?'

'I did. And stuck my neck out.'

'What did he say?'

'Nothing new as far as you're concerned. The Wamai, he feels, are out of step with the present. They should not be allowed to hamper future development. They are only a handful. That was the expression he used. A small handful.'

Bulmers was clenching and unclenching his fists. 'Numbers,' he muttered. 'Always the same. Bloody numbers!'

'Bear up,' I said. 'Plenty of time yet.'

The petrol trailer had moved off from the nose of the aircraft. One of the engines coughed, then burst into a staccato roar. Exhaust smoke whirled back in the slipstream. Beyond the 'plane the brown-dry field quivered, dustily hot under the low sun.

'Pole,' said Bulmers, pitching up his voice, 'is this scheme going through?'

'Early days yet. And as I tell everyone, I can't answer for the Board.'

'But you reckon H.E.'s determined to press ahead?'

The port-side engine bellowed. The noise was now deafening.

38

'Gardener didn't exaggerate. It's true that he's set his heart on the Project.'

'Food for the hungry millions!' he bawled.

'Food and partnership. Partnership's what he really seems to be after. African unification.'

'Unification?'

'Medicine for their souls.'

Both engines cut off instantaneously. The propellors ticked to a stop. An airport official began to gather together the passengers. I settled my brief-case under my arm and in the unnatural silence held out my hand and said goodbye. I looked back from the steps and saw Bulmers still standing where I had left him, stocky and sunburnt, conspicuously laundered, his shadow a black finger pointing across the bleached cement.

39

III

SMITHVILLE, capital of Equatoria, was a flourishing, modern city of stunted skyscrapers, traffic lights, endless lines of parked cars, emporiums with plate-glass windows, and pavements crowded with a polyglot population clothed without exception, black and white, shabby and smart alike, in European dress. There were very few trees, and as the plateau from which the city had sprouted was flat, this resulted in a landscape man-made in its entirety, from the smooth walls of the office blocks to the golden and geometrical mine dumps that rose, surrealistically, at the far end of the long, straight streets. Thanks to the altitude (Smithville is very nearly two thousand feet higher than Banda) the air was crisp and invigorating. The pace of life was consequently brisker. Patricia was quite right about this. I noticed the change at once.

I was taking a first walk along the principal shopping street. I had crossed three identical intersections and had reached the fourth when an extremely large and untidy man, approaching the same spot on a course at right-angles to my own, stopped abruptly, lifted his hand in a gesture of astonishment and cried '*Frump!*'

The nickname jerked me back nearly twenty years. Turning, I stared up at the immense red face under the brim of the stained pork-pie hat, the shoulders padding the worn and weatherbeaten tweed coat; a coat linked, by a single and protesting button, across a massive diaphragm.

'Good God,' I said. 'Sneezer!'

'And what the blazes do you think *you're* doing in Smithville.'

'Preparing to climb to the top of Tower House.'

'What the hell for?'

'To get a view of the place,' I said. 'I've half an hour to kill.'

'View of the place! Can't you see enough from street level? Come and have a drink.'

'Are the pubs open?'

'The pubs in Smithville,' said Sneezer, bringing down a hand heartily upon my back, 'are *always* open.'

The bar boasted a chromium façade and a neon sign. The interior was a gloomy and twilit facsimile of an oaken beer parlour. Sawdust and brass spittoons upon the floor and a white man to serve us.

'One fine day,' said Sneezer, smacking his lips dubiously, 'they'll learn to make beer that tastes like beer.'

'How's your hay fever?'

'Gone! Haven't had an attack these ten years. One of the reasons I emigrated. Couldn't stand the English summers.'

Poor old Hardcastle! I could recollect him as if it were yesterday, a bulky boy in white flannels chasing a square cut to the boundary and sneezing as he ran.

'Are you in business here?'

'Do I look like a business man? I'm farming. Fifty miles out. Come and stay.'

'Good of you,' I said, 'but I don't see that I can manage it. Only staying a night or two and I've put my bags at the Berkeley.'

'Take 'em out again,' said Sneezer promptly. 'I'm driving back later today. I'll pick you up. What time would suit you?'

'That will depend on Mr. Groot.'

'Groot? The Minister?'

'I have to see him this morning. And one or two other people.'

'Look here. Tell you what! I'll park as near as I can to old man Smith, you can't mistake my crate, and give you till four o'clock. If you don't turn up I'll conclude you're not coming.'

'Good enough,' I said. 'But where's this place I'm to meet you?'

'Statue of Doug. Smith. Parliament Circus.'

'I'll find it.'

'So you're calling on Groot!' Sneezer tipped back his beer and grunted. 'Moving among the mighty.'

'You're not growing any smaller, old chap,' I said, eyeing his paunch.

'Putting on weight. Keep putting it on.'

'Married?'

He shook his head and stared mournfully into his glass.

'Could do with a wife to help me with my accounts. Clear-headed girl with a grasp of double-entry. How about yourself? Family man?'

'On the contrary,' I said, 'still single.'

'By the way, my domestic arrangements are primitive. Might call 'em haphazard. Ought to have made that clear before I asked you out. I leave everything to my boys.'

'They don't appear to starve you.'

'Plenty to eat,' said Sneezer with conviction. 'If I've not made much money, farming Africa, at least I've filled my belly! Good to see you again, Frump!' He stretched out an arm and without warning, impulsively, clapped me on the shoulder. 'Never thought to have one of the old form turn up in Smithville! You're looking prosperous, old fellow.' He fingered the sleeve of my coat. 'Tell us about it. Done well for yourself?' He beamed and leant across, affectionate, overpowering, as much of a puppy as ever—a young St. Bernard.

'Not badly. I work for the Halliday Trust.'

'You do, do you? And I thought you were going to be a pianist.'

'For that matter, Sneezer, you were setting out to rival Chaliapin. What's become of your voice?'

'I trot it out on a lead now and again. Frump!' roared the big man, 'what a mess we've made of our lives! We had our futures settled before we left school. A farthing for our ambitions. Look where we've landed! Farming and finance! Speaking as one musician to another, we've made a proper muck of things.'

'The war didn't help.'

'You're right there,' he said. He shook his head sorrowfully and sighed, pondering life's missed opportunities. He had not changed one bit. Sneezer had always wallowed in lost causes, his own and other people's.

The Ministry of Native Affairs, where I was due to interview Mr. Groot, was a modern block, eight floors high and, one small detail apart, indistinguishable from the cement cubes on either side. The detail was a stone relief set over the central doorway. This long frieze was a pæan; its theme, the humble labourer, the African. He was here shown at work, on the farm, in mine and factory and as a servant, bending his body to the simplest and least skilled of tasks. Inside the building he was represented in the flesh by two, and as far as I could see, only two individuals, one small and the other large. The large black man swung open the heavy iron and glass door that leads into the entrance hall and, after I had given my name to the white clerk at the desk, the small black boy shot me aloft in the glass and metal cage of a lift.

I was shown into a comfortable room. Tubular armchairs, shelves of books, colourful matting on the floor. The wall facing the window had been painted a bright shade of blue. A gilded parrot cage cascaded green creepers; a framed

43

drawing above the bookshelf defied interpretation. I was adjusting myself to my surroundings when a striking girl with fair hair entered through another door.

'The Minister is ready to see you,' she said, and I followed her into the presence.

Julius Groot was tall, white, bald. His brow rose loftily, receding into a blur of fine hair, once gingery, now colourless. His hands were very white, his rings nipped my fingers, his eyes challenged all comers. He was almost ostentatiously pale. Green blinds muted the sunlight flashed across the street canyon from the cement walls beyond the gulf. As we sat down, one of the telephones buzzed upon his desk and he picked up the receiver.

The conversation ended, he pressed a bell and to the fair girl who re-appeared said, 'Take my calls for the next fifteen minutes, will you. I don't wish to be interrupted.'

'Now, Mr. Pole.' He was at once friendly and masterful. 'Before we go any further, I want you to feel this.' He was thrusting a bulky file across the desk. 'Just take it in your hands. I'd like you to feel the weight.'

Bewildered by his request, I took and tested the giant dossier. Inconsequently, my mind leapt back to an afternoon the previous summer. In the cool shade of a tent I had balanced, just so, in my hands, a large fruit cake. A lady with pencil and notebook gazed at me enquiringly; a shade impatiently. 'Well, Sir? And what's your guess?' My brain numb, I had guessed; the other ladies grouped about the table and the plate of sixpences had burst out laughing; I had fled.

The Minister leant across the desk and took back the file. The exertion caused him to flush a faint rose pink.

'This,' he said, 'is the assembled correspondence relating to the Nwambe Desert Project. For two years every aspect of the problem has been thrashed out, inter-departmentally and with the administration of Bandaland. By rights you should read this through, but I won't ask you to. I haven't read it through myself and I have no intention of doing so. Some people work this way. *I don't!*'

The last words were accentuated by the crash of the dossier upon the floor. The impact shook the room. The door behind the desk opened a crack, revealed a strand of bright, sunshine-coloured hair, then closed again silently.

'You can inform your Trustees,' he said, 'and it all boils down to this in the long run, that we don't give one damn for Sir Christopher Mountclair's little scheme; not one damn, Mr. Pole. There are half a dozen sound reasons for our non-participation buried in that—that rock of correspondence. . . .' He stabbed his finger at the file lying on the floor. 'I won't burden you with them unless you want me to. But we like to play fair with our neighbours. Let the Governor go ahead with his waterworks and much good may it do him. This is small fry, little more than a pilot scheme, and in my opinion we'll never be called upon to co-operate on a large scale. I give the Nwambe Project three years. I don't know about the Bandala, but the Renduyu are as bad as a plague of locusts. The world's worst farmers. Three years and Sir Christopher will be right where he started—face to face with the desert.'

'Thank you,' I said, taken by surprise, 'for being so frank.'

'Frank!' he exclaimed. 'Think I'd hold my job for five minutes if I pulled my punches? This is a hard-working, plain-spoken country, Mr. Pole, as you'll find for yourself. Airs and graces may go down in Bandaland but they cut no ice with us! The root of the matter is simple enough—a lesson we've learnt to our cost time and time again. You can't help the black man until he's learnt to help himself.'

From the Nwambe Project we passed to more general matters. Before long he was asking me why the English Press was so critical of Equatoria. 'Critical,' he said, 'and misinformed.' He used almost exactly the same phrases as

45

Patricia. The effect was uncanny. 'I'm fed up,' he shouted, thumping a freckled fist, 'with shooting half-a-dozen native slaves on my way to work each day! Go home and knock a little sense into your editors' thick heads, Mr. Pole. Tell 'em to come out here and see the country for themselves. We're not brutes and sadists.' He had risen and was advancing ponderously round the corner of the desk. 'We're men honestly and decently doing our best for our country. More than that!' (His voice lifted slightly.) 'We're the standard bearers of white civilization. White civilization in a dark continent. Easy enough in England, Mr. Pole, to treat the odd native student as a blood brother. Don't forget that here in the Republic he outnumbers us by five to one.'

He stepped to the window and pressed a catch. With a click the blind flew up; light flooded the room.

'Come and look here!' he said, beckoning me across. 'There's a normal busy scene for you. White and black citizens going about their business, side by side. A background of solid prosperity common to both races. Are your newspapers fair in what they say?'

Together we gazed into the crowded street. The curved tops of cars glinted below like the shells of beetles. I sensed that a comment of some sort was called for.

'Why are so many Africans queuing outside the shops?' I asked.

He turned, puzzled, then amused. 'You, an Englishman, what d'you find so odd about a queue? They're waiting their turn, as you can see. They'll be called in time.'

'But the white customers are able to pass freely in and out.'

'And why not? The shops are our shops.'

'Don't the Africans have shops of their own?'

'Of course. In their housing locations. The natives you're looking at are houseboys, servants purchasing for their employers. And here's something you people overseas, with your false, sentimental reasoning, will never understand.

You know we have segregation laws? Your editors make a song and dance over them when they're hard up for copy. You'll find separate benches in the parks, native and white buses, black and white counters at the Post Offices, all as it should be. But there never has been a law passed that enforces separation inside the shops. What you're seeing down there, Mr. Pole, is established *custom*. The native has learnt to wait in the street until the shop is empty of whites. Mind you, I'm not prepared to argue that it's an efficient arrangement. These things cut two ways. If I should want a box of cigarettes, say, and send out a boy to buy 'em and the shops were busy, he'd be waiting an hour, perhaps longer. My secretary would bring them back to me inside five minutes. But there you are! In a multi-racial society like ours you'll find that segregation is instinctive. If there doesn't happen to be a law, then it's necessary to invent one.' He held out his hand abruptly and I realized I was being dismissed. My time was up. 'Regards to Sir Christopher. You can tell him we haven't much faith in his solution but we're neighbours. We don't want to be unreasonable. Tell him we're ready to help.'

I arrived in Parliament Circus soon after half-past three that afternoon. A boy followed me, carrying my suitcases. Conspicuous among the gleaming Lincolns and Cadillacs parked at the foot of the stone plinth was a battered and rusty safari truck which, from his description, I recognized as Sneezer's. In the wire cage at the back crouched two Africans, shabbily dressed and squatting apathetically, hunched forward with their heads sunk in their shoulders. I tipped the boy and sent him away. Then, aiming to stow my bags, I tried to open the rear doors but found them padlocked. The boys inside the truck were prisoners. They did not answer or look up when I spoke to them. Gloomy, listless, they stared out through the mesh with entirely expressionless faces. Forty feet above their cage doves fluttered and jockeyed for position on the broad, bronze shoulders of Douglas Smith, pioneer, founder and first President of the Republic of Equatoria.

I kicked my heels in the circus, growing steadily more impatient, for three-quarters of an hour. Twenty minutes after four, Sneezer rolled into view, voluble, contrite. He clapped me on the back, brought out a ring of keys, fumbled with the padlock until I could have shouted, opened the doors and piled in the suitcases.

'Why d'you keep your boys locked up?'

'Convicts, old man.'

'*Convicts!* What are they doing in your truck?'

'Farm workers. We all employ convict labour.' Sneezer snapped the padlock shut, pocketed the keys.

Before we climbed into the cab I looked up again at the rugged, bronze face silhouetted against the sky. From this slight swell of land it was possible to view the mine dumps to the south of the city and on them Douglas Smith appeared to have fixed his gaze. His shirt sleeves were rolled up, his forearms bared; bronze braces supported his baggy bronze trousers. Here was a man temporarily distracted from the job in hand. A simple man of humble education and great faith who had shaped a country.

'Smug old bastard, isn't he?' said Sneezer. 'White workers' promised land, that was his dream. Preached the dignity of toil. All very well, you know, but most of the fellows here leave the toil to the natives.'

The truck tipped alarmingly as he clambered aboard. We bounced backwards, rounded the circus and pointed a wavering course up the most northerly of the roads that radiate like spokes from the hub of the statue.

'And how did you find Mr. Julius Groot?'

'In excellent form, I should say. Now and again he

addressed me as if I were a public meeting. I got on better afterwards, with the technicians.'

'He's got a big mouth,' said Sneezer and hauled the truck, which was straying, back to the left side of the road.

'D'you know him?'

'Who? Me? Why should I? Know *about* him. Mind you, he's doing a good job.' The truck was straying again. We swerved dizzily to avoid an oncoming car.

'Dropped a front wheel into an ant-bear hole,' said Sneezer. 'Tendency to drift.'

We were leaving the city behind. Without warning, the tarred road gave place to a rough and dusty surface and the noise grew deafening as we hit the bumps and rattled on. The open, treeless expanse of the high plateau came into view. Fresh, bracing air rushed through the window. A great wind seemed to be scouring the pale blue dome.

Ahead, a wide encampment of shacks and shanties sprawled across the horizon; a slum mercilessly exposed, lying over the open land under the clear sky. Roofs were sloping sheets of corrugated iron anchored with large stones. Walls were fashioned from petrol cans and flattened oil drums, or roughly constructed from poles and strips of hessian. The grass all round was threadbare, the brown earth showing through. Ribby donkeys and skinny, pot-bellied children wandered among the hovels. An ancient bus groaned down the road in a dust cloud, open-sided, bulging with sombrely-dressed black passengers travelling to the city centre.

'One of your native housing locations?'

'That? No. Squatters' camping ground. No place to put 'em. They won't stay in the reserves.'

We passed to one side of the shanty town and settled to a long judder and roar along a straight and empty road through the tawny, quietly undulating, empty land. Small stones rattled continuously on the wings, the steering wheel kicked and vibrated, dust seeped inside and I was forced to close the window. Very occasionally we passed a side turning and the junction was marked, not by a single signpost, but with a cluster of boards and old harrow discs, each bearing the name of a settler or a farm. We had been driving for nearly an hour when Sneezer slowed at just such a turning and we pitched and tossed along a track that in England would almost at once have petered out into a field, and which we followed for eleven miles.

The word 'farm', with all its inevitable associations, had not in any way prepared me for what was to come. Facing the full glare of the low sun we arrived suddenly at the end of a ridge, the land fell away and we began to drop into an immense basin, a sunset-coloured depression scooped from the fiery earth and smoking with a peculiar dry haze. On every side a cross-hatch of spiky cactus plants shaded the rose-red soil. A few bordering the roadside had grown immense and blossomed crazily, their twenty foot spikes dwindling in perspective like vegetable telegraph poles. Regiments of smaller plants marched across the slopes. Mass-produced, their pale-green fleshy leaves sprouted with precision over what seemed square miles of country. The landscape was dominated by these cacti. There was literally nothing else to be seen.

'Sisal,' said Sneezer, steering between the potholes.

'All yours?'

He shook his head. 'Only wish it were. I'd be making a fortune!'

The bungalow, shaded by a group of tall gum trees and hemmed about on every side by the sisal plantations, was a low, wooden building with a large, wire-meshed verandah. We shot round into the open space before the steps and Sneezer jammed on the brakes. As we stopped our dust cloud overtook us and for a moment everything was obliterated. I heard the sound of barking and as the dust cleared and I struggled with the door, which was not easy to open, I faced the friendly but disconcerting charge of three gigantic dogs. Two were honey-coloured, built like golden retrievers but with small, bristling manes—ridgebacks. The other was the largest and shaggiest wolfhound I had ever set eyes on. Sneezer came round at the double and hauled them off, gripping them by their scruffs and throwing them around like puppies.

'Abraham!' he bellowed. '*Ab-ra-ham!*'

There appeared in the doorway of the verandah a tall, gaunt, unprepossessing African, his coal black face lined and pitted, his brow deeply furrowed. He did not smile nor make an obeisance. He stood at the head of the steps—clad in a stained and dirty khaki shirt, on his head the ubiquitous embroidered white skull cap—and waited for orders, his arms hanging at his sides.

Sneezer issued instructions loudly in Swahili, gesturing at the truck (where the two men crouched, covered in a thick layer of dust) pointing at myself, fending off the dogs, fanning himself with his pork-pie hat. The air, though dry, was warm and stuffy and coats had again become an encumbrance. The shadows of the gums had touched and were climbing the wall of the barn across the bare earth yard. The sun, swollen and red, stood on the smooth rim of the basin and prepared to set.

'Now,' said Sneezer, seizing my arm and propelling me forward. 'Which comes first? A bath or a drink?'

In the end we had several drinks, sitting in cane chairs on the verandah and watching the lilac shadows creep over the plantations and deepen swiftly with the approach of night. We chatted in a desultory way. Now that we had arrived and were pigeon-holed in our compartments, I the guest, he the host, Sneezer's manner had altered. He had become constrained, a little over-anxious to put me at my ease, to refill my glass, to agree with everything I said. At

51

school, I remembered, in spite of his size, he had always been a shy, even a timid boy.

Our talk was interrupted by the noise of shuffling feet and the jingling of light chains and across the yard in front of us, dim in the dusk, slouched a long and straggling procession of Africans, walking two by two like a crocodile of schoolboys. With a shock of surprise I saw that the men were chained together in couples, wrist to wrist. On either side of the procession marched African guards, swinging long sticks. Bringing up the rear, bare-chested, carrying himself with assurance, strutted yet another black guard, an antiquated-looking rifle sloped over his shoulder.

The procession passed by and we sat, for a short while, without speaking. I found it impossible to relate what I had just seen to the present; to connect what appeared to be a flash-back—Virginia, Carolina, the historical past—with the man Hardcastle who had been at school with me, and with an African farm in the middle years of the twentieth century. Sneezer, I think, must have been aware of my embarrassment for he leaned across, splashed more beer into my glass and said, as if answering an unspoken question. 'We don't keep 'em chained while they're working, old boy. Just one of these government regulations.'

Soon afterwards I went and had a bath and, lying in the tepid water, thought the matter over. But it was hard to reason objectively, for people were passing backwards and forwards along the passage and there was no lock or catch on the bathroom door. Sneezer's bungalow, I was rapidly becoming aware, was alive with Africans. They were not all servants, for there were women and children amongst them. Abraham's family, perhaps, or the cook's relations, together with odd followers and hangers on. I was accustomed, by this time, to black servants. The service at the Government Guest House at Banda, for example, was faultless and quite above reproach. The boys were noiseless and discreet. They came and went like shadows. Everything was done for you, your wants, if possible, anticipated. Out in the desert, too, we had been extremely well looked after. But then Bulmers was a disciplinarian. Sneezer, I had the feeling, was perhaps not quite so successful when it came to handling his staff.

The furniture in my bedroom was of the scantiest and a large part of the floor space was occupied by stacked crates, tin boxes, chests and cabin trunks. A bare bulb dangled on a short piece of flex from the centre of the ceiling and glowed brown. I could trace patterns in the dust on the dressing table with the tip of my finger. I came in from the bathroom just in time to catch a glimpse of a gaudily-coloured skirt as a visitor vanished, not quite quickly enough, through the opposite door. There was laughter and a great deal of scuffling outside. In the distance I could hear Sneezer stamping about, roaring intermittently. As he trod, the floors everywhere creaked and windows throughout the building rattled. The kitchen and staff quarters, I learnt later, were separate little thatched houses behind the bungalow and a certain raising of the voice was essential when transmitting orders. I dressed, tried to lock the door behind me, found there was no key and resigned my belongings to their fate. Sneezer, under another brown-glowing electric bulb, was pacing impatiently up and down the verandah.

'Ah, there you are. Let's have some grub. Famished. *Lete chakula!*' he bellowed. "*pese*, *'pese!* Have a drink while it's coming. Doesn't seem to be any ice. Blasted fellow Abraham gets lazier and lazier. One of these days he'll find out what's coming to him.'

Dinner arrived, after repeated calls, half an hour later and was well worth waiting for. I enjoy good cooking and Sneezer's cook was an artist. We began with ripe avocado pears, eaten with pepper, salt and Worcester sauce. The main dish was a haunch of roast kid, basted in wine. The sweet was a creamy blend of banana and passion fruit crusted with meringue. Abraham waited on us and I never once saw his solemn, rather frightening face relax. Sneezer's conversation dried up completely. He was accustomed to eating in silence and devoted himself, with absorbed concentration, to the task in hand. I saw Abraham, handing round the vegetables, at one point nudge him with the dish. Certainly, it was a meal to remember.

'You've a French chef hidden away in your back premises,' I announced when we had finished.

Sneezer was delighted and insisted, then and there, on sending Abraham to fetch the cook. A substantial interval elapsed ('washing himself, I should hope,' Sneezer grunted) and we drank our coffee. Abraham reappeared at last, pushing in front of him a skinny, bent little African in an ironed white shirt that had clearly been donned for the occasion. He flashed a quick, shy grin at Sneezer, then put his palms together and bobbed his head in my direction.

'That's no good,' said Sneezer at once. 'He's only given you the usual greeting. I'll tell him you're a *Bwana Mkubwa* and he must give you the greeting reserved for a chief.'

I watched the little cook's intent expression as his master turned to explain, the mouth on the brink of a grin, the eyes darting from Sneezer's face to mine. In the end he nodded calmly and without fuss or protest stretched himself full length on the floor of the verandah and clasped his hands in the air above his head.

'After the meal he's just given us,' I said, '*we* should be kneeling at *his* feet.' I was not too happy to have him lying there.

'*Mzuri*!' said Sneezer, relenting, and rewarded him with cigarettes.

The table was cleared and Abraham and the cook boy vanished behind the scenes. Sneezer unlocked the small cupboard in the corner and dug out a bottle of brandy. He was in high good humour and surprised me, suddenly, by jumping up (the flimsily-built verandah quivered) and crying, 'Frump, old chap, let's have a *Ngoma*! Lay on some beer and give the poor devils out there something to dance about!' He was off, roaring, into the back quarters, to return a few minutes later and subside again, with a grunt of satisfaction, in the chair next to mine.

'I reckon to give 'em a binge if they work hard enough,' he said. 'Between ourselves, this last lot's a bunch of lazy so and so's.'

'Sneezer,' I said, returning to the charge. 'Can't you farm without using convicts? Surely there's free labour available.'

'Not as cheap and not as reliable. My boss happens to prefer it this way.'

'Your boss? But I thought this was your own place!'

'No, old fellow. I'm only the manager. Had a farm once but had to sell up.' He hesitated a moment before adding, 'Ran into trouble.'

'I'm sorry, Sneezer.'

'No need to be. This job suits me all right. Less to worry about in the long run.'

The verandah was a dimly-lit oasis of quiet in a noisy desert of sound. Sneezer chewed the stem of his pipe, I lit another cigarette. Feet padded past, voices spoke throatily from the night. The dogs lying at our feet shifted and growled, their heads on their paws. The tension outside could be felt where we were sitting. Excitement was mounting rapidly.

'Like it out here?'

I looked up. The question was unexpected.

'Yes and no,' I said. 'I've not been long enough in Africa to adjust myself. I wouldn't want to settle, if that's what you mean.'

'No,' said Sneezer, and heaved a sigh, 'I didn't suppose you would. Not the type. I'd go back, you know. Sometimes

55

think I'll make a clean break, tomorrow, or next week or the month after, but I can't make up my mind to it when the time comes. Mind you there's a lot to be said for a young country. You can get on. You're not crippled with taxes. But it's no use coming out with your head stuffed full of ideas that don't fit in. Mistake I made. You're up against it at once. Kicking against the pricks. I've learnt my lesson, but it's late days now. If I were still in my twenties, I'd start again. . . .'

'What ideas, Sneezer?' I asked him. I could guess easily enough but was interested to know how he would express them.

'Civil rights,' he said, biting on the stem of his pipe. 'Equality. Democratic principles. Whatever you may feel about them you can't start applying them out here. Slapping 'em on wholesale. Just doesn't work. All you can do, Sebastian, believe me, is to play fair to yourself and keep your own nest clean.'

This was the first time, to my knowledge, he had used my Christian name. His red, full-moon of a face was solemn and a little pathetic. He leaned forward, tapped me on the knee.

'I employ convict labour. Agreed, I might—I say, I *might*—persuade my boss to change his ideas. More likely, I'd get the sack. Either case, who's better off? The men *I* take are handled well, I see to that. I'll show you their quarters tomorrow, I'm not ashamed of them. I'd eat the food they're given. And I stand no truck from the boss boys. I could take you to farms, old fellow, where the men share sheds with the cattle. I've known 'em to be locked up for the night in an outhouse without sanitation and left to sleep in their own muck, like swine. This isn't England, Frump. You can't change these things.' He muttered something under his breath, then grabbed my arm. 'Come on,' he said, 'give you an evening to write home about! Crude but genuine. They put everything they've got into it, the poor bastards. Dance from the heart!'

The night was warm, stars powdered the clear sky. As we came round the corner of the bungalow we saw firelight gleaming on the barn walls, shining on the blotched pillars of the gum trees. A bonfire of old sisal stumps had been lit in the centre of the level space between the huts and out-buildings clustered behind the house, and here fifty or sixty Africans had already gathered, most of them squatting silently on the ground, their faces turned towards the flames. Two men holding big cowhide drums were arguing heatedly and a group of women giggled, raising their arms with a trembling and fluttering of their fingers as Sneezer loomed into view at the back of the circle.

Almost at once there was an unfortunate incident. I never heard the rights and wrongs of the affair but I was told afterwards that not all the convicts had been released for the occasion. A few so-called 'intractables' were still locked up. The boss boy responsible was surly and, when pressed, not only refused to loose them but was insolent into the bargain. (He may, for all I know, have been acting within his rights.) I was close by when it happened. Sneezer lost his temper, swore at the top of his voice and hit out. The blow was clumsily produced and badly timed but landed with all the big man's eighteen stone behind it and the boy went down and stayed down. He was dragged by his heels along the ground and left to recover by the wall of one of the huts.

'Sorry about that,' said Sneezer, turning shamefaced and rubbing his knuckles. 'Haven't knocked a native down for getting on three years. As if,' he exclaimed, 'they'd try to run for it when there's beer around!'

The beer, at that moment, was being doled out of a large iron drum and circulated in a variety of utensils—cracked china cups without handles, tin mugs, empty food cans, gourds and hand-carved wooden bowls. I sampled the brew, against Sneezer's advice, and was not impressed. The stuff tasted to me like thin, sour porridge.

The drummers were beginning to thump tentatively upon their instruments, breaking off now and again to resume their arguments. A thin, graceful youth with a long neck and thin long arms, wearing a white singlet that contrasted vividly in the firelight with his shining ebony flesh, strolled about plucking with delicate fingers at the springy steel strips of his timbila. The men sat stolidly upon their haunches and drank beer. A few tapped in listless fashion their hands on the ground beside them.

'They'll start in a moment, don't worry,' said Sneezer. 'Always takes 'em a while to warm up. The drummers have got to get going first.'

We hung around at the back of the crowd for ten more minutes. Then Sneezer said, 'They're off to a slow start tonight, that's clear. Let's leave 'em to it. Like to come and look at the decorticator?'

The decorticator was a mile from the bungalow and we drove there in the truck, the headlights conjuring up from the blackness the spikes and spires of the sisal along each side of the track. Once a pair of green eyes flashed ahead, Sneezer accelerated and a gazelle leapt nimbly out of our path and streaked away into the night. We arrived to find the big iron shed, open-ended, a blaze of light. The electric plant here, at least, seemed to be functioning efficiently. Inside, the noise was deafening. Wheels wobbled, belts span, machinery thundered and trembled as the huge jaws devoured an endless belt of sisal leaves, chewing them up and spewing out flaccid heaps of blond fibre. Streams of water washed the useless pulp out of the building. The night shift was at work, Africans all of them, feeding their noisy charge and carrying away, draped over long poles, the fibre that was like flaxen hair. On the cement floor

58

smouldered two or three wood fires; small cooking fires such as Africans always seem to light wherever they work, and the smoke drifting about and the sight of the bare-torsoed black figures swarming among the roaring belts and wheels made a primitive inferno of a commonplace industrial scene.

We stayed and watched them for a quarter of an hour. Sneezer made a few small adjustments to the machinery, exchanging as he did so good-natured asides with the men, and we drove back to the farm. As we stopped and climbed out of the truck we heard the dogs howling inside the bungalow and the thudding of the drums, gruff sounds of chanting and the occasional blast of a whistle informed us that the *Ngoma* was on. The light from the fire was blocked by a ring of swaying, shuffling, gesticulating figures. The pattern of their movements changed with the whistle; the drummers were leaning forward, pounding flat-handed, heads shaking. Hoarse voices made sudden, emphatic statements, the women shrilled, the earth vibrated under the piston-like kick of iron-hard heels. Shoulders and chests ran with sweat and shone in the flickering, uncertain light of the flames. The ground smoked with dust.

There were no spectacular costumes to arrest the eye, no fanciful head-dresses, no spears and shields, and as the evening progressed it became abundantly clear that very many of the dancers were reeling drunk. Why should I try to pretend that this was other than a sordid little *Ngoma* in the labour compound of a sisal farm in the back-blocks of Equatoria, where a mixed bunch of Africans—house servants, farm workers, boss boys, and criminals from the slums of Smithville—whipped themselves up hysterically, drunk with much beer, drunk with the turbulent rhythm of the drums? Their movements were repetitive and often ungainly, their voices harsh; the disagreeable smell of perspiring bodies filled the air.

This, I told myself, was an experience to remember. My first native dance. Sneezer, I was pleased to see, appeared to be thoroughly enjoying himself. In amongst them he moved, stirring a wake of excited calls and laughter, towering above the tallest of his subjects, the white sleeves of his shirt flapping as with abrupt, dramatic gestures he urged on the revellers. Now and again the bass boom of his voice rang out as he shouldered a staccato chorus. Watching him, I felt instinctively that this abandonment in the face of frustration was as much his surrender as theirs.

We had returned to the bungalow and were talking about bed (the dance continuing, livelier, more disorganized than ever) when Sneezer, pouring out a night cap, said suddenly, 'I hate that fellow's guts, he's a sulky bastard, but I'm sorry I hit him.'

'He's recovered, I take it?'

'Didn't you see him out there? Drunk as a lord!'

My room under the low, iron roof was very stuffy and I lay with only a sheet covering me, hearing, muted, the throb and stamp, the shouts and shrill screams from the compound. My bed faced the window and I was lying in that drowsy state between sleep and wakefulness when the door creaked and I distinctly heard a soft footfall on the floor. I opened my eyes but still lay as if drugged, unable to break the spell, unable to react and move, although convinced that someone was in the room. I listened intently, staring rigidly ahead, and across the oblong of faint starlight, silhouetted against the barely perceptible radiance, I thought I saw the figure of a woman pass. At that I found my voice, shouted 'Who's there? What d'you want!' threw back the sheet and jumped out of bed. I heard a nervous little crow of laughter as I fumbled up and down each side of the door, hunting for the electric light switch. Then I found it and nothing whatever happened. There must have been a breakdown—or possibly Sneezer had shut off the plant for the night. At all events the bedroom remained impenetrably dark. I remembered I had a torch in one of my suitcases and stumbled round the bed, guiding myself with a hand on the mattress. As I crouched over the case, which I had left on the floor, and felt through my clothes, I could hear quick, uncertain breathing behind me. All this occupied less time than it takes to write. I turned with the torch in my hand and shone the light full at the intruder.

I was not mistaken. A native woman was standing a yard away, without a stitch of clothing on her body. She stepped back with a gasp, and her pink palms flashed as she put up her hands to hide her face. She was neither young nor, by our standards, attractive. As she twisted away from the beam of the torch her big breasts swung against her chest. They were long and pendulous, the shape of marrows, and her milk-chocolate nipples—this I noticed and remembered afterwards—stood out prominently, paler than her jet black skin.

'Outside!' I said. I spoke, perhaps, more brusquely than I need have done. 'Go on, get out of my room!' She looked frightened, stared at me with large eyes, but made no move. Impatiently, I stepped across to the door, flung it open and flashed the torch into the passageway. She understood then and moved towards the opening, but while still in the room hesitated, saying something in a low voice. 'Go on!' I said again and she passed close by me, so close that I felt one of her breasts brush against my hand. I gave her a quick push into the passage, closed the door and pulled across two or three trunks and boxes from the pile and stacked them against it, wedging them, as I thought, securely with the end of the chest of drawers. I was sweating by the time I had finished. My hair sticking to my forehead I crawled back into bed, where I lay and laughed weakly. I had certainly stumbled into a crazy corner of Africa!

Abraham forced an entry with the early morning tea.

The noise of toppling trunks woke me and I looked up into his scowling morning face. Without a word he placed the cup on the chair beside the bed and methodically set to and cleared the doorway.

Later, at breakfast, after we had exchanged good-mornings and were squeezing lemon over our slices of paw-paw, Sneezer glanced across at me and said, 'Sorry you were troubled last night, Frump.'

'Quite all right,' I said.

'We don't often have guests staying here and these things will happen.'

I noticed the 'we' but said nothing and allowed the matter to drop.

Another peculiarity of the bungalow was the telephone. This rang continuously, for Sneezer belonged to a party line shared with other farms. They each had their own call. 'Mine's two short and a long,' he told me. 'You get so that you don't hear the others.' His particular ring sounded before we had finished breakfast and Sneezer got up and left the table. He returned in a few minutes—I had heard his voice booming away in one of the small rooms off the verandah—and said, 'George Peck wants me to go and look at a cow. Feel like coming?'

I said I would. 'What do you know about cows?' I asked.

'Not much,' he said, 'but more than George.' He added wistfully, 'I had a dairy herd and fifty head of stock in the old days.'

'Look here, Sneezer,' I said, 'what made you take on this job. You don't like sisal. . . .'

'Who does?'

'Chuck it in, be sensible, and manage a mixed farm instead.'

'At the time, old boy, there was precious little choice. My boss didn't happen to be too particular. Now—well, for a start I've no capital left. Moving around can be a chancy game.'

As we drove across the basin that morning we saw men working up and down the sisal lines, hacking at the plants with steel choppers. The stumps they left behind looked like giant pineapples. Small railway tracks criss-crossed the estate, linking the plantations with the decorticator, and along them rolled open trucks, stacked high with the sword-shaped leaves.

George Peck's farm, however, was up on the plateau, ten miles away, and once we had left the basin behind us the air grew fresher and the wind that sweeps over the high, bare land flattened the dry, brown grasses. The wooden farmhouse stood right up on a ridge, with no trees to shelter it, and all around a horizon-wide view of treeless, tawny hills. By the time we arrived the sun had disappeared over-head, sparkling in the cloudless sky. But the heat was strangely tempered and as we stood talking by the truck (our shadows crouching between our legs) the wind smacked and buffeted, and I for one was glad of my coat.

George was a soldierly type, good-looking, I thought, in a sun-burned way. He spoke with a slightly exaggerated accent, wore a neat moustache, a red checked shirt and a wide-brimmed straw hat decorated with a narrow snakeskin band. His shorts were girdled with a snakeskin belt, his legs and arms were tanned the colour of mahogany and he carried a small, bone-handled knife in a leather sheath. After introductions the three of us marched to the brick-built 'cow palace' (as George called it), the animal was exhaustively overhauled and pronounced upon and we all marched back to the farmhouse to 'meet Lydia and have a drink.'

Lydia Peck was a tall, handsome, discontented-looking girl who greeted us distantly, cold-shouldered Sneezer and showed plainly that she was put about by our arrival. The

63

first few minutes were sticky. Then George happened to ask what I was doing in their part of the world and I mentioned the Halliday Trust. After that, his wife relaxed a little and consented to talk to me. An uncle of hers, apparently, had once been a Trustee. I told her about the Nwambe Project and added that I had not yet visited one of Equatoria's native reserves.

'You've come to the right place,' she said, 'if that's really your ambition. We're unfortunate enough, on this farm, to border the native lands. Ask George to drive you out to the boundary, it's no distance, and you'll be able to see the mess for yourself.'

'Mess?' I said.

'They don't farm, they murder the land. Their cattle are the size of goats—only numbers count with the Renduyu. The Government keeps trying to cut down the herds, but they refuse to co-operate. D'you know what one of their chiefs said the other day? "When a dirty old pound note's worth as much to you white people as a new one, how can you ask us to destroy *our* wealth?" I thought that was a clever reply for a native.'

'Very clever,' I said. 'And what's the answer?'

She shrugged her shoulders. 'George says that one day, fairly soon, it'll be them or us. So we go on living on top of a volcano—if you can call it living.' She glanced across at her husband, who was contentedly discussing cows. 'George doesn't seem to mind. We've been here for four years now, miles from our nearest neighbours, with just a wire fence between us and the natives. I can't leave my child, I haven't seen Smithville for months. George gets around a good deal but all I do is sit at home and listen to the drums. Sometimes at night, when I hear them, I think this is it, now they're coming. If only they weren't so close I believe I might forget them. As it is, they seem to press up against me. Shut out the sunlight like a black wall.'

64

That morning George Peck posed the same question. We were standing by the boundary of his farm, George, Sneezer and myself, looking over into the reserve, when he turned to me and asked, 'What's going to happen, Pole, when there's a desert on one side of this wire and tall grass on the other?' There was no easy answer; we all knew it. But from my point of view, the moment was an exciting one. For the first time since my arrival in Banda, I was faced with the crux of the problem. I could tell myself that I was here, in Africa, for *this*.

The rolling hills across the border were astonishingly neat and tidy. The grass, cropped close as a billiard table by the herds of goats and cattle, was powdered as thickly with round, whitewashed clay huts as an English meadow with mushrooms. From a distance the slopes looked like runkled, browny-green felt. There were no barriers, no hedges, no trees, nothing but huts and cattle and an occasional herd boy, scattered like toys on a smooth and immaculate carpet.

'Cover's wearing thin,' said George, and indeed, if you looked closely, you could see the reddish earth showing through the grass. I was reminded of a suburban lawn after a dry summer. 'No sponge soon to take the rains. Top soil's going already. I could show you some classic erosion gulleys. At the rate things are sliding I don't give this reserve a great many years. The land's crying out for a rest. You can see that for yourself. No fences, no attempt at rotational grazing. . . .'

'Why don't the Government step in, take a firm line?'

'Easier said than done,' said George. 'The native's stuck in his old ways. Go ahead, give orders till you're black in the face, but how are you to see they're carried out unless you come in and do the job yourself. And even then he'll sabotage you if he can.'

'Horse to the water,' said Sneezer. 'They don't work our way and they never will.'

'This,' said George with certainty, 'is the load that's going to sink the country, and all the gold in Smithville won't float us again.'

George, I learnt, was driving into the city that afternoon. The chance of a lift back was too good to miss and before we left I arranged with him to pick me up at the bungalow. But when it came to saying goodbye, I realized that Sneezer was genuinely sorry to have me go so soon.

'See you in England,' I said. 'You must look me up, next leave.' He promised he would do so. He gripped my hand in his enormous fist and pumped my arm up and down and tried to say something more but the words refused to come. Looking up into his face I suddenly had the feeling that the huge man was on the brink of tears and tore myself away, horrified and embarrassed. The dogs barked and bounded beside the car as we swirled out of the dusty yard.

George Peck did not speak until we were climbing from the sisal basin. Then he said, in his clipped voice, 'As man to man, Pole, would *you* find it easy to sleep with a native woman?'

'I don't think,' I said, 'I'm inclined to try.'

'Appalling idea,' he said. 'Simply can't understand a fellow like Hardcastle. Lets the side down all round, I say. Why, Lydia can't bear to be in the same room with him, and I don't blame her. Wouldn't have brought him into the house this morning, only you happened to be there and Lydia doesn't see many new faces. Lonely life,' he confided, 'for a woman.'

And sometimes for a man, too, I said to myself, thinking of Sneezer.

'This is the first time I've come across him since we left school,' I said. 'We were in the same form.'

'He'd have been well settled by now if he hadn't played the fool,' George said. 'Proper Bolshie type when he came out to Equatoria, or so I gather. Put his foot into things right, left and centre. You hadn't heard?'

'I knew something must have happened.'

'Tipped his first bunch of convicts over the border into the Reserve. Well, I mean, can't do a thing like that and expect to get away with it, can you? Fellow must have been crazy. Mark you, this was years back. He'd sobered up by the time I came out. But I've heard the old stagers talk. That was only a start.'

'Really?' I said. 'And what else did he do?'

'Now that you ask me, damned if I can remember. But I know what finally ditched him. There was a chap, name of Varden I think it was, farming in this district. One of the real tough eggs, bred in the country. Fellow was in his cups one night and beat up a boy and the boy took and died. Bad show all round, you might say. We all have to discipline a boy now and again, but we do it when we're sober and we don't reckon to kill him. And now I'm on the subject, Pole, here's a tip worth having. If a native comes for you, never punch his head. Skulls like iron. I cut my knuckles open on a boy's teeth, first year I was out, and the place went septic.' His voice took on an aggrieved note. 'Weeks before my hand healed up. No, just you forget the Queensberry rules and give him a jab in the solar plexus. Believe me, they can't take it. The nigger's stomach,' George concluded with immense conviction and a sweeping disregard for the cruder points of anatomy, 'is his Achilles heel.'

'Thanks,' I said. 'Now I know. But what happened to Sneezer?'

'As I was saying, this chap Varden was up before the courts and convicted. I forget the exact fine. I think it was nine pounds and costs. Something of the sort. This was evidently too much for Hardcastle's Bolshie principles and the damn great fool went straight across to Varden's place and improved on the sentence.'

'What exactly d'you mean by that?'

'He beat him up,' cried George excitedly, slapping the

steering wheel. 'And, by God, his name's still mud for it among the older settlers. They're five to one as it is and if we don't stick together . . . I'm an easy-going bloke myself, prepared to live and let live, and I'm one of the few round here who'll speak to the man and have him across to my place. Not that I see much of him, because of Lydia. And if your big friend's not bloody careful, Pole, he'll be heading for trouble again.'

'How's that?' I said.

'You've just stayed with him. You've seen the disgusting way he lives, pigging it with native sluts. And I'll tell you why he's been able to carry on that way for so long.' George lowered his voice. 'The sisal estate he's managing is owned by an Indian!' He glanced at me triumphantly, as if everything had been explained. 'But he's on the wrong side of the law, these days, is Hardcastle. They've made it a criminal offence to consort with a native, and quite right too. And a man with enemies can't be too careful.'

'You haven't made it clear to me,' I said, 'how he came to lose his farm.'

'They burnt it down one night. Varden and a few buddies. Set fire to the buildings over his head. He was lucky to get out of that one. He wasn't meant to.' George must have noticed my expression for he gave a short laugh, like a bark, and said, 'This isn't England, you know, Pole.' A phrase, I was to find, that soon acquired a certain cachet through constant repetition.

We changed the subject and George occupied himself happily during the tedious drive to Smithville describing in detail the finer points and inner workings of his new, self-designed, hand-built and (needless to say) efficiently-serviced septic tank.

Fetching out a handful of small change from my pocket,

I let fall to the floor a scrap of paper. The waiter picked it up and handed it back to me. I paid for the drinks, then read the address scribbled across the slip. *84, Highwood Avenue, Fairview Estate*. Pat Jensen's mother.

'Fairview Estate?' said George. 'Twenty minutes east of Main Street. On a bus route. Not going that way myself or I'd take you. I must get cracking, old chap. Late as it is.'

I stayed in the lounge and ordered another beer. It was a relief to be alone for a moment. Mrs. Jensen, I thought, might or might not be able to help me, but she was someone to whom I could turn. Groot had not chosen to take me up and I needed a contact in Smithville.

The air was cool when I came out of the Berkeley, the stars brilliant. The bus rushed swiftly through deserted streets. Alighting at one end of the estate, I found Highwood Avenue without difficulty. The houses were small and set close together and seen at night the dormitory area might have belonged to Wembley or to Wimbledon. Looking closer, I saw that the sharp spears of palm leaves bristled over garden gates. Fronds of jacaranda trailed shadows across pavements; the Southern Cross showed between chimney stacks and gables. Now and again I passed a house starkly floodlit, a battery of headlamps, mounted upon the roof, suspending over windows, guttering and garden an even canopy of light. I met two—and only two—passers-by, walking together. They were policemen.

The door of number eighty-four was opened, on a chain, by an elderly African boy in a white linen suit. My appearance must have reassured him, for he let me in before I had explained myself or the purpose of my visit. As I stood in the narrow hall a voice called out, 'You're very early, dear. Why have you come so early?' and the boy led me into a small drawing-room where Mrs. Jensen was playing patience, the cards spread on a board laid across her lap. My entry so flustered her that she made a move to get up, and before

69

I could stop her, had tipped board and cards on to the carpet. The boy went stiffly down on his knees to retrieve them.

'I've ruined your game!' I said.

'I'm glad to be rid of it. Nothing could have made it come out. But who *are* you?' I was about to speak when she held up a hand. 'Don't tell me. I know. Looking at you, I know. You're Elsie Sorrell's nephew. How nice of you to call round!'

'I'm no one that you know. My name's Pole. Sebastian Pole. I've met your daughter in Banda.'

'You're a friend of Pat's? Sit down and tell me all about her. Mark, leave the cards where they are and fetch us some coffee. When you came in and I saw you, Mr. Pole, I thought of Elsie at once. You're very like her. I can trace a distinct resemblance. But you say you're no relation. . . . How long have you known Patricia?'

Mrs. Jensen was trim, faded, but still vivacious. She wore her hair piled up on her forehead. Her eyes were bright; her sharp little nose decisive. She sat in the centre of the small, cluttered room and chattered away like a bird. Caging her, the silver frames of a bewildering number of photographs flashed from walls and tables. They were ranged along the mantelpiece, arrayed on top of the upright piano.

'I hardly know Pat at all. Only met her a few times. She seems to be enjoying herself as Press correspondent.'

'Oh, but Mr. Pole, she was doing so well, here in Smithville. It was a tragedy, yes, a tragedy that she had to leave. Please don't misunderstand me. Naturally, I would have been sorry to see her go. My only daughter. But in such a *hurry*! And under such a *shadow*! And all the fault of that outrageous woman! The affair was mismanaged from the start. A prominent public man, he should have known better. And Mrs. Goldstein married, with a young family. . . .'
She put her hand to her mouth in sudden consternation.

'There!' she said, 'I've mentioned her name.' As if trying to extenuate her error, she added. 'The papers were full of it. Photographs, too.'

'Pat has never told me anything.'

'Of course not. And one day it will be all forgotten. She could have come back before this, but she's a stubborn girl, is my Patricia. I daresay you've found that out for yourself. She had a most trying time, a humiliating time, before matters came to a head. She was loyal to the last. After three years she had grown very attached to the Minister. She felt, we all felt, that it might be a passing phase, that things might go on as before, but no, that was not to be. She suffered, poor child. He treated her shamelessly.'

The servant knocked and came into the room with a tray. Mrs. Jensen gave me a significant look and pressed her lips obtrusively together. She re-arranged the cups and saucers and the moment the door had closed, leant forward and tapped my knee. Her small hand glittered with rings.

'I shall never forgive the Minister. At the time of his unfortunate attachment Patricia was still his secretary. He took her into his confidence! Yes, you may well be astonished, Mr. Pole. *She* arranged their clandestine meetings. Acted as their go-between. Black or white? I expect you like sugar.'

There was a pause while Mrs. Jensen poured out coffee. She handed me my cup, then picked up a small poker and stirred the coals in the grate.

'I do like to see a fire,' she said.

'I hardly think you would in Banda.'

'No, Pat tells me that it's very stuffy. Are you from England?'

'London,' I said. 'I'm out on business.' And I began to tell her about the Nwambe Project and my work for the Halliday Trust. I brought up the matter which had been troubling me since my return.

'Representative Renduyu opinion?' she repeated when I

71

had finished. She stared at me blankly. 'I don't know what to say. I'm not the right person to advise you, I know so little. Surely the chiefs, the tribal chiefs, live out in the Reserve?'

'But the Africans in Smithville? What do *they* feel? Let's not generalize. Take your own houseboy. I expect he's a Renduyu.'

'*Mark!* Why yes, yes, of course he's a Renduyu. He's a good boy, too. He will have been with me for ten years next April.'

'His opinion might be worth having.'

'I hardly think so. Mark's opinion? Oh no, Mr. Pole, you're not serious.'

'He may have something useful to say. Shall we ask him?'

'Dear oh dear,' said Mrs. Jensen, pink and flustered. 'I'm afraid he'll disappoint you. He's not a reader, my Mark. He takes no interest in the newspapers. He listens to a chapter of the Bible on Sunday mornings. . . .'

The bell was rung. The servant tapped, entered, stood by the door.

'Come over here, Mark. The Bwana wants to ask you a question.'

I saw the boy stiffen apprehensively. He took a faltering step forward. He did not turn his head, but when I spoke to him his big eyes rolled in my direction.

'Answer the Bwana, Mark.'

Mark had nothing to say. It was clear that he had never heard of the Nwambe Desert Irrigation Project.

I tried another angle. 'Your Minister for Native Affairs, Mr. Groot. . . .'

The boy reacted exactly as if I had struck him.

'Mr. Groot no good man,' he said violently. 'Because of that man, Bwana, Missie Pat go away, never come back. He make my Memsaab cry like a small girl.'

'That will do, Mark. You can go.' Mrs. Jensen waited until

he had left the room. 'After ten years he feels himself one of the family. They become very faithful.' She was smiling unsteadily, clenching in one hand her handkerchief squeezed into a tight ball.

I was profoundly embarrassed.

'I'm sorry,' I said. 'Forgive me for having insisted.'

'No, no, I am sorry. I wish so much I could help you. I'm sure Pat would know what to suggest. I do feel, you see, that in Smithville you are likely to get the wrong impression. The natives here are urbanized. They have become town-dwellers. You need to go out to the Reserves and speak to the chiefs.'

'Then I've missed my opportunity. There's no time to arrange that now. I'm due to fly back tomorrow afternoon.'

We sat in silence. Mrs. Jensen, head on one side, stared at the small fire.

'You had better see my son,' she said at last. 'You will have time to do that. I'll write him a note. He is in charge of a small Mission and Health Centre in one of the native townships.'

'How very good of you.' I glanced at my watch. 'Can I visit him tonight?'

'No, no! You mustn't think of such a thing. Olaf himself never moves outside the Mission after dark. He would not be safe if he did. Do you realize that in none of the native locations—and we are surrounded by them—is there a street light of any kind. Not a single lamp-post. I often sit here in the evening and frighten myself, thinking of Olaf down there in that enormous overcrowded slum. Smithville is ringed in darkness.'

'You're frightened here, too. Out on the farms it's the same. I was talking. . . .'

'Listen to me, Mr. Pole. This country has taken a wrong turning. Pat may not think so but I've lived in Equatoria for a great many years, yes, for more than thirty, and I have watched it happen. When I first came out we were happier

73

because we were not too *proud*. The young people today are proud and have lost the power to love. Look at our children! Children reflect the change. I had a five-year-old boy in this room, with his mother. "There's a man coming up the garden," I said, and the boy ran to the window to look. "Not a man," he told me scornfully. "It's a native." Sometimes I think we have all gone mad. People are growing harder, more bitter, more and more ruthless. A winter of pride. Everyone obsessed by the colour of their skins. I pray, Mr. Pole, each day and with my whole heart for the sun of love to shine.'

The front door bell rang. I heard Mark's step in the hall. Mrs. Jensen's hands lifted instantly to her hair. Then she stood up, smoothing her skirt.

'That note to your son,' I said.

'Of course! You shall have it.' She gazed round vaguely, as if, just at that moment, her eyes could not focus. I felt that it would be tactless of me to press the matter.

'I'm staying at the Berkeley.'

'Then I'll write later. Willoughby can hand in the letter at the hotel tomorrow morning. I'll not forget.'

I thanked her, said goodbye and went into the hall. The door of the little cloakroom was open. Inside, a short, elderly gentleman with wavy grey hair was drying his hands on a towel. As I appeared he turned his back, the better to examine his face in the mirror above the basin. His hair under the electric bulb had the sheen of gunmetal. Passing the doorway, I found myself transfixed by the reflected stare of pale and unexpectedly hostile eyes.

The letter was in my box after breakfast. I surprised the reception clerk by asking him how I was to get to Northtown.

'You'll have to drive. There's no other way.'

'What about the bus service?'

'All native buses, sir.'

'Then you'd better fix me up with a car.'

The location lay five or six miles from Smithville. We drove through the mine dumps and then out across the bare plateau. The hillside ahead was stippled with grey dots. As we drew closer I saw that the dots were small cement cubes, hutches rather than habitations, each with a door, a chimney and no window. They were identical, massed closely together, without a tree or strip of grass to break the monotony. There were thousands of them laid out over the slope, arranged as symmetrically as graves in an army cemetery, and the whole of the built-up area was surrounded with a barbed wire fence.

My white driver stopped outside the location and refused to go any further. He did not intend, he said, to have his paint scratched or his windshield starred. He was uncouth, preposterous and not to be persuaded.

A dozen or more Africans were lounging about by the gateway. Yes, they all knew Olaf Jensen. Eager hands pointed up the road and I walked on into Northtown, alone.

I followed what passed for a main thoroughfare of trampled dirt. There was no pavement, no gutter, and the surface was scarred with dry water courses. The cement boxes dwindled over the slope ahead. At the top of the rise I had my first view over the centre of the township; a vast circle of the same box houses, rusting iron roofs, straight roads and a single brick building the size of a cinema.

Here, at an intersection, was an open space, a market crowded with Africans. Men and women turned away as I approached. Only the dirty, ragged children gathered, to stand and stare.

As I hesitated, a man in a worn but neat suit, a spotless collar and a chain across his waistcoat, approached. He raised his hat and stopped a few yards away. 'Sir, why do you watch us? The people are anxious. They hope you are

75

not come here to make trouble for them.' His eyes never left my face. They were alert, the eyes of a dog on the defensive, standing, paw raised, ready to run.

'I'm trying to find Mr. Jensen. Olaf Jensen of the Northtown Mission.'

'You friend of Mr. Jensen, sir?' There was no mistaking the lift of relief in the voice.

'Yes, I'm a friend of his,' I said to reassure him. 'Can you show me the way?'

A young African left the crowd and slouched across, hands in the pockets of his blue canvas trousers. He was wearing a red and green checked shirt, a yellow scarf, pink-rimmed sun-glasses and an orange jockey cap. His manner was as truculently self-assertive as any spiv's, anywhere.

'Why you walk so far? Where you left your car, boss?'

'Don't listen, please, to this man, sir. I take you to Mr. Jensen myself.'

'No need to do that,' I said. 'I only want directing.'

'Mr. Jensen lives far from here. Way, way down the hill. Maybe you can see the roof of the Mission. . . .'

'Not that brick building, is it? The large place in the centre?'

The young man, laughing raucously, explained that I was making a big mistake. The building in question was the Municipal Beer Hall.

By this time a group had gathered. A half-moon of black faces hemmed me in. I could not follow at all clearly the older man's involved and repetitive explanations.

'It would be better, sir,' he said at last, apologetically, 'if I were to go with you.'

'You're right,' I said, and told him to lead on.

My guide—his name, so he informed me at the first opportunity, was Mr. Mero—led me for half a mile down a steady slope between the dwellings. We passed a great many people and they all saluted him respectfully. Women came to their doorways to call after us. Children looked up from their games with small stones in the dust. We were now in the heart of the location and I felt the easier for his presence.

He walked, always, a few yards ahead and with the stick he carried flicked neatly from the roadway scraps of refuse that might otherwise have fouled my feet. At one point he came upon a shining empty tin and this he bent to retrieve, stuffing it into the pocket of his coat, careless of the bulge it made. The action slightly shocked me. (Once, in London, I had seen a well-dressed man stoop to gather up the stub of a cigarette.) Not far from the beer hall, which now loomed over us like an aeroplane hangar, we reached a crossing. Mr. Mero turned at right angles, took a few steps down this new—and to all appearances, exactly similar—street, and then stopped abruptly, planting his stick on the ground and staring ahead.

'We must go back, Sir,' he said when I came up with him. 'Much trouble this way.'

I saw that two open trucks were parked a few hundred yards along the street. White men in uniform were standing about near them.

'What's happening down there?'

'Police make raid, sir. Maybe search for weapons. Maybe want to take some people away. You don't know about police raids, sir?'

'Whereabouts is the Mission?'

'Mr. Jensen he lives other end this street. We go back, then round. Today not possible to go straight to his home.'

'The raid's no concern of ours,' I said. The sun was already high and hot and I felt I had walked far enough. 'You think the police have sealed off the area? I'll ask them, they'll probably let me through. No need for you to come any further.' I thanked him and held out a coin but he drew back, looking hurt, and again insisted that it would be foolish to go on.

'The police aren't after *me*,' I said, and left him.

Everything was very quiet. The men ahead lounged in the road. Doors were closed. No children played outside the houses. The African families of the neighbourhood had gone to ground.

I was within a stone's throw of the first truck when the police started a hare. There was a shout and a man dodged out from between two of the houses and ran up the street towards me, his frayed trousers flapping round his ankles. He ran clumsily, his head thrown back, gesturing with his hands as if urging himself on. Swerving, he vanished again among the houses, the police in pursuit. The next few moments were noisy and confused.

There were suddenly men in uniform everywhere, rounding up and driving towards the trucks a shouting, struggling group. Women were wailing, children screaming. I heard the thud of blows. Sticks cracked against skulls as the police laid about them. Out of the mêlée ran a girl of seven or eight, holding her face in her hands. She stumbled, pitched forward and lay where she had fallen. Feet pounded and trampled the earth not a yard from her body. I could not stand by and leave her lying there. Trying to pull her clear I was kicked violently on the side of the head.

I came to my senses perhaps a minute later. My head throbbed as I sat up. There was an arm against my back and looking round muzzily, I saw that Mr. Mero was on his knees in the dust behind me.

'You have recovered, sir?' he said. His voice was dismayed and anxious.

There was no sign of the girl. Everything was quiet again. Two policemen were coming down the street with the fugitive between them. They had their man securely handcuffed and were engaged in getting their own back. He was pushed without ceremony into the first of the trucks— already crowded with Africans. The arrest was over.

78

Casually swinging their truncheons, a few of the police sauntered my way. I stood up unsteadily to face them.

They were a tough-looking bunch, youths rather than men, loutish, coarse-grained. Though puzzled by my presence, they asked me politely enough how I felt. Then I was shouldered to one side while, six or seven strong, they closed round Mr. Mero in a menacing ring.

White men in Equatoria (as I had already had cause to realize) possess two quite distinct voices. One is normal. With it they conduct reasonable conversations with their fellow whites. The other is a snarl. On the whole, the blacks in the Republic are hectored, ordered about, sworn and shouted at by their white masters; rarely conversed with. I heard Mr. Mero plaintively endeavouring to put his case.

'Sir, I came in order to help this gentleman. Here is my Exemption Pass. My papers are perfectly in order. Please examine. . . .'

'You can use your eyes, can't you? You knew that Police Operations were in progress? You bloody educated nigs. . . .'

'Yes sir. I tried . . .'

'D'you live in this street? No! Then what the hell d'you think you're doing around here? Don't answer back, you white-collared bastard. It's the Station for you, this time. Into the truck!'

'But sir, I only came . . .'

'Did you hear what I said? Into the truck!'

I thought it was time I intervened. 'The man's done nothing wrong,' I said. 'He was showing me the way to the Mission.'

No one took the slightest notice. Mr. Mero stood in the centre of the group, still holding his wallet in his hand. Desperately, he looked from face to face.

'I never broke the law. I'm a respectable man, sir. Why you want to send me to prison?'

One of the young policemen took a pace forward and stood

very close to Mr. Mero, staring down at him, hands resting on his hips. There was a moment's silence. Suddenly and without warning, the man jerked up his knee and jabbed Mr. Mero in the fork. Mr. Mero doubled up and writhed on the ground, moaning quietly. The wallet and his papers were scattered in the dust.

'You damn swine!'

The man turned in amazement. He did not seem able to credit what he had heard. Slowly, his expression changed. His face reddened.

'Say that again.'

'I said you damn swine.'

'So that's the way it is! Nigger's friend. Stand up for the black bastard, would you?'

He walked in, his arms hanging loosely, his head thrust forward. The others closed round, barging and jostling.

'If you knock me about,' I said, 'there'll be trouble.'

'Where's your permit?' he asked abruptly. 'You're in a Native Location. I'll check your permit.' He saw me hesitate and nodded, satisfied. 'Got you, my beauty! Bring him along.'

There was a scuffle as the men on either side of me gripped and twisted my arms behind my back. I struggled, protesting. 'Shut your bloody mouth, will you?' said the same young policeman and hit me across the face.

'Steady, Jack! Not in front of the nigs. Wait till we get him to the Station.'

Mr. Mero drove in the back of one of the trucks, jammed in among the African prisoners. As the races had to be kept apart, I sat in the cab beside the driver. We arrived to find that the Officer in charge of the Station was out. This, perhaps, was unfortunate for the Sergeant.

I never saw what became of Mr. Mero and the others. As a white criminal I was given precedence and hauled, more roughly than was necessary, into the office where the

80

Sergeant sat behind his desk. He was a small, unprepossessing man. I remember that his breath stank and that the whites of his eyes were yellow. A bottle of digestive mixture stood on the desk beside his inkwell. His voice was querulous, permanently aggrieved. I cut short his initial bluster by demanding to be put through to the Ministry of Native Affairs.

Fortunately, the Minister remembered me. I held the telephone receiver a few inches from my ear and let the Sergeant have the benefit of the assured and masterful crackle.

'On the contrary,' I said, 'I'm not enjoying myself in the least. At the moment I'm under arrest. I'm talking to you from the police station attached to Northtown.'

There was a heartening explosion of surprise.

I explained that I had failed to apply for a permit to visit the location. I was unaware that such a regulation existed.

The regulation, said Mr. Groot, was purely a matter of form. There must be some mistake. He would like a word with the police. This was outside his department, but he could promise me that I would be released at once.

I described, briefly, what had happened. He tried to pass the matter off. A few of the latest recruits to the Force were, he agreed, over-enthusiastic in the performance of their duties. Disciplinary measures were taken, where necessary. I told him that they were admirable young Storm Troopers. Neither Mr. Groot nor the Sergeant liked this. I did not intend that they should.

I discovered that I was a free man. All most irregular, as the Sergeant was at pains to emphasize. I was guilty of a technical offence and in the circumstances it was his duty to charge me. However, the Minister was the Minister, and for once. . . .

I sat tight and demanded the immediate release of Mr.

Mero. For a quarter of an hour I argued, threatened, wore the Sergeant down. I had the young policeman fetched and questioned. In the end Mr. Groot's influence won the day and the Sergeant capitulated. There was, as yet, no written record of the morning's arrests and he fastened, for re-assurance, upon this particular aspect of the situation. I asked for transport and after a short struggle he agreed, grudgingly, to provide a car.

Mr. Mero entered the office in a rush, no doubt kicked from behind. He was dishevelled, breathless, one wing of his collar had broken away from its stud, his tie was screwed round and hung over his shoulder. A moment later and his hat, battered and shapeless, followed him through the open door.

The Sergeant, his face a ferocious mask, gave Mr. Mero to understand in the course of a prolonged and rhetorical diatribe that he was a filthy nigger, a lousy, lying black sodomite and an educated ape and warned him that unless he wanted the skin flayed off his buttocks he'd be wise, in future, to steer clear of trouble. . . . 'We've got our eyes on you, now, you low-down, dirty bastard. D'you understand that?' he shouted, banging the desk.

Composing his features, automatically moderating his voice, the Sergeant then wished me an unemphatic good morning.

The police car, acting on my instructions, drove us back into Northtown and dropped Mr. Mero by the market, at the point where I had met him rather less than an hour ago. I got out and we shook hands in the road. Mr. Mero was plainly overcome. I had to remind myself that, far from granting him a privilege, I had done the man an irreparably bad turn. The police were unlikely to forget that he had slipped their clutches.

'Goodbye sir,' he said, raising his battered hat. 'I cannot describe what this means to me.'

82

'Where's your stick?' I asked him. 'Don't tell me you've lost your stick?'

'My stick, sir!' Mr. Mero laughed, shrugged, waved an arm. The matter, he implied, was a bagatelle, a trifle not to be considered. He took my hand again and gazed into my face with absurd, unreasonably devoted eyes. His voice, when he spoke, was husky.

'I shall never forget your kindness to me this day,' he said.

I climbed back into the car, slammed the door. The driver let in the clutch with an unnecessary jerk and, bumping and jolting, we shot off down the slope towards the gate. (There was no time, now, to visit Olaf Jensen at the Mission. My 'plane left that afternoon at two o'clock.)

'It's types like you from overseas who spoil our niggers,' said the policeman at the wheel. He spat contemptuously through the open window.

IV

I WAS back in Banda late that afternoon and 'phoned Patricia from the Guest House. I was feeling curiously light-headed. Our conversation soon went off the rails.

'I don't understand,' I said, 'why you never told me you were once Groot's private secretary.'

'But Sebastian, *you* never told *me* you were going to interview the Minister.'

'Didn't I? I suppose I only knew at the last moment.'

'Did you have a good time?' she said, brightly conversational.

'Not particularly. One of your policemen kicked me on the head.'

After this, I had to explain what had happened. 'You never even mentioned that you *had* a brother,' I said, aggrieved again.

'Olaf,' she said, 'is a crank.'

This annoyed me.

'You'd rather he'd joined the police force?'

This annoyed her. Our exchanges grew crisper. In the end, she slammed down the receiver in a huff. I remembered, then, that we had not arranged to meet. I stood and looked at the telephone and debated whether to ring her again. But in my detached state it no longer seemed particularly important whether we met or not.

I left next morning, unexpectedly, for Hoyu, a hundred miles west of the capital, where I was to live for a few days, alone, at the Governor's bungalow on the shore of Lake

William. The idea was Lady Mountclair's. She had made the arrangements and I was only too glad to fall in with her wishes. The rest, I was told, would do me good and I would be free to concentrate on my report. The perfect place to work. Quiet. No interruptions. Lovely scenery and fresher air. . . .

The bungalow was all that Lady Mountclair had made it out to be, but I was not left in peace there. Soon after my arrival I learnt that Patricia had come to stay with the local District Commissioner, McDermott, whose wife, apparently, was an old schoolfellow of hers. Though I had the excuse of my work, it was inevitable that we should spend a good deal of time together. She kept off politics and put herself out to be charming.

The day before I was due to return to the capital, the McDermotts sprang a party. The invitation was carried from the District Commissioner's office by an African runner, who arrived on the terrace in front of the bungalow, panting noisily, a short stick in his hand. Wedged securely into the cleft was a folded piece of paper. I looked up, dazzled, from the blue water, took the stick, plucked out the paper, opened it and read the message.

Jollifications this evening. Mary feeling sociable. Come along at eight if you feel you can stand the racket. On no account tip the postman more than thirty cents. Wish to avoid inflation in my district. Alastair.

The runner stood beside me, his sweaty black chest lifting and subsiding, his breath coming less noisily. I went inside, rummaged through my pockets, could find only a Bandala florin, hesitated (there are a hundred cents to the shilling in Bandaland) then recklessly came out and pressed the silver coin into the man's hand.

'Don't you let on to Mr. McDermott!'

The runner, suitably overcome, popped the florin for

safety into his mouth and set off, loping steadily away along the lakeside path, each soft pad of his feet sending up a little spurt of dust from the sun-warmed ground.

A chain of clouds were towing their shadows over the green and bronzed slopes of the hills on the right, across the twenty-five-mile shining width of the lake—dwindling distantly to a narrow horizon, water without visible end—and hauling their anchors up the forested crags of the higher mountains to the left. I sat and watched them. The silence was complete.

After a while, 'Job,' I called, without looking round.

The head houseboy appeared in the doorway.

'I'll be going up to Hoyu after sundown. Tell Elias to have the car ready. Drive myself.'

'But Bwana, Elias gone Hoyu fetch Memsaab.'

'Of course he has! I'd forgotten I'd arranged that. And Job, is the water hot? I'd like a bath.'

'Not yet, Bwana. Soon ready.'

Job disappeared and not long afterwards a youngster, carrying a bundle of wood upon his head, ran down the path from the outbuildings. The blue surface of the lake deepened steadily as the sun dipped, falling towards the serrated edge of the Western Highlands. The hills were hazy in a cloak of gold.

I was still in the bathroom when the car returned. I came out on to the terrace, changed and fresh after the heat of the day, and found Pat sitting in one of the cane chairs. Under the trees it was already dark.

'I shouldn't have come,' she said. 'I ought to be helping. You can imagine what the house is like—upside down. You know, I can't understand Mary.'

'Why, don't you believe in parties?'

'You'd think she'd have her hands full enough, with the children and everything. And then to decide on the spur of the moment, like she does.'

86

'In my opinion, festivities need to be spontaneous.'

'But, Sebastian, we'd arranged to watch the fishing to-night.'

'Time for that too,' I said. 'Now that you *are* here. No point in arriving at the McDermotts until half-past eight or nine.'

'Good,' she said. 'As long as you hadn't forgotten.'

Job came out with the drinks. One of the servants carried from the bungalow a hissing pressure lamp. He hung the lamp on a nail hammered into the largest of the trees that in daytime shadowed the level grass terrace, and the intense white light turned the underside of the boughs into a cavern of green glass, vivid and unreal. The evening wind had sprung up, rustling the leaves.

'And how's Terence? Still feeling neglected?'

She shrugged impatiently. 'Why do you always have to drag in Terence?'

'If he wasn't so polite to me,' I said, 'I'd like him a great deal better.'

'Shut up, Sebastian! You're too damn pleased with yourself.'

'There go the boats,' I said, pointing. 'Here's to the night's catch.'

Moving slowly some distance beyond the band of trees at the lake's edge, a ball of fire burned on the blue-black water, vanishing behind a trunk, emerging again, keeping up a slow but steady progress from left to right. Another followed, and then another. The fires alone were visible. It was already too dark to distinguish the boats themselves.

'My favourite moment of the day. I shall find it hard to leave this place.'

'I wouldn't live here by myself if you paid me.'

'Why not, Pat?'

'Too lonely. Why, unless you went up to Hoyu you'd see no one, only natives, from one day's end to the other.'

'That worries you, doesn't it? I remember talking to a

87

girl on a farm next door to one of your Native Reserves in Equatoria. The drums kept her awake at night. Something to worry about, there. The haves and the have-nots. The old struggle. But here they're peaceful, well-behaved, polite. They've got their Father-Confessor in Alastair McDermott. The white man always has been a friend and ally. They're unnaturally respectful. I've never before been treated with such deference! I'm not used to it. Jack, in England, has been as good as his master for many years now. When I was sitting by the side of the road, this morning, before you came along, an African—sorry, native—pedalled up on his bicycle. As he drew level he jumped off, let the bicycle fall in the dust, bobbed and clapped hands and said his little piece and then pushed his machine yards down the road before mounting again. There's courtesy for you! Courtesy you take for granted.'

'It's not so bad for a man,' she said.

'Listen Pat! Can you hear them? Concert hour again.'

Through the hiss of the lamp and the soft shrilling of insects sounded the far dip and throb of music. In the village along the lake shore the young girls and boys, the children, were gathering together, had started to sing. Soon they would straggle up the path to the bungalow, group themselves below the terrace, out of range of the lamp, and serenade the Governor's guests. This was their custom.

'I heard them when I came back last night. Half-past eleven and going strong!' (Singing by the ashes of their cooking fires, too happy for sleep.) 'Someone really ought to collect their songs. Now that's a job I should enjoy! A trek through Bandaland with microphones and recording equipment. I've jotted down one or two of the tunes from memory. They come into my head when I'm trying to apply my mind to that confounded report. I wonder if I could interest anyone influential? What do you say? Pat, what a paradise this is! I can feel myself growing, putting down roots. I don't want to leave. I can't face the thought of Banda again, let alone London. I'm no longer fitted for pandemonium. You can laugh, but you know life here gives the ordinary man like myself stature, position, the feeling that he's somebody, that he's arrived. There are a lot of us in England, all scrambling competitively, fighting for money, position, fame, all cooped up on an island hardly longer than this lake. It's hard to emerge, feel yourself. And here! Why, position's flung into your lap! You're someone immediately, by virtue of one simple fact—the fact that you're white. I'm beginning to understand a little about your attitude, Julius Groot's attitude, the attitude of your country. Something I didn't understand before. What you have, obviously you want to hold. I can understand—but that's not to say that I excuse. There's no excuse for a great deal that goes on in Equatoria, as I've said before. The fact is—and the closer I get to working things out the more reactionary I find my standpoint—it takes *gentlemen* to make a success of race-relations. And the tragedy over there is that you don't appear to be breeding gentlemen. You're breeding toughs.'

'You're unfair,' she said. 'You're judging superficially. But at least you've grasped that there are two sides to the problem. As for the natives round this part, they still seem to know their place, I'll say that for them.'

'We're living in a backwater. If it was all like this, then there would be no problem. Sooner or later, the current will wash these people out into the main stream—and the more's the pity. I don't believe in progress any more. I want the African to stay simple and happy, contented with his station. As thoughtlessly happy as those children.'

The boys and girls had arrived below the terrace. Their voices were husky and untrained, they lacked crispness and attack, but while we listened there was always the feel of the great black lake lying out behind them, broad and long

89

as an inland sea and hung with a bright chain of fires. There was the smell of sunbaked earth exhaling after nightfall, the touch of the cool night wind that stirred the warm darkness. Their songs heightened my sense of the richness and mystery of tropical Africa. Without artifice, poignantly youthful, the children's voices spoke from the heart of the continent.

When at last we persuaded ourselves to move, a servant went ahead, holding up the lamp, and we negotiated a steep track that led from the boys' quarters, through the trees to the small beach. Our canoe was a gigantic dug-out, forty feet long and hollowed out of the trunk of a single tree. The crew rose to their feet—they had been squatting patiently on the shingle by the lake's edge—and lifted the leaf-shaped blades of their paddles. The fussy little lamp threw chests and shoulders into shining prominence. The shadowy dug-out, grounded on the beach, prolonged itself into the darkness.

There was an altercation among the paddlers. Voices were raised, the bright blade of a chopper winked in the light. Dropping his paddle, brandishing the weapon, one of the men leapt up the path and vanished. We heard him crashing and smashing about among the undergrowth and in another moment he returned holding an armful of freshly cut foliage. The fronds were arranged as cushions on the hard floor of the canoe, we clambered aboard, four of the paddlers jumped after us and two heaved at the flattened stern, leaping in at the last moment. We were afloat and the big dug-out was as steady as a rock in the water. Sitting on our cushions, it was barely possible to see over the inward-curving, smoothly worn wooden walls. Six paddles dipped, the men perched sideways on the bulwarks, the water rippled, the light of the lamp receded. With the third thrust of their blades, the paddlers began a rhythmic chant. One of the men startled us by extemporizing in a shrill falsetto, not unlike a cock-crow, and deep in their chests, vibrant as plucked bass strings, the others answered.

Minutes passed and the fires of the fishing fleet looked as far away as ever. The wind blew strongly now that we had left the shore and we could feel the rock and lift of the waves. Ahead, across the black water, glittered the chain of lights. The mountains were buried in the night, their slopes hidden, but where they crouched round us the sky was empty of stars.

'I was talking to one of the fishermen this morning,' I said. 'He came up to the bungalow to speak to Job. Job was able to translate. We discussed marriage and I found his point of view original. He told me he had four wives.'

'Is that a good idea?'

'There's a lot to be said for it. He was most enlightening. Two take charge of his house, cook his meals and bear his children. Incidentally, he inferred that it would be gross mis-management on his part if they became pregnant together. The others are business partners and help him with the fish. They empty the boat, spread out the catch to dry, fill the sacks. He sleeps most of the day. He gives them a commission of one sack in twenty to sell for themselves.'

'And what would you do with four wives, Sebastian? You haven't made up your mind to marry *one*.'

'Perhaps it's a question of safety in numbers. A lone wife is a gamble. With four—you can cover up your mistakes.'

As I spoke I saw my hands, her cheek, lit palely. The light from the fires had reached us. The shape of the canoe, the heads and shoulders of the paddlers, our own sprawled bodies slowly materialized out of the dark.

The crew thrust once more, then raised their paddles and momentum carried the dug-out in so close to the nearest of the fishing boats that we could smell the wood smoke and hear the crackle as the gusty breeze flattened the flames. An iron brazier jutted from the prow, a brazier filled with burning branches, and behind the fire, upright in a smother of sparks and smoke, stood the fisherman with lifted net. As we watched he struck, driving the net deep below the surface. Banging the pole across the side of the boat he levered up the catch, straining, pressing down, to tip aboard a glittering stream of fish. More wood was thrown between the prongs of the brazier, the flames leapt up, red-hot embers fell and sizzled in the lake. Round us reflections bobbed crazily and, as the fleet followed the shoal, the blown fires scattered across the water stippled the black night.

The District Centre of Hoyu is built like a citadel upon a hill. There are, however, no defences. The red-tiled homes and offices—linked each to each by a web of neat gravelled drives bordered by gum trees, jacarandas and scarlet flamboyants, drives efficiently signposted at each junction, so that no confusion is possible—are set out in the open and surrounded by smooth and pale-green acres of shaven grass. Every evening before sundown the slopes and swellings of this park-like hilltop echo to the click of golf balls and it is dangerous to venture out along the exposed avenues. African children wait their turn to be employed as caddies and amuse themselves knocking stones about with sticks shaped like clubs. At the foot of the hill, several hundred feet below the golf course, the main street of the town, lined along one side by a row of flat-roofed stores, slashes a dusty scar through the inevitable banana groves.

Pat and I drove the three miles up from the lakeside. A car was travelling ahead of us. Our headlamps made bright tunnels of the arching trees. Other cars were parked haphazardly outside the McDermotts' house and I turned the Humber and left it facing back the way we had come. On these occasions I prefer to take no chances. Windows were open, the verandah was brightly lit, the hum of many voices filled the warm night air. Mary McDermott caught

92

sight of us as we stood in the doorway and pushed her way through the crowd. She was plain, plump and cheerful, born in Smithville, a devoted mother of sons.

'I'm so glad you've come! How nice the two of you look together! What would you like to drink? I saw Alastair just now. . . . The eats are in the small room at the back, the cook-boy and I have been slaving for hours. Such fun! I recommend the vol-aux-vents, they're my creation entirely. Come through. You can help me find my husband.'

'Is Terence here?'

'Did you want to see him?'

'No, Mary. I wanted to avoid him.'

'Oh dear, I'm sorry.' A shadow crossed Mrs. McDermott's face. 'Always the same with Pat,' she told me, smiling up, her brow smooth again. 'She's much too attractive. The men *will* run after her. Never mind, darling, I don't think Terence will be a nuisance. I'm sure Sebastian will see to that.'

'Why,' I said, 'there's Douglas Cameron!'

'Yes,' she said. 'That's right. Mr. Cameron. The new Veterinary Adviser. Do you know him?' She lowered her voice. 'He's rather dreadful, isn't he?'

'I've met him in Banda. I'd no idea he was working down here.'

'He's come about our cattle. Alastair! *Alastair*!' she called, catching sight of her husband's shock of red hair. 'Say hullo to Pat and Sebastian. I've been so busy talking I haven't given them a drink.'

The District Commissioner was a reserved man, shy with strangers, dryly humorous if he knew and liked you. He took us each by an arm and propelled us towards the table under the window. 'Good to see you,' he said. 'Now, what's it to be?'

The room was hot and hazy. My shirt had already clung to my skin. Looking round, I saw nobody else I knew. Flies with inch-long bodies buzzed clumsily about the ceiling light, flopped between the bottles and glasses. Further up the table one of these insects had up-ended itself in a pool of spilt beer, where it wriggled until a fair youth who had been talking to Cameron flicked it over disinterestedly with the stub of a burnt-out match.

'Met a leopard on the Muboya road this afternoon,' McDermott was saying.

'Did you, Alastair?' said the tall, thin girl with a lined face, standing beyond Pat. 'I *wish* I could persuade Dick to shoot me a leopard.'

'I'm losing too many balls,' said a golfer behind us. 'It's my belief the caddies swallow them. The market rate for a mint ball has risen to ten stems of plantains. Enough to keep a family for a fortnight.'

My elbow was jogged. 'How's life?' said a fat red-faced man, squeezing himself to the table. 'You're H.E.'s guest, aren't you? What d'you do with yourself all day, down by the lake?'

'Writing,' I said. 'Not getting on very fast. Too many distractions.'

The fat man caught sight of Pat and winked. 'Was it the pair of you I saw trailing a line on the lake yesterday?'

'Sebastian wants to meet a crocodile.'

'Plenty up the creek by the island. Lying out on the mud banks. You want to go quietly. They're fast movers.'

There was a sudden diversion. A small and terrified monkey was loosed on the gathering. Squealing shrilly, the animal made a leap for a painting hanging on the wall, landing, paws together, to clutch the corner of the frame. But the picture tilted and the monkey leapt again, with a wail, far out into the crowd. Women screamed and put up their hands. A glass smashed on the floor. There was a moment's panic, then the crowd parted to let an elderly man pass through. The monkey was perching on his shoulder, thin long arms wound, as if for reassurance, about his neck.

'Such a shame,' said Mary McDermott, appearing beside us. 'Tiny was behaving beautifully and then some silly person offered him a lighted cigarette. Of course he went and grabbed it by the wrong end. Pat, my tummy's rumbling. Shall we encourage everybody into the next room?'

I was moving after them when Cameron came across and greeted me. 'How goes it, Pole? Heard you were in Hoyu. How long have you been around?'

'Five days,' I said. 'I'm staying by the lake.'

'Governor's got a bungalow down there, hasn't he? I've only seen the lake in the distance. My work takes me up into the hills.'

'They look very pleasant from water level.'

'Just like Scotland,' said Cameron. 'Wonderful country. Wish I could say wonderful people. Don't care for the African.' He drained his glass and helped himself to another drink. 'In no hurry to eat, are you? Between ourselves, things here are in one hell of a muddle. Can't understand what they've been up to.'

'What are you doing?'

'At the moment, cattle check. First things first. Dipping's been neglected. I was speaking to one of the Headmen only this afternoon. I told him straight. I said, "Your cattle haven't been dipped in a twelvemonth, they're lousy with ticks." I'm new to this country, Pole, but I know India and believe me, this is one stage worse! An eye-opener! The African peasant's bone-idle. Maybe they don't eat the right food. Maybe they are riddled with T.B. and hookworm, but the fact remains that from what I've seen of them they're a slack, incapable, gutless lot. There's just one thing they appear to respond to—and that's a kick on the backside.'

I told him he had made a mistake and come to the wrong

95

country. 'You'd get on like a house on fire in Equatoria. They speak your own language.'

He looked at me suspiciously over the rim of his glass and finished his drink. I stubbed out my cigarette and we followed the guests into supper.

Mary seized me, immediately afterwards.

'Bring your coffee with you,' she said. 'We must have a peep at the children. They're such cherubs when they're asleep.'

She led me along the bedroom passage. An African girl in a blue jersey, wearing an apron, was knitting in the middle of a room. She jumped from her chair when we came in. 'All quiet, Sophy?' The girl nodded, smiling awkwardly at the carpet. 'Then you'd better lend a hand in the kitchen with the washing up.' We put our cups on the chest of drawers and tiptoed into the room beyond. A band of light slanted through the open door and I could see the two small beds and the cot standing round the walls. Duncan, aged five and a half, Robert, three years old and Donald, eighteen months, were sleeping peacefully.

I knew this freckly crew, had played noisy and disorganized games with them on the family verandah. They possessed voices like bullfrogs, screams like engine-whistles, the shades of their hair ranged from lemon yellow to Titian red. They were destructive, uncontrollable, three wayward particles of the elemental life force. Quietly sleeping under their sheets they looked like angels. Their faces were pale—as all English children in the tropics are pale. Freckles powdered their waxen skin. Their cheeks were crumpled, their lips pouted, they breathed steadily through the swell and fall of voices at the other end of the house. 'I took three jiggers out of Duncan's toes, today,' Mary whispered. 'They will run about without shoes on!' We tiptoed out of the room again and carefully closed the door.

'Don't they need nets?'

'Not up here. Look at us, all our windows open. It's different down by the lake.' We had retrieved our coffee cups but Mary made no move to go. Instead, she shut the other door and turned to face me. 'Sebastian, I want to have a word with you. It's about Patricia.'

'What about Patricia?'

'Now don't jump down my throat! I've known Pat a great deal longer than you have. She's a dear, but she can be as stubborn as an old mule. . . .'

'So her mother said.'

'Her *mother*! You've met Mrs. Jensen?'

'I looked her up when I was in Smithville.'

'Then *that's* all right. I expect she told you about—about Pat's background. All she's been through.' She paused, as if waiting for me to say something. 'Pat's been unhappy enough and now there's a chance, perhaps—why, I thought it would be too cruel if for want of a word from me. . . .'

'A chance, Mary?' I looked down into her face. 'What *is* all this? Are we going around looking like an engaged couple?'

She stared up, dismayed. 'Sebastian! I've not made a fool of myself, have I? But you looked so happy together, I've never seen Pat more radiant. Alastair remarked the same thing.'

'All right, we look happy. That's fine, isn't it? What more d'you want? You married women!' I said, half joking, half in earnest. 'Your one ambition in life is to see your friends wedded off and comfortably settled. You're match-making, Mary. Admit it!'

'I'm doing nothing of the sort. I'm not trying to hurry you or make up your minds for you, but I did think it was my duty to help. Match-making indeed! I've got eyes in my head. I'm sure you're bluffing, Sebastian. Why did you arrange to meet her in Hoyu?'

'But I did nothing of the kind.'

'Well, all I can say is, she came because of you. We've never managed to persuade her before. Until you arrived. Then she sent me a wire and was here almost before I had time to open it. Why, Sebastian, I've scarcely *seen* her these last few days.'

There was an awkward silence. I fiddled around with my coffee cup.

Mary McDermott was angry. She walked up and down the room, taking short quick steps. Then she sat heavily on the chair in the middle of the carpet and propped her head in her hands.

'I suppose I was silly to build castles in the air. I've always felt sorry for Pat, she's had a rotten deal one way and another, and we both liked you. You're so good with the children, and somehow it seemed natural that the right man should have come along at last. She was in love with Groot all the time, you know. And now there's this boy Terence. I've never felt he had a chance. . . .'

Her shoulders were hunched. She was utterly deflated.

We returned to the front room, smokier and noisier than ever, and I poured myself a drink. I saw Pat's blonde head in the crowd and hovered on the fringe of the party, marking time. Cameron came up again and ostentatiously drew me aside.

'Just had a chat with the Jensen girl.' After a pause, he added, 'Personally, I like a woman with some meat on her. Still, she's a nice little thing. You've done well for yourself.'

I asked him what he meant by that. He stared into my face and laughed. He had bold good looks. Thick eyebrows, dark cheeks and chin. I realized that I had always disliked him.

'You've played your hand better than I have. I'll admit to you, Pole, I'm in a damned awkward spot.' I tried to interrupt, but he cut me short. 'For Christ's sake, isn't it plain the way things are with you? You've got her where you want her, haven't you? Ready to sit up and beg?'

98

I put my hand on his chest and shoved him against the wall. 'Go to hell,' I said and went through the open door and out on to the empty verandah.

I stood on the verandah and looked into the garden. Under the lace canopy of a pepper tree, hard by a hedge of rampant plumbago, stood a couple as silent as statues, locked in one another's arms. They did not move as I walked along the path and turned down the road to the car.

I had smoked two cigarettes and Job had brought me a nightcap when, from the terrace, I heard the sound of a car travelling fast down the hill. The headlamps swept a sword of light over roof and tree tops, there was a screech of brakes violently applied, the slam of doors, the sound of voices. I waited, wondering who had arrived. I might have guessed. Douglas Cameron came stumbling down the steps from the bungalow and advanced across the grass with Pat on one arm and a woman of his own on the other. He was Macheath to the life. I waited for the opening bars of *Thus I stand like the Turk, with his Doxies around*, but instead, 'So this is your Lakeside Love Nest,' he shouted. 'Put 'em down on the table. *Lete soda, ice. And lete bilauri ine. 'pese!*' This last impatiently to the boy who was following behind them, a bottle in each hand.

'Why did you run away, Sebastian?' said Pat, disengaging herself and sitting beside me.

'Snug little place,' said Cameron, staring about him. 'Suit us down to the ground, wouldn't it, Janet?' He slapped her bottom and Janet laughed rather breathlessly. 'Is there a bathing beach? Good swimming?'

'If you don't mind sharing it with the crocodiles,' I said.

'What are all those lights across there? A pier?'

'Good heavens, man, where d'you think you are? Southend?'

'Ndagaa fleet,' said Pat. 'They fish with fire. We went out to watch them before the party. In a canoe.'

'Did you, too? Must do the same, one evening. Where's that blasted boy?'

He bellowed and the boy came running. Then Job hurried out with cushions for the cane chairs. I looked at them in surprise. I had never seen those cushions before.

'Very nice, too,' said Cameron, relaxing, stretching his legs. He opened a silver case, offered round cigarettes. Pat took her lighter from her handbag.

'Half a dollar it doesn't work first time,' said Cameron at once. Pat snapped back the catch. There was a click. 'Thanks,' he said, reaching out his hand. 'Easy money.'

'Douglas,' said Janet, 'I'm sure you oughtn't to have taken those bottles.' She was a timid girl with large, dark eyes.

'Why not? We'd have drunk as much if we'd stayed.'

'But that's not the same thing.'

'Plenty of drink down here,' I said. 'No need to have lifted McDermott's.'

'Good. It'll come in handy.'

'I suppose it will,' I said, 'if you intend to make a night of it.'

Cameron grinned and pinched Janet's knee.

Moths were whirling about the lamp and the spots of their shadows flickered over the table.

'I'll have water with mine,' said Pat, as he knocked the cap off a soda bottle. Cameron bellowed for *margi baridi*.

'You haven't wasted much time picking up Swahili,' I said.

'Languages are never any trouble to me. Same in India. Soon had a smattering of Hindustani. Mind you, I peg away.' He pulled a small green phrase book from his pocket. 'Some of the exercises are damn funny. Listen to this!'

'Anything the matter, Sebastian?' said Pat quietly.

'Of course not.'

'Sir, I am ill of fever, at night I vomited and gave off much perspiration, sleep did not hold me.'

'You might have told me you were leaving.'

'Boy, my razor is spoilt, it will not cut even a little and my scissors likewise, they are still dirty with your black hairs.'

'I found myself on the verandah and slipped away while the going was good.'

'Put some lemon juice and water into a tumbler, stir it well and give it to the policeman. The latrine is full of fleas. His porters have eaten meat until they were completely gorged. The European pig—how's that, eh?—the *European pig* has fallen into a pit. A hippopotamus has destroyed our hut. Sir, give me a safety-pin to take the insects out of my feet.'

Janet and Douglas Cameron were leaning back and shaking with laughter.

'Another car,' I said. 'Who's this coming?'

We watched the beam of the headlights.

'I have an awful hunch,' said Pat, 'that it's going to be Terence.'

She was right—it *was* Terence. He came down the steps, hanging his head sheepishly, disconcerted to find the four of us sitting round the table. 'Quite a party,' he said. 'Mind if I join you?' He was a tall, thin young man with a finely-cut, mournful face, a dejected stoop.

'Come along, Bug-hunter,' said Cameron. 'Take a pew.'

The servant, without waiting to be asked, brought an extra glass and more ice on a tray and retired to hover in the background, between the trees.

'Smoke?' said Cameron. Terence accepted a cigarette, brought out his lighter. 'Half a dollar it doesn't work first time!' Terence paused, stared from under his forelock, thinking it over. 'Right you are,' he said. There was a click and a guffaw from Cameron.

'How much d'you make a year?' I asked.

We were a curious quintet, all at sixes and sevens with each other. For a while I did my best to talk to Terence. The young Pest Control Officer was as punctiliously monosyllabic as usual; as usual he never looked at me but kept his head averted. Cameron grew steadily rowdier. Janet laughed and gasped, wriggled and squealed hysterically, but her round dark eyes were anxious. Pat, who was bored by Terence, had not yet forgiven me for abandoning her. I had a conscience as far as she—and Terence—were concerned and hated Cameron's guts. There was really nothing to do but to drink.

Cameron pitched the second empty bottle into the darkness. 'Governor stands treat!'

I called for Job.

'*Lete chupa whisky, chupa gin,*' said Cameron. 'That should do for a start. We'll drink the old boy's health, blast him.'

'Job,' I said, 'understands English.'

'How d'you get on with Sir Chris?'

'Barely,' I said. 'I scrape home.'

Janet took advantage of the lull to escape from the table. 'Bathroom's third door on the right, along the passage,' I called after her as she followed Job into the bungalow. Cameron looked up absently, leaned sideways.

'Know what he said to me?'

Terence had crossed behind my chair, sat himself down on Pat's far side. Cameron cleared his throat and in a whisper exaggerated the Governor's precise, pedantic manner of speech.

' "Mr. Cameron, although there is still, unfortunately, a great deal of work for you to do at headquarters, I am sending you to a country station where, I feel sure, you will be able to indulge your social proclivities to the full." You know those hooded eyes of his? He looked at me like an octopus.'

'So you've been thrown out of Banda for being too sociable?'

'I've been edged out,' he said, 'and I wasn't to blame. He should keep that woman of his on a lead.'

Job arrived with the drinks. As soon as he had retired, Cameron glanced round, pushed his head towards mine, lowered his voice dramatically. 'I tell you, Pole, she bitched me.'

'Very nice for you,' I said.

Cameron fingered his glass, strangely subdued. 'Yes and no,' he said. 'Got to think of my career.'

'Mind you, I can't speak from experience, but I always assumed that the element of risk involved was part of the attraction.'

'Risk!' said Cameron. 'I've taken a few risks in my time and I'll take 'em again if there's a sporting chance I'll get away with it. But in my frank opinion, mucking about with the wife of the man who's governing the country where you happen to work isn't a risk—it's suicide.'

'I'm absolutely with you,' I said.

Cameron looked at me morosely.

'She's damn fascinating. I was ready enough for fun and games, stand by the rules. Saw the red light. . . . Did you hear about Blackett?'

'Blackett?'

'He was pitched out of Bandaland. Right out on his ear. No fun, that, you know. I'm in my early forties. Made a go of things.' And he muttered something offensive about the young wives of old men. 'If she's not careful she'll have me selling matches in Piccadilly Circus.'

'What are you doing with Janet?'

He looked surprised. 'She's all right, isn't she? Picked her up at the party.' His face in the pale glare of the pressure lamp was the face of a screen hero past his prime. He held out his glass. 'I've always wanted women,' he said blusteringly, with a return of the old manner. 'And I'll make no bones about it, Pole. Women have always wanted me.'

Janet came back. We went on drinking and the subsequent events of the evening are hazy. I remember that Terence came out of his shell and did some extraordinary things with a box of matches and that he then performed so brilliantly upon the mouth-organ he pulled from his pocket that we had the entire staff of the bungalow and their wives and relatives standing round in an enchanted circle. Across the lake the fires of the Ndagaa fleet grew red and dim; the boats turned for home. The wind lost itself among the thick leaves of the trees. Then the lamp suddenly started to burn bright and dim, bright and dim, like the beam of a revolving lighthouse and Job took it away and brought out candles. Their soft light suited our mood. Pat's head was resting on my shoulder, my arm was round her waist and we talked drowsily until Cameron dropped a piece of ice inside Janet's dress and groped to retrieve it while she flapped and twisted like a landed fish. Her screams must have roused the village. I beat back the mists, struggled against inertia, decided that it was time the party came to an end.

We wandered round the bungalow, gathered by the cars. 'Can you drive yourselves back?' I said. They were a long while saying goodbye, climbing aboard. Before she got in, Pat put up her face to be kissed. 'Sure you're all right? I can wake Elias.' No one paid any attention. Engines hummed and they jerked forward, one behind the other. Standing alone in front of the bungalow I watched their tail lights smothered by quickly rising clouds of dust.

I walked carefully to my room and after a brief and inconclusive encounter with the mosquito net succeeded in getting my legs up. I must have fallen asleep almost at once. The sun woke me. My mouth was dry and there was a pain behind my eyes. Sitting up, I found that for the first time in my life I had gone to bed with my shoes on.

V

ON my return to Banda I was informed, through the P.R.O., that the Omuvomo wished to meet me.

'Had to promise to get in touch and fix something up,' said Gardener. He sounded, I thought, most dubious. 'Mind you, Charles is a delightful young fellow—but irresponsible. University education's gone to his head. With any luck he'll marry and sober down in time.'

A large white envelope, heavily embossed, was brought round later to the Guest House. I was invited to tea at the Palace at four o'clock that afternoon.

The Palace at Banda, prim and properly Edwardian, tries to ignore its surroundings of elaborate basket work. I had driven up the winding approach from the city, swept through palisades of woven reed (barefoot sentries leaping to attention, each in his thatched box), and Elias, standing between the stained-glass windows of the porch, had pulled the knob of what, incontestably, was a most ordinary looking door bell. After the neo-classical pretentiousness of Government House, this was a change for the better. A servant opened the door. Behind the servant stood the Private Secretary, inclining respectfully forward. And behind the Private Secretary stood a slim, lanky, chocolate young man in a flannel suit. Modest, entirely self-possessed, his accent impeccably Oxford, this was Charles M'Toki, King of Bandaland.

I was led into a room filled with period furniture. There were enough pieces here to stock a dealer's gallery. The Omuvomo ran his fingers along the polished mahogany lid of a serpentine commode.

'I have a weakness for antiques,' he said. 'As you see, I made the most of my years in England. Your shops are magnificent. Such a mass of lovely old things.' He sighed. 'We have nothing like them in Banda. There were many in Oxford, but on my travels I visited a town called Bath. Perhaps you know Bath? You do? Then you will understand. I stayed there a week and after that I had no more money. Luckily I had a return ticket to Oxford.' He jingled the loose change in his trouser pocket, pleased to remember how foolish he had been. 'That Tudor chest I bought in Bath, Mr. Pole, and the Queen Anne secretaire and the Sheraton card table against the wall over there. The mirror between the windows is reputedly Chippendale.'

Brass handles shone, carefully tended woods glowed, but curiously enough the legs of the tables, tallboys, chests and secretaires were each set carefully in a small, earthenware crock.

'The ants,' said the Omuvomo. 'We have to take our precautions. The palace is not immune. One would hardly expect it. They've had the nerve to invade Government House!' And he jingled his change again and grinned like a schoolboy.

Tea was carried in on a tray by a tall servant. A boy followed behind with a cake stand. There were tomato sandwiches, biscuits and two kinds of cake. The teapot and cups looked as if they would be happier inside a display cabinet.

The servant poured out, then fell on his knees to hand tea to the King. He rose from the carpet to give me my cup and the boy in his turn dropped to the floor with the plate of sandwiches. At that moment the door opened to admit the Private Secretary. He said something in Landala which annoyed the Omuvomo.

'*Really!* We've hardly begun our tea! It's the Prime Minister. He suggested that you might like to meet a few of his colleagues. I particularly told him, not before five.' He glanced at his watch. 'They're early. Most unusual. Tell them they must wait.'

The Secretary turned to deliver the message. The movement was misinterpreted. A phalanx of elderly Ministers broke through the doorway. Abruptly and of one accord they fell forward and knelt in the centre of the carpet.

'Quick!' said the Omuvomo as the servants hurried across to remove the tea things. 'Have a slice of cake before it's taken away.'

Introductions were soon over. I noticed that only one or two of the Ministers were dressed like the King in European suits. The rest wore robes. One and all they radiated an air of portentous solemnity. They grouped themselves, plates and cups were cleared from the tables (the Omuvomo hurriedly munching chocolate cake), and a short speech of welcome was addressed to me in hesitant English by the larger of the two men on the sofa. I thanked them, the large man turned to the King and relapsed into Landala, gesturing with his hands, and the business of the afternoon was on.

'The Chancellor,' the Omuvomo translated, 'wishes you to know that the Bandala Cabinet is not happy about this proposed irrigation project in the Nwambe desert. They do not feel that the Governor has given them sufficient opportunity to air their views. They are strongly of the opinion that the project is not in the best interests of Bandaland. For several reasons. Better ways can be found of spending the money, here in this country. We need another cotton ginnery, more schools, a technical college. If the Renduyu are hungry, then the Republic must feed them.'

'The Renduyu must learn to grow thin,' said the heavily-built Minister in the dark blue suit.

His remark, translated, was well received. Heads nodded round the circle.

'Have your Ministers nothing more constructive to say?'

Apparently they had not.

'There have always been lean years, years of famine,' said the same Minister. His English was almost as good as the King's. 'Hunger is nothing new.'

The Chancellor spoke again, as rapidly as before.

'There is another reason for their dislike of the project,' said the Omuvomo. 'They feel that the desert is an essential barrier between this country and our neighbour, the Republic. To allow the Renduyu to inhabit the Nwambe would, in effect, bring Equatoria and a white administration of which we do not approve within the very gates of Bandaland. Already the people of Smithville talk of Federation. They demand that our countries should be united under *their* flag. For our people, this would be an irreparable disaster. We should lose what small measure of freedom we possess. Our crops would go to feed the Renduyu. We should be plunged into slavery.'

'Tell them,' I said, 'that Parliament will never hand over Bandaland. They can forget the idea. Such a thing could never happen.'

The Omuvomo translated. The assurance was received sceptically with shoulder shruggings and restless movements.

'Britain is no longer all-powerful. Equatoria has modern weapons, guns, tanks. . . . We have a few battalions of the Queen's African Rifles.'

'There is no sense in this talk,' I said. 'Equatoria is an independent Republic. Her army and air force are for her defence. She would never declare war on a peaceful neighbour. Why should she wish to invade your country? There is no gold in Bandaland.'

'But there is food.' The fat Minister spoke again. 'Bananas, corn. Corn is our gold.'

The conversation that followed added nothing to what had been already said. The fear of Equatoria, the instinctive dislike of the Bandala for the Renduyu, the reluctance to see money spent outside the country, these were reiterated. Solemnly they gyrated in a waltz of ideas that was becoming tedious. In the end the Omuvomo struck a new note and on this note the gathering broke up.

'What we have to consider, I feel, is this,' he said. His voice, now that he was not merely repeating the phrases of his Ministers, took on a quiet tone of authority. 'Hunger, as Mr. Kigoma expressed it, is nothing new. No more is danger. Today, we live in the presence of both. There is little that is certain in this world, but I agree with Mr. Pole that while we remain a Protectorate within the British Commonwealth we shall not be sacrificed to the Republic. Nevertheless, there is still the point—and how I wish some of our impatient young politicians would take note of the fact—that during the last riots in Banda two Republican battalions and their armoured brigade were alerted and disposed along the frontier.

'We must ask ourselves, therefore, a question. Will the settlement of the Renduyu in the Nwambe disturb our own political equilibrium and precipitate a rising? Some say it will, but I say not necessarily, provided the causes and the reasons are sufficiently well explained. We shall not always remain a Protectorate. One day we shall be masters in our own house.' (He was translating his remarks, sentence by sentence, and for the first time the frowns, the dubious pouting of thick lips, the wrinkled foreheads relaxed and heads were vigorously nodded.) 'But is that the summit of our ambitions? The situation must be faced realistically and if the phrase "Africa for the African" is to be something better than a pipe dream then the sooner we can forget our

109

differences and help one another forward, the better. We have just had presented to us by the Governor an unique opportunity of assisting our neighbours, the Renduyu, to raise their standard of life. Food, in this instance, must come before freedom; but if we act wisely, one day freedom, perhaps, may come as well. I will leave you, gentlemen, to think the matter over.'

'I shall not move them,' he confided to me as soon as the Ministers, falling upon their knees once again and retreating in a group backwards, had left the room.

His modesty was disarming. What had the Governor said to me? 'You cannot, Mr. Pole, persuade a train of mules to negotiate a difficult trail by walking a hundred yards ahead of them. The Omuvomo has not yet learnt to get behind his Ministers and *whack their rumps*.'

I was sitting in the garden of the Guest House that evening, with Patricia, when Martha Bifabishu was announced. I was not expecting her, she had sent no message, and her sudden arrival took me by surprise. I suppose that, slightly flurried, I did the wrong thing. I told the boy, why yes, she had better come out to us. Pat did not say anything. Soon afterwards the boy reappeared, walking across the grass in front of the tall Miss Bifabishu, who topped him by several inches. I stood up as she approached, greeted her, turned to introduce Patricia. Patricia still did not say a word but lifted her light basket chair, swivelled round, sat down again with her back to us, picked up a magazine from the grass and began to flip over the pages. Her rudeness was controlled, deliberate —and impossible to disguise. Miss Bifabishu, I thought, behaved extraordinarily well.

We sat down together, a short distance apart, and to break the silence I asked after the children.

She said that they had not forgotten my visit, adding that she would always be happy to see me at the kindergarten. But this was not the reason why she had called.

'You may remember,' she said, 'I told you about my brother, Samueli. Since then I have spoken to him. You must know, Mr. Pole, that he mistrusts the English here in Bandaland. But you, a visitor, a guest in our country, he is ready to see. I would like you, if you would consent, to meet him. It is important for Samueli to exchange views with a man like yourself, a man from London, detached from our background. He is too much with excitable young people. He is their leader. Because he has suffered imprisonment, because he has been deported. . . .' (She was speaking so quietly that I could only, with difficulty, catch her words.) '. . . he has become their hero. To be a hero for one year, for two years, is bad for a man. Samueli has suffered. But he will listen to you. Perhaps,' she said, her eyes on the distant landscape beyond the feathery plumes of the gum trees, 'you will be able to teach him moderation.'

I said I would be pleased to meet her brother, but that she must not expect too much. At the same time I remembered Lady Mountclair's strictures and decided that it would be tactful to keep this visit dark. We arranged a time and place. Three o'clock at her house on the following afternoon. She wrote out the address carefully, adding in Landala a few instructions for the driver; then got up to go. I walked with her to the Guest House and before saying goodbye, apologized for what had occurred. Then I went back into the garden.

Pat was still reading. She did not raise her eyes from the magazine and I stood over her, staring down at her smooth, blonde head.

'You monstrous little savage,' I said at last. 'How can you do such things?'

She would not look up.

'What goes on in this country,' she said, 'is none of my business, but I *don't* shake hands with natives.'

'Pat,' I said, 'there are certain civilized standards of behaviour. You could make an effort to be polite.'

'*Polite!*' She looked up at last. Her face was pale and pinched. I saw that she was quivering with anger. 'Why did you ask that girl into the garden? *I* was here, wasn't I? You could have talked to her inside.'

'Never occurred to me. Why Pat, you sat in the same room with the African editors at the Press conference. I don't recollect that you put yourself out to insult them. And if you objected so strongly to Miss Bifabishu's presence in the garden, you could always have got up and gone.'

'The Press conference was not a social occasion. My position there was made perfectly clear. And now you're asking me to make way for a native? How dare you, Sebastian! You've no right to suggest such a thing.'

I stared at her hopelessly. 'Pat,' I said, 'you must try to learn. . . .'

She jumped up at that, her face twisted. 'Learn!' she cried. 'It's for you to learn—how to behave! You *don't* ask natives to sit down with whites. You *don't* talk to native girls in front of white women. You've just insulted me, can't you understand? Rubbed me in the dirt.' She suddenly crumpled up the magazine and flung it at my head. 'I'd have sooner you'd slapped my face!' she shouted and stamped a foot.

'Pat,' I said, 'control yourself.'

'Don't come near me,' she said, retreating. 'Don't touch me. Take your filthy hands away. If you touch me, I shall scream.' We stood a yard apart, looking at each other. Her eyes were brilliant. Her small, sharply-pointed breasts lifted as she breathed. 'You'd dare to paw me after touching that black ape! You're disgusting. I wish to God I'd never met you. All along you've made me feel cheap, Sebastian, and now I hate you for it. Hate you!'

Her mouth puckered. She turned and walked quickly away across the garden.

'Pat!' I cried. 'Come back. Don't be ridiculous. *Pat!*'

I took a few steps after her; then stopped and watched her go.

Although we followed her instructions, Martha Bifabishu's house was difficult to find. Elias was confident enough when we left the Guest House. He flashed his white teeth, gave me his usual salute and assured me that we should be there in fifteen minutes. Twenty-five minutes later we were still searching.

He had left me in the car while he investigated a narrow lane on foot. There was little motor traffic in this quarter of the city, but a great many cyclists went by. Husbands pedalled soberly, wives in their long gowns draped sideways over the carrier. Sometimes three, once four, men passed, piled on to a single machine. Two buxom Bandala mothers, babies strapped to their backs, loitered by the side of the road. The curly heads of the children lolled from the coloured scarves that supported their bodies, rolling from side to side as the mothers shook and humped themselves and walked up and down outside the window, peacock-coloured skirts sweeping the dust. Pleased as Punch, they seized every opportunity to show off their infants, calling out to each other, laughing, putting fingers to big lips, peeping at me coyly before relapsing into giggles again.

I remembered I had in my wallet a photograph of my nephew, my sister's year-old boy, and not to be outdone I brought it out and pressed the picture against the window. The mothers were intrigued; approached, however, with the greatest caution. Their broad, glossy faces shone like dancing pumps. They wriggled their bare, plump shoulders and edged forward. Their skin glistened in the sunlight like black satin.

Elias, in his smart khaki-drill uniform and peaked cap, came striding down the lane and scattered them like farm-yard fowls.

'House this way, sah. Road too small for car. Bwana must walk.'

The women followed behind. I could hear them still chattering and laughing and at one point Elias, evidently stung by a taunt, turned and answered them back. The sun burned through my coat and shirt. The heat bounced up from the red earth, rippled off the mud walls. Old people sat in the shade, leaning back against the eastern sides of the huts, and stared at us as we passed. Small children ran to their mothers and peeped round their skirts. Men greeted me politely, lifting topees or trilby hats. '*Jambo, Bwana. Jambo.*' The smooth green leaves of banana palms arched over thatched roofs. Hens squawked and scratched. There were pools of grey ash on the ground, strewn cooking pots, home-grown tobacco neatly laid out to cure.

Then the lane opened into a space—I cannot describe it as a square—surrounded by much larger huts and some small houses with netted verandahs and windows. A few dusty flamboyant trees grew on the open ground between the houses and an attempt had been made, with stones and plants and netting, to make a garden. Everything here was primly neat and tidy, in distinct contrast to the cheerful squalor lower down the slope. And the third house on the left was Martha's.

The small square room behind the verandah was crowded. I had expected to see Martha and her brother, but here were ten or eleven young men and three young women. The men were dressed casually, student-fashion. In spite of the heat they wore hairy tweed coats, roll-top jerseys. The girls wore bright cotton frocks, modern style. I hardly recognized the sober Martha Bifabishu in her off-duty dress.

114

Samueli was an older man than the others and he alone was fluent and entirely self-confident. He at once took charge. Everyone was standing about awkwardly. The atmosphere was constrained.

'Glad to meet you. Take that chair please. I must apologize for bringing you this end of town, but I have to be careful where I go and with whom I'm seen—no offence, I assure you! We shall talk freely here. You'd better perhaps meet Jacob Mankele.' One of the young men bobbed forward. 'He's engaged to my sister Martha. She's busy with other people's children, too busy to marry him, so Jacob has to be patient. No need to trouble about the rest. How shall we describe them? *Comrades*? Or possibly that doesn't suit your political tastes, Mr. Pole?'

I was faced with a circle of wide grins.

'You're at liberty to call yourselves what you like,' I said, and Martha rounded smartly on her brother and told him not to be provocative.

A table, a plain sideboard, a few upright chairs, two basket chairs (in one of which I was sitting); what furniture Martha possessed had strangely little character. The books in the small bookcase, a pair of coloured reproductions (a Raphael Madonna and a Van Gogh cornfield), some small pieces of carved wood, through these belongings, and inadequately, she impressed her personality upon her surroundings. I felt that I had strayed into a room in a students' hostel; into furnished 'digs.'

We talked, at first, about London. Samueli knew Bloomsbury. Malet Street, Gower Street, Charing Cross Road, the Y.M.C.A., and the Tottenham Court Road Corner House—these were his old hunting grounds.

'I can still feel the fog,' he said, putting his hand under his chin. 'The fog in the throat. Because of the cold I did not do much work. I was lucky to get my degree. When I heard that I had passed I went up to Oxford and celebrated the event with the Omuvomo, who was then in his first term. We got gloriously drunk together.'

I told Samueli I had met the King.

'Charles,' he said, 'is a very agreeable fellow. We have a nickname for him in our own language. We call him the looking-glass man. Not because he is proud of his appearance, but because he so perfectly reflects the Governor's moods.'

This sally earned a chuckle of laughter from the young men gathered round.

'Samueli,' said Martha, 'you know that is not kind.'

'When Sir Christopher smiles, Charles smiles. When Sir Christopher is angry, then Charles also is very angry. He is a dear chap and absolutely useless and, what is more, he knows it. I believe he considers himself an expert on antique furniture. You found his taste good?'

'His taste,' I said, thinking of the crowded drawing-room, 'is catholic.'

'That is only natural. In these fields you can hardly expect us to be selective. Not yet. Look at my sister's pictures! I do not pose as an authority, but tell her, Mr. Pole—she may believe you—that it is not really done to place together in the same room the work of two artists of different periods and conflicting styles.'

Martha glanced up at the wall, then looked at me anxiously.

'What is done or not done,' I said, 'seems beside the point. This is Martha's house and she must live with the paintings she chooses to live with. They may not always satisfy, her taste may change, but it's not for anyone else to try and change it for her.'

'Admirable,' said Samueli, rolling his large and prominent eyes to the ceiling. 'You English have the knack. You're natural diplomatists. That's why you so often drive us hopping mad. You make your unreasonable demands sound so disarmingly reasonable.'

116

He spoke with a certain significance. To prompt him I asked for chapter and verse.

'I take it,' he said, 'you've met the Public Relations Officer? An old ass called Gardener.'

I said that I had.

'Have you ever spoken to any of our editors?'

'Only at a Press conference. Not individually.'

'With Gardener present?'

I nodded.

'Then you will have learnt nothing. And I want you to be under no illusions. Our Press is shackled. The editors of our Landala language newspapers are gagged and bound. Not literally—that wouldn't be fair play—but quite as effectively. Let us take the case of my friend Mr. Lobole.'

'Lobole?' I said. 'Wasn't he among the men I saw?'

'Very likely. Now Lobole is not a moderate. He owns and edits our most advanced paper. As an Englishman I would not necessarily expect you to subscribe to his views, but if you knew him as well as I do you would recognize his qualities. He is, above all things, courageous and enterprising. He has a nose for corrupt practices. A short while ago he conducted a most interesting enquiry into aspects of our cotton industry. The state of affairs he revealed was deplorable. He was doing an excellent service to the country. But he published a number of allegations, not all, in the opinion of the Governor, justified. When this happens, as it frequently does, the editor is asked to visit the Public Relations Officer for an informal chat. At Lobole's interview, taking up a copy of his report, Gardener said something like this.'

(The young Africans were leaning eagerly forward. The room was quiet.)

' "Look here, my dear fellow, you know this won't do, won't do at all. You must remember your responsibilities. Your attack is malicious and unjustified and—and not cricket. You really mustn't abuse your position to this extent. The power of the Press is a trust, see that you guard it," etc. and etc., in much the same vein. The five minute lecture over, the P.R.O. pushed across a sheet of typescript. This was the refutation of the published report, containing the true facts as seen by the God-like eye of the administration. Lobole was requested to read it through. Attempts on his part to protest, to argue, were summarily brushed aside. There was no appeal possible. "Well, my dear chap," said Gardener. "Goodbye, nice to have seen you. I'm sure you'll play the game and be more careful in future not to overstep the mark." So Lobole was sent back to his office with a flea in his ear and the copy of the denial in his brief-case. *Every word of that denial, without a comma altered, had to be printed in the next issue of his paper and given exactly the same prominence as the original statement*. That is the position of our Press today in Bandaland.'

'How you do talk, Samueli!' said Martha. 'Would you like something to drink, Mr. Pole? Shall I make a pot of tea?'

'Yes, yes,' said Samueli with a flash of irritation. 'Go into the kitchen and make the tea. Leave us in peace.'

There was a lot of noise in the room. The young men were arguing excitedly, shouting across to one another.

'Notice,' said Samueli, 'the reasonable way in which you impose your censorship. Everything so logical, so well regulated. You don't requisition the front page to state your case. You match type for type, headline for headline. Your handcuffs are so smooth and comfortable, who could object to wearing them? Only a few so-called agitators! Only a few irresponsible malcontents like Lobole and Bifabishu!' The veins were standing out on his forehead. His eyes bulged. 'When will you stop treating us like children? When are we to be allowed to manage our own affairs? Why should we be thwarted, snubbed, forbidden to do this and that, disciplined, handed out prizes and punishments according

118

to your lights? Your administration, Mr. Pole, favours the boot-lickers, the sycophants, the yes-men who do as they're told and don't make trouble. Merit, real ability, gets you nowhere. This is no place for the able. We try to stand up.' He lifted his stocky, powerfully-built body from his chair. 'And before we have straightened our backs, our head hits the ceiling!'

He was playing to the gallery. He had the covey of young men, silent now, hanging on every word.

'I appreciate you British. This may surprise you. Yes, I admire the way you get things done—in England! But you've finished your work here and it's time for you to clear out. Leave us, if you like, a team of technical advisers with whom we can discuss our problems *man to man*. Why should we continue to allow ourselves to be patronized, lectured, criticized? Every time your senior officials open their mouths they infuriate, because they have never ceased to think of us as children. There are far too many men like the P.R.O., who have outlived their usefulness. They must go, go, go!' said Samueli, his big lips drawn back from his teeth. 'Or we will rise and throw them out!' And he flung himself into his chair.

One of the girls came in with cups and mugs on a tray and immediately afterwards there was a second interruption. A shabbily-dressed African, his trousers patched, his shirt torn, arrived panting on the verandah. Blood from a cut over one eye had congealed on his cheek. I watched him from my chair. He did not come into the room but stood outside, answering the quick fire of questions directed at him, pointing back across the square. Samueli grunted impatiently, heaved himself up again, went out on to the verandah. The two men stood talking together at a distance, pre-occupied, heads bent.

Jacob Mankele walked across and sat down by my side. 'This is a little unfortunate,' he said. 'There has been a

gathering of the Band of Brothers, we were not informed. . . .
However, we learn that they are now marching in procession
through Banda. They will shortly enter our quarter of the
city. It is believed that their aim is to demonstrate outside
Government House. The police have moved to intercept—
so far without success.' He sighed and pouted; clicked his
tongue. 'Meetings, religious or political, and processions
involving more than a dozen persons are, as you probably
know, Mr. Pole, forbidden in this country by law.'

'Who are the Band of Brothers?' I asked.

Jacob hesitated.

'You could compare them,' said one of the young men,
'with your Salvation Army.'

'But Erifazi, that is stupid,' said Martha, entering the
room, teapot in hand. 'They are not Christians.'

'No,' said Jacob slowly. 'The Brothers are not Christians.
Nevertheless, they are finding their way to God. To the one
true God.'

The man outside had gone. Samueli returned from the
verandah. His step was springy, his manner electric. He
stood in the middle of the room with his hands in his
pockets.

'You are witness to our trials, Mr. Pole. Freedom is a
mockery in Bandaland. There is no Hyde Park in *this* capital
city.'

'Now, Samueli,' said Martha, 'pass Mr. Pole his cup. Do
you take sugar?' she asked.

When tea had been poured for all, she took up cudgels
again with Jacob.

'How can they hope to find their way to God,' she
demanded, 'if they do not worship Jesus Christ?'

'Martha,' said Jacob, rubbing his nose, 'does not understand how it is possible. We have had discussions together.
But while in the old days the Missionaries made many con-
verts, it is now becoming increasingly difficult for the mass

120

of our people to feel close to Jesus, Son of God. There are obstacles in the way of our faith.'

'Christ,' said Samueli, turning impatiently, 'was a white man.'

'His teaching,' retaliated Martha, 'is universal.'

'That may be so, but to the Brothers He is the white saviour and they have no use for Him.'

'Many of us,' said Jacob earnestly, 'prefer to approach God not through Jesus any more, but through the Holy Ghost.'

They were drawn deeper into argument, close-cropped bullet black heads poked forward, black fingers encircling thick white china mugs, faces solemn and intense. I sat slightly apart, watching each speaker in turn. I was conscious the whole time of a confused murmur, a far-away throbbing, a rise and fall of many voices. The sound seeped into the quiet room. The carefully-measured phrases of the students were superimposed upon this whisper of distant disturbance, and my attention was strained. The murmur was as gentle and as menacing as the sea.

'Another cup, Mr. Pole?'

I thanked Martha and suggested that I had better be going. Samueli assured me, most emphatically, that I would be wise to stay where I was.

'They will disperse,' said Jacob. 'All will be over in perhaps half an hour.'

The discussion lapsed. We were listening. The distant uproar was now not so distant. Tension was mounting and our voices, when we spoke to each other, were forced and unreal.

Someone ran past the house. The man nearest the window swung open the casement and shouted. The runner stopped, answered, then ran on.

'The police are making another attempt to turn the procession,' said Martha. She put down the cup, pressed her

121

fingers against her cheeks and gazed unseeingly at the floor.

Samueli and the students were talking together in their own language. They sounded angry, urgent. Led by a bulky young African in a canary-coloured jersey, a small group stormed out of the house. The others crowded round the open window, listening and waiting, while the girls cleared the mugs and cups from the table and carried them through into the kitchen. More and more people were hurrying up the narrow lane and running past the house. Some had chickens tucked under their arms. Old men hobbled by, leaning on sticks. Women led children by the hand. This was the bow wave of the procession. Above the sound of rapid footsteps, growing louder and more insistent, whipping up the panic, we could hear the disorganized, the frightening multiple voice of the crowd.

'Miss Bifabishu,' I said, 'I must go. My driver is waiting down there with the car.' Until that moment I had not thought about Elias.

Martha told me again that I must not move from the house. 'It would be madness. Your driver will not have waited. He will return for you when the procession has passed.'

Samueli continued to pace round the room, smoking a cigarette. He was nervously on edge, keyed up by events. The drone of motor-cycles brought him again to the window, where the students made way for him. One of the machines back-fired. Everyone started and Samueli swore in English and pitched his half-finished cigarette into the street. That distant crack like a rifle-shot, punctuating the murmurs and grumbles of the crowd, marked (as far as we were concerned) the climax of the afternoon.

People had stopped running past the window. The open space between the houses remained empty and, as we listened, the noise from the road below very gradually grew less. Samueli abandoned his vantage point, perched himself the wrong way round on one of the upright chairs, rested his arms along the back and began to hold forth. The theme of his extempore discourse was freedom. Freedom for the oppressed and downtrodden black races of Africa. Now and again I tried to interrupt, but he had the bit firmly between his teeth and nothing that I said could stop him. Even Martha's sharp asides proved ineffectual.

'You British,' he said at one point, fixing me with a finger, 'are the architects of the new Bandaland. You have broken down our original way of life. Now you presume to build it up again, to your own pattern. We resent, justifiably resent, your presence and your activities.'

'Samueli,' said Martha for my benefit, but loudly, so that the others could hear, 'enjoys dressing up. He still hankers after a spear and a chief's lion-skin kaross.'

'Do you realize,' I said, 'that over the border in Equatoria they talk of Bandaland as the black man's paradise?'

'I am not a member of the Band of Brothers,' said Samueli, 'but I am with them. I am with every movement, however humble, however abortive, which undermines—or attempts to undermine—the established rule in Bandaland. I need hardly say that I am against the Governor. I am against the police. I am against the Omuvomo and his cabinet of pompous and inefficient fools. I am the enemy of every white official, because he is supernumerary, of every white trader, because he lifts his profits from the black man's pocket. You British would not remain here in Bandaland if it did not pay you handsomely to do so.'

'The British taxpayer . . .' I protested, but Samueli was already ranting on. The back legs of the chair thumped the floor as he tipped his seat, driving his points home.

There was no more noise outside. The procession had passed. A breath of air freshened for a moment the stifling atmosphere of the room. First one of the students, then another, turned to glance out of the window and remained staring. Looking round I saw for myself, beyond the dusty, metallic fronds of the palms, high above the thatched roofs of the houses, the column of smoke that had risen like a menacing black arm and was hanging, motionless, against the misty sky.

I was walking along the terrace of the club at sundown that evening when Glyn-Jones hailed me. He was sitting at a table with two other men and was not, I noticed, drinking tonic water.

'Come and join us,' he said. 'What'll you have?' He clapped his hands, shouted for the boy. 'See anything of the troubles? James, here, had windows broken and Dick's car was damaged. Haven't heard of any European casualties. Frankly, I don't stick my neck out on these occasions. Put up the shutters and go to ground.'

'Was telling Bob, had a stone through the back of my car again,' said the larger of the two men. He spoke with considerable heat. 'Seven weeks ago, that's to say the last time stones were flying around Banda, I had one bang on the same target. They haven't the nerve to shy at you until you've passed. I'm fed up.'

'Did you see Elizabeth Street? Bad as an air raid. I heard they were standing by with tear gas.'

'Who was it said religion was the opium of the people?'

'Call 'em religious if you like. They're a vicious lot when roused.'

'Don't forget, Dick, sects like the Band of Brothers form a rallying point. Hold a prayer meeting, start a procession and every young lout with a grievance looks about for a brick to break windows.'

'The missionaries,' said Glyn-Jones, 'should have taught them to love their neighbours. Too busy proselytizing. That's always been the trouble,' he said, turning his back on the others. 'Overdid the team spirit and right from the word go we've paid for it. This all ties up.' He turned abruptly back. 'Remember the old Sunday free-for-alls, Dick? Black Protestants and black Catholics starting in to convert each other with bricks and broken bottles?' He gave a mirthless hoot. 'Day of rest? Day of casualties!'

'If the Governor gives them their heads, as he's threatening to do. . . .'

'Then we're finished. Mob rule. Our one chance is to keep these demonstrations small.'

'If we British have to sit on the lid, in Bandaland, in order to stay here at all,' I said, 'then it's high time we packed up and left.'

'And abandoned the decent majority to the hooligans?'

'Look here, old fellow, we're not sitting on any lid. We're rolling a boulder up a hill. You're asking us to ease up the pressure, stand out of the way? The moment we do that, down she goes. Down to the bottom, where we took over in —when was it?—nineteen hundred and something. Another twenty, thirty years and with any luck we'll have reached the top. The Bandala will be able to stand on their own feet.'

'You think so, James?' Glyn-Jones drained his glass, shouted for the boy. Then he gave my arm a pinch.

'Look at it this way. Bandaland's a good, old-fashioned public school. White staff, black prefects. Now and again we have a spot of bother. Fifth form try to burn down the Chemi Lab. Or the School Magazine blows its top off— that's often happening, I assure you—and prints an attack on the gym master. What's to do? Haul the editor up before the Head.' He gave another of his hoots. 'And the Head won't play. The Governor's one of these modern chaps and likes to let the boys rip.'

'Something could be done, surely,' I said. 'For a start, we should gain their confidence.'

'We've been trying to do just that for fifty years.'

'Which, if I may say so, seems to prove our methods wrong.'

A hand clapped me on the shoulder. I looked up. The P.R.O. was staring anxiously into my face.

'*Pole*! Are you all right?'

'What's bitten you, Jack?' said Glyn-Jones.

'Of course I'm all right,' I said. 'I was never involved.'

'But I heard they'd overturned the car. Set it alight?'

'I wasn't around. Nor was Elias. That's the trouble. The whole thing was unnecessary.'

Gardener swung a chair across from a neighbouring table and sat down between Glyn-Jones and myself.

'I don't understand. You weren't around?'

'I'd left the car in Mbonde Avenue.'

'Mbonde Avenue!' said Glyn-Jones. 'You're a dark horse. What were you doing down there, in the thick of things?'

'I'd gone to visit some people. A private visit, nothing official. I stayed in their house while the procession passed. If Elias had stood by the car he could have made an easy get-away. But he'd dropped in to see a friend and when the balloon went up, decided to stay where he was. The police turned the main body of the procession about half a mile up the street. I learnt afterwards that they'd marched past the car, first time, and left it alone. Dealt with it on the way back—and made a job of it, too.'

The P.R.O. whistled thoughtfully.

'Mbonde Avenue. You were in the heart of an African district. I don't know of any Europeans. . . .'

'I was not visiting Europeans,' I said.

Gardener grunted, fingered his moustache.

'So they rolled over one of the Governor's runabouts?' said Glyn-Jones. He played with his glass and looked positively amused.

126

'This was a private visit you were paying?' said Gardener coldly.

'Entirely my own affair,' I said, 'which makes it the more awkward.'

(As could be expected, I was not looking forward to sorting things out with Sir Christopher.)

'Frankly, I should have been kept informed. I would have warned you to avoid that area of the city. You must remember, the administration are responsible for your safety.'

'Pole,' said Glyn-Jones cheerfully, 'has blotted his copy book.'

I had, as I had anticipated, an embarrassing interview with the Governor. I was making my escape from the precincts when Major Wakefield intercepted me with a message from Lady Mountclair. She would be glad to see me if I could spare the time. I felt like a mouse scuttling between the paws of a pair of omnipotent cats.

She received me in her drawing-room; a room full of the most theatrical-looking flowers. The air was heavy with their scent. Banks of blossom were massed in every corner; trumpets crimson and moon-coloured, deep blue mops, yellow and orange petals curling like congealed flames. Too many flowers. Hospitals, funerals, prima-donnas' dressing-rooms. . . . She greeted me distantly and did not take my hand or smile.

I could hear the tick of the ormolu clock on the mantelpiece. She stood with a hand on the lid of the piano, looking away. A violin case, scores, loose sheets of music littered the polished top.

'My husband,' she said quietly, 'has cares enough as it is. How could you be so thoughtless?'

I did not attempt to defend myself.

'Why,' she said, rounding on me, her skirt swinging, 'did

127

you go there? Curiosity? Because I deprecated the suggestion?'

'Martha Bifabishu invited me to her house.'

'To meet her brother?'

'To meet Samueli.'

'And what is Samueli to you? Was it wise? You could have spared us some anxious moments, Mr. Pole.'

'I took a cup of tea with a group of students. Nothing more. But for the procession. . . .'

'What do you think of him? Your candid opinion.'

'An excellent man for the opposition party. A poor choice for the Government front bench.'

She smiled; moved from the piano to the sofa; pushed across an inlaid box of cigarettes. We sat down. The ordeal was over.

I suggested that the African Press deserved better and more imaginative treatment. She agreed at once. Her husband, she said, was not happy about the situation. Lobole's name cropped up and I spoke of his enquiry into the cotton industry. Leaning forward, earnest, emphatic, she tore Lobole's case to shreds. I watched her while she talked of graft and corruption, bribes offered and taken, cheating at the scales, cartels and monopolies. I remembered the evening by the lake and wondered again—was Douglas Cameron her lover? I tried, and failed, to push the idea out of my mind.

To think of Rose Mountclair, not in terms of a First Lady, inviolate, beyond criticism, but as a fallible human being, was a physical wrench. That she was young and lively, an intriguing—and forceful—personality, I had recognized from the first. That she might be vulnerable had simply not occurred to me and I had overlooked the fact that she was a woman to be desired.

'Lobole,' she was saying, 'is unreliable. He is fighting the Nwambe Project, as he would fight any far-sighted, enlightened plan. We are all of us entitled to our views, but

128

his alarmist propaganda has all along been harmful to the country.'

We exhausted the topic. I stubbed out my cigarette; rose to go.

'One moment,' she said. She waved me back into my chair, crossing the room to the small desk under the window. 'I must talk to you about your report.'

'My report! I'd expected Sir Christopher. . . .'

'He's not yet seen the draft.' As she spoke, she unlocked and opened a drawer in the desk.

'But, Lady Mountclair, it was delivered the day before yesterday.'

She turned, smiling slightly. 'You must forgive my interference. You see, I read through the report myself and felt —what shall I say?—that it would be unwise to pass it on in its present form. There are various small improvements you can make. Please don't be alarmed! I know that the report is confidential. I realize that my husband is an interested party. But you were good enough to consent when I suggested he should glance through the draft. . . .'

'To make certain I had not slipped up on detail,' I said. 'That was one thing. This is quite another.'

'I agree. The points I wish to raise are not factual. They are concerned with mood. I have made a note of them. Would you care to go through them with me, now?'

She had sat down in the chair next to mine. I saw that she held my typescript in her hand. Clipped to the top sheet was a small piece of pale lilac writing paper on which she has listed her suggestions neatly in green ink.

'You've informed Sir Christopher you're holding up the report?'

'No,' she said. 'I thought it best to say nothing until we were able to talk the matter over. Now and again you write a little flatly, a little discouragingly. A brisker, more enthusiastic presentation . . .'

'Lady Mountclair, you are asking me to take sides.'

'To judge from this, you have already taken sides.'

'I have no business to be talking to you at all. But since you have accused me . . .'

'No, no. Hardly accused. Suggested.'

'Since you suggest that I am prejudiced, let me put my case. The report is for the information of the Trustees. I know the members of the Board personally. They are not philanthropists but hard-headed business men. They do not appreciate enthusiasm. They want security.'

'Quite,' she said. 'Security. You must have seen the estimates. I have no head for arithmetic but it was clear to me that those figures stood up and talked.'

'Lady Mountclair, it is not as straightforward as simple £ s. d. There is such a thing as a climate of opinion.'

She sat up a little straighter. 'Opinion? Will you allow yourself to be influenced by people's fears, their conventions . . .'

I told her I had met three, perhaps four men in Banda who were wholeheartedly in favour of the Project. They were all specialists, technicians, looking at the matter from their own narrow angle. I agreed that, technically, the project was feasible, a sound proposition. The estimates, I said, were based on what could be called the *tangible* element of the scheme. The dam would cost this, the value of the food produced in the irrigated area would be that. But we were up against the *intangible* element. The human uncertainties. That was the side that worried me.

She shifted restlessly; tried to interrupt.

'And don't forget,' I said, 'that the problem of food production can be tackled from the other end. Reorganization of the Reserves. Stronger measures in the Republic. The native lands over there could produce twice, some say three times the quantity of food, if they were intelligently farmed.'

'If!' she said, roused in her turn, 'and the population will

130

double in the next twenty years and we shall be back where we started. Of course there are drawbacks. Of course everyone is against the Project. Can't you understand that people are *always* against whatever is bold and far-sighted and venturesome and new! Would you and your Trustees have dared a stake in the development of the American continent? Or would you have shilly-shallied on the east coast and talked about the reaction of the Red Indians and favourable climates of opinion?'

She jumped from her chair and began to walk up and down, the pages of the report fluttering in her hand. She was magnificently angry.

'You men make me sick. You're so cautious, so unimaginative. My husband, thank God, has imagination, has fire, has the strength and the will to hammer through opposition. That's the reason I married him. Because I recognized and loved his spirit. This,' she said, steadying her voice, 'is his last great work. He cannot, he *must* not end his career on a note of failure. That would be too dreadful. Not to be borne. Think again, Mr. Pole.' She stopped beside me and put a hand on my arm. I could feel the pressure of her fingers through the thin sleeve of my coat. 'Be courageous. Dwell on the opportunities rather than the drawbacks. Opportunities far too important to be missed. There is just one thing the matter with your report. It was conceived and written in a mood of defeat.'

She sat down, dropped the typescript on the floor, put up her hands to smooth back her hair. The movement of her arms distracted me. Her dark blue dress left her shoulders uncovered. I did not seem able to escape the white embarrassment of her flesh.

'Let's talk of something else,' she said. 'I've not seen you since you returned from Lake William. Did you enjoy yourself at the bungalow . . . ?'

*

I took the report back with me to the Guest House. Next morning I studied Lady Mountclair's suggestions, satisfied myself that they were harmless, revised the text to please her, typed out the corrected pages and sent the draft to Government House. That is the bald summary of events. In fact, I fought a battle with myself that morning, and every amendment, every qualification, every deletion made to the original draft was (as I dimly realized at the time) my defeat, her personal triumph.

VI

THE report was airmailed to London, to be considered by the Trustees. I was to stand by and wait their decision. More details, further information, might be required. I found myself suddenly stranded in Banda with nothing particular to do.

Patricia made no move; left me severely alone. In fact, I was not sorry things were working out that way. At the best of times, I felt, looking back, ours had been an uneasy relationship and, as she had chosen to make the break herself, I could (I reassured myself) face even Mary McDermott with an easy conscience.

Sir Christopher departed on tour and in his absence the pull of Government House grew steadily stronger. The pressure Rose Mountclair continued to exert was a challenge I no longer felt inclined to resist. I allowed myself to be drawn into her orbit. I accepted the ordered, organized hours, the minor irritations of etiquette, realizing that the artificiality of the small court was organic. The constant, growing stimulation of her company was what really mattered—and, in a sense, the formalities reassured for, knowing as much as I did, had I wished, I could have known more. I did not wish; chose not to see her plain; to respect her, I soon found, was a necessity—not for convention's sake but for my own.

Moments of escape were rare, but one sultry afternoon we went with a small party to swim in a crater lake. We drove ten miles out along the main road to the west; then turned

133

and bumped our way down a side-track, stopping in an open space, a slab of sunlight walled about by palms. We tumbled from the cars and gathered in the shade at the side of the clearing. The instant we arrived a group of totos appeared from nowhere (the African landscape is invariably peopled) and appropriated our wraps and bathing towels.

When we were ready Rose Mountclair (who had dressed sensibly for what was to prove a minor expedition and was wearing khaki trousers and a faded bush shirt with military-type pockets) led us off along a narrow path that wound into the green gloom of a banana grove. Spirits were high and there was a good deal of talk and laughter. The atmosphere was refreshingly intimate.

'This sort of thing never used to be done,' said the solemn, bald young man from the Irrigation Department. 'Quite irregular. What the Old Guard would say is anyone's bet.' He spoke in a breathless undertone, his head bent. 'Not been a First Lady like *her* before, that's certain. It's up to us—up to us to remember our place, I say. Trouble is——' He glanced sharply sideways, as if summing me up. 'She lays herself open. There's always the fellow with no manners waiting to push in.'

He hurried on and left me to think it over. The heat was intense. Giant fronds blotted out the sky; pagodas of fruit hung solid where the stalks sprang.

We entered a narrow valley. A frieze of girls mounted the track from the stream-bed, polished brown gourds balanced upon their heads. Looking up, startled, they saw us coming and gave way at once, melting into the shadows, moving easily and gracefully in their long cotton gowns. But the crone in a tattered skirt made no attempt to run. Naked to the waist, gnarled and withered, she grew out of the ground by the path like the stump of a tree, her old breasts dangling over the cage of her ribs like leather straps. She did not respond to our greeting but stood and watched while we crossed the valley and entered the plantation on the further side.

Now we began to climb. Ahead, as we emerged from the dense cover of the groves, rose a steep and sharply-pointed crest; the grass slopes singed and dry. This, I realized, was one of the lion-coloured hummocks I had seen from the club terrace, pimpling like islands the lazy dip and swell of the emerald sea.

Out into the open we moved, striking across rough ground at a tangent to the track, small and exposed under the angry eye of the sun. The slope grew steeper. The climb was exhausting; we panted and sweated; struggled up the final crest, too hot and breathless to speak. The summit, I found when we reached it, was no summit, but the lip of a crater. The hill was hollow and we stood upon the rim of a grassy bowl. Far below, the sun bounced back from a disc of black water; a lake fringed with palms and woven about with a tangle of vegetation, a jungle in miniature. Disturbed by our appearance on the skyline, an ibis croaked mournfully and flapped from a tree, bronze wings burnished, weird cry echoing inside the crater, while ducks swam out from the lotus-starred banks and drew a skein of ripples across the glassy surface. So the hundred hummocks dotting the banana groves were long-dead volcanoes and each hill hid within it a rich tropical garden and a lake like jet!

The totos were rewarded. They grinned shyly and scampered away down the outer slope, running jerkily on their thin, dusty legs; a trio of agile black grasshoppers.

The descent into the crater was abrupt, precipitous. We slipped and slithered through the long grass and I thought of snakes. There might be—who knew what?—lurking in the riot of foliage at the water's edge. Thorns scratched, creepers prodded at my face, and we came out on to the lake shore and stood on a rib of smooth rock; slabs of pumice rising like the backs of hippos from the sun-sprinkled surface near us.

We split into groups and sought cover. Tree trunks tapered to the cloudless sky, dwarfed by the rim of grass, cathedral-high above the mist of leaves. One by one, as we were ready, we padded out along the half-submerged ridge of worn lava and jumped or dived. The water was not cold and ran over our bodies like silk.

We all forgot ourselves, shouted, splashed each other's faces, swam violently in short bursts and then lay on our backs and thrashed with our feet, sending up fountains of spray. The Assistant Secretary became excited, ducked and turned somersaults, grabbed his wife by the ankles and tried to pull her under. Her screams made the hollow hill ring like a wineglass.

Rose Mountclair was a good swimmer. I admired the neat little twist of her hands as they curved over her head. Her legs churned a wake like a motorboat's.

She challenged me to a race. I did my best but was outclassed. Defeated, treading water, I saw her pull herself on to the bank just where a wild banana dipped a leaf to the surface, a ten-foot glossy frond like a feather. Leaf and reflection sounded in the sunlight a trumpet note of vivid green.

She was big, as I have said, and her shoulders and thighs were startlingly white. She stood up there on the bank, full and round as a white peony. I swam on slowly and she knelt and stretched down a hand; pulled me up and out to stand dripping beside her. The wooded bowl enclosed us. We were ringed about by the towering, silent trees.

The moment was curiously detached from the reality that was Banda. We were alone—but we were also apart. Unthinkable, back at Government House, to speak simply, directly, without embarrassment.

'If I had my way, every child would be taught to swim as

136

soon as it learnt to walk. When I was a girl, I was afraid of water. I ask you—actually afraid!'

'You should have children,' I said.

'My stepson,' she stared at the heads that bobbed on the broken surface, 'is ten years older than I am.'

'Don't you find it hard to be adrift from your own generation?'

'Of course it's hard. But I wanted to shape my life, achieve something positive. I was eager for results in those days. Too eager, perhaps.'

'In other words, you're not happy?' (She turned and looked into my face.) 'I want your happiness,' I said.

'Who is entirely happy? The future offers this—or this. A choice has to be made. You look at my life from the outside and find it artificial, pompous. . . . Oh, it's all that, I agree but—can't you understand?—it's also so much more. Remember, I took a short cut, had to adjust myself and learn a great deal, very fast. My family were appalled at the responsibilities I was preparing to take on. I was young-and-twenty and threw everything overboard to become midwife to the new African era. But I wasn't blind, I knew what I was doing. I believed in the future. No, no, you misunderstand me. I'm extremely fortunate. I love my husband. The trouble is, a year or two's discipline is a poor substitute for a career of service and dedication.'

Unexpectedly, she laughed and touched my hand.

'Don't be so startled and so solemn. If only you knew how I sometimes crave to be amused!'

That night, Captain Gardener gave a party.

I arrived at the P.R.O.'s bungalow shortly after nine o'clock. The evening, from the first, promised to be one of those thoroughly organized affairs and guests were not encouraged to sit about and talk. There was *vingt-et-un* at a long table in one room, dancing to a gramophone in another. I knew most of the people—I had ceased to feel a stranger in Banda—but was a little disconcerted to run straight into Terence. An unexpected encounter. Shortly afterwards, again to my surprise, I spotted Cameron's girl friend, Janet. I went up and asked her if all Hoyu was in Banda that night. We danced together and I enquired tactfully after Douglas. She looked at me out of the corners of her eyes and said that, as far as she knew, he was getting along fine.

'Funny you should say that. I'm quite sure I saw his car this afternoon, and he said nothing to me about coming up. Mind you, I haven't had much to do with him since—since that evening by the lake. He's not,' she added, looking over my shoulder, 'my cup of tea.'

A single turn round the floor was enough for both of us. The heat was overpowering. We went next door and tried our hand at *vingt-et-un*. Terence was sitting across the table, playing intently, accumulating a pile of counters. Then Patricia arrived and wanted to join the game, but by now all the counters were in circulation.

'Here,' said Terence gruffly, pushing across a generous half-share of his winnings. 'Take these. I was playing for you.'

'Keeping her hand warm, eh, Terence?' someone said, and raised an easy laugh.

When I left the table, an hour and thirty shillings later, an engineer from the Public Works Department caught me and asked for news. He was devoted to the cause of the Project; a fanatical admirer of the Governor's; one of the few 'Governor's men' I had discovered among the permanent officials. I told him that we were still waiting to hear from the Trustees.

'Don't rely on a decision at once,' I said. 'They'll need time for discussion before things are settled, one way or another.'

138

He blinked at me through his powerful spectacles. 'There's only one *possible* decision,' he said.

'I hope for your sake you're not disappointed.'

I became aware, at this point, that one of Gardener's house-boys was hovering beside us, a letter in his hand.

'Mr. Pole, sir?'

'Yes?'

'Boy just bring this for you.'

I took the envelope and glanced at the name. I did not recognize the writing.

'Thanks,' I said. I pushed it into my pocket, looked round. The engineer had moved on; joined another group. I was suddenly face to face with Pat.

'Hullo!' I said. 'Thought you were playing.'

'Lost everything. I've left Terence to pay my debts. He's making money. He can afford to.'

'Lucky at cards . . . ' I said, and then immediately wished I hadn't.

'You were very glum at the card table. How much did you lose?'

'Thirty shillings and fifty cents.'

We appeared to have run out of words. She looked up, a slight frown netting her forehead. Her gaze was searching, solemn.

'Well, Sebastian, what have you been doing with yourself?'

'Keeping out of your way, mostly. Hadn't occurred to me that we'd made it up. How about you?'

'Same old round. I've been watching out for you at the club.'

'Never seem to get to the club. Haven't had a moment to myself for days.'

'Glad to see me?'

'Why, of course, Pat! You're looking delightful. Would have been a pity to have quarrelled for good.'

'Let's move over into a corner. And try to be serious. I really do want to talk.'

We pushed our way into the corner. Counters, scattered from the table, skidded underfoot. The fuggy air was solid with smoke.

'You might have rung me before this,' she said. After a small hesitation. 'Sebastian, aren't you seeing rather more of Lady Mountclair?'

'Yes,' I said. 'If it comes to that, I suppose I am.'

'You're a fool, you know. She'll only get her claws into you.' Her light blue eyes were fixed on my face.

'I hardly think so. There's nothing particularly perilous about our relationship.'

'Give me a cigarette. I've run out.'

I opened my case. She took her lighter from her bag and I thought of Cameron again and that absurd interlude outside the Governor's bungalow.

'Half a dollar it doesn't work first time.'

She laughed and then flicked up a flame with the first snap of her thumb.

'I won't take your money.'

'How *does* the fellow do it? Cast a spell over them?'

'What's she got that's so wonderful,' said Pat dreamily, inhaling, her eyes half closed. 'I'd like to know.'

'Do we have to discuss her?'

'Don't you find the subject interesting, Sebastian?'

I side-stepped. 'I understood this was to be a light-hearted evening.'

'Is Lady Mountclair such a solemn subject?'

'She's the First Lady.'

Patricia glanced at me doubtfully. 'If that's the way you feel, you're safe enough.'

'Meaning . . .'

She blew a cloud of smoke into my face. 'Lady Mountclair has a weakness for men.'

'So had Eve. So have most women. Life would be dull for us if they hadn't.'

'She doesn't attract you?'

'For Christ's sake, let her alone!' I wanted to cry. I pushed my hands into my pockets and stared at the floor.

'Let me explain,' I said. 'I'll tell you why I like her. She's England. A breath of my own England—you can understand the pull. I'm in a strange continent. I'm walking the tight-rope between white and black. I'm at sixes and sevens and often bewildered. She gives me security, relief. I find her reassuring company. She's also an enthusiastic amateur musician and her husband can afford the best. Her piano is a Bechstein, her violin an Amati. She has persuaded—how she managed it I cannot imagine—an eminent musician to head the faculty here at the University. She is insisting that I attend a rehearsal of their orchestra tomorrow. I shall go, of course. I would go a long way to listen to Dr. Schütz.'

'Are you fond of music, Sebastian?'

'An understatement. Sometimes I think that music makes sense out of life. That it's the only thing that fundamentally matters to me.'

'And what about your work? The Halliday Trust?'

'I have to earn a living. I could teach small boys to murder the piano. Not a very satisfactory alternative.'

'I can see,' she said, 'that you two have a lot in common.' She turned impatiently away. 'I must bore you to tears. I don't share your background and I haven't a note of music in my head.'

'I'm quite aware of that.' Before I could stop myself, I had added, 'But, you know, yours is a very lovely head.'

She exclaimed beneath her breath. 'Why do you always have to flirt with me? Can't you ever take me seriously?'

'Is that a snub?'

'Yes. I think you need snubbing. I dislike your implied superiority.'

'And what have I got to be superior about?'

'That you're musical—and an enlightened Britisher, I suppose, and talk with the right sort of accent and—and that you're one of the gentlemen you say we don't breed in Equatoria. Oh, I've said it before and I'll say it again. You're too damned pleased with yourself.'

'Pat, there's no point in quarrelling.'

'Then try to behave.'

'Don't you like to be told how good you look?'

'Not the way you do it. You're insincere. Aiming to be clever. You respect Lady Mountclair. I can tell that, the way you talk about her. You don't respect me. You never have and I've been a fool all along to expect it.'

'Pat, what can I say? Quite honestly, I respect your courage. The way you stand up for your convictions, however misguided. Don't run off with the wrong impression.'

'What's it matter anyway,' she said after a moment's silence. 'You'll be going back to England in a few days. We'll never see each other again.'

'You never know, Pat.'

'You never know. But I don't think it's likely.'

'And we've had some grand times together. I'll not forget Hoyu.'

Her expression softened. 'What d'you say, Sebastian. Let's get out of here sometime soon and go on to my place.'

'Well, we could. But your friend—you know, I forget her name. Won't she mind?'

'Olive's away.'

'Away, is she? You mean . . .'

'We shall be on our own.'

'That makes quite a difference, doesn't it?'

'Just as you like. I've asked you, haven't I?' she said, not looking at me, turning her head and drawing impatiently at her cigarette.

To my relief, before I had to answer, Terence interrupted us.

'Wondered where you'd hidden yourself, Pat. I ended up twelve bob to the good after settling your account. Hullo Pole.' He gave me a wan smile and took her arm to lead her away. 'Let's go and find ourselves a drink.' She did not resist but glanced back with a brusque little nod. 'Think it over,' she said, as clearly as if she had spoken.

I was still standing where they had left me when Gardener approached, hesitantly, his long face rosy with embarrassment.

'D'you mind stepping into my den? Bob Lucas has turned up. Wants a word with you.'

Lucas? I had met the Commissioner of Police at one or two functions. He was affable, a good talker, a first-class shot. We had never discussed anything of the remotest importance. I could not conceive why he should suddenly want to see me.

The P.R.O.'s den was a small room largely occupied by a desk. The map of Bandaland on the wall was identical to the map that hung on the wall of his office. Lucas, in a crumpled khaki uniform, was standing with his back to the door, staring up at this map. He was broad-shouldered, grey-haired, looked older than his years. He turned as we came in and I saw that he was sweating. The drops stood out on his temples.

'I shan't keep you,' he said, giving me his hand and then perching himself sideways on the edge of the desk. 'Don't usually work these midnight hours, but as it happens this particular tangle-up won't wait. Get down to brass tacks, shall we? You'll help us if you're frank.' He brought out a handkerchief, dabbing at his forehead, wiping round his neck. 'This fellow Bifabishu. I don't have to remind you that you saw him on the afternoon of the 21st. Seen him since?'

'No,' I said. 'I've not seen him again.'

'But you're in touch with him?'

143

I stared at the Commissioner. 'In touch?'

Lucas swung his legs, leant forward. 'Look here, old fellow, I'm not trying to frame you. This is entirely between ourselves, you, me, Jack here. Your loyalty's not in question. But you're new to the country and it's possible—I don't say it's likely but it's possible—that without your suspecting it you're being used as a tool. And believe me, I'm in no position to take a chance.'

'I'd like to help you,' I said, 'but you're making a mistake. I saw Samueli Bifabishu on the 21st. I've not seen or heard from him since.'

The P.R.O. shifted restlessly behind me. Lucas picked up from the desk and began to twist this way and that in his fingers, an ivory paper knife. I could feel the tension between them.

'Look here Pole, my dear man, you really must come clean with us. Half an hour ago a letter was brought to this house. The messenger was shadowed. He is known to have worked for Bifabishu . . .'

'A letter!' Light dawned at last. I fumbled in my pocket. 'That's absolutely right. I *was* given a letter. Forgot all about it—never even opened it.'

The Commissioner's face relaxed. Gardener coughed gratefully. The atmosphere was suddenly easy again; the tension pricked like a balloon.

Lucas handled the envelope; turned it over and over.

'Go ahead. Open it,' I said. 'I don't know who it's from. After what you've told me, I'd prefer not to deal with the thing.'

Lucas slit the envelope neatly with the paper knife and drew out a thin piece of notepaper. The same copperplate handwriting filled one half of one side of the sheet. He read the message without the flicker of an expression. Then he handed it across.

The letter was from Martha Bifabishu. She needed to see

me. The matter was of the most urgent importance. She entreated me to come to her house at once.

I had to stonewall the Commissioner's questions. I could not guess what had prompted her letter. I was unprepared for such a request. Taken completely by surprise.

'What do you want me to do?'

'Why, there's only one thing you *can* do. Go and find out what the woman wants.'

'Now? Right away?'

'The sooner the better. There may be no time to lose. Can you get to her place in the dark?'

'No,' I said. 'Almost certainly not. And I'm without my driver. He went off duty this evening.'

'I'll sketch you a map. By the way, no need to park the car where you left the last.' He gave me a sharp glance, leaning over the desk and scribbling on Gardener's writing pad. 'Fork right by the market. Bring you nearer. This is Mbonde Avenue. Town centre down here.'

I was surprised he knew the area so well.

'Bifabishu's headquarters for three years,' he said drily. He showed me the map. 'Is that clear?'

'Good enough.'

'Don't leave the car outside the house. Drive to this point, no further. And remember to lock the doors.'

'Then I walk up here?'

'Martha's is on the left.' He made a mark on the paper and wrote in her name.

'Look here, Lucas, what d'you think this is about? Might be something personal. I'm certain Martha's all right.'

'Might be a personal matter, I agree. But I don't think so.' He stretched across, flipped the letter with his finger-nail. 'Take it from me, this means trouble.'

'You're very sure of yourself.'

'I've my own sources of information, most of 'em reliable.

And I have an idea this ties up. I'll tell you for what, Pole. The country's running into a squall and if we don't reef and make ready we'll be keel up before we know what's hit us. I'll say no more at the moment.'

'You don't feel that I'm likely to involve her . . .'

'She's asked you to come, man! She's willing to take the risk. Now I want you to report back to my office. You know the building? Across the street to the Post Office. I'll be waiting for you.' Lucas slid off the desk, touched me on the shoulder. 'Keep your mouth shut and slip away quietly. Find out what you can.'

Nothing in the least like this had happened to me before. The sensation was not disagreeable. I said goodbye to the P.R.O., left his bungalow, met no one and was walking down the road to the car when I heard steps behind me. Quick, light footsteps. Then my name was called. I stopped and turned.

'*Pat!*'

'Where are you going? Running away again? Sebastian, this is becoming a habit.'

I looked at her and hesitated, wondering what to say.

'I was fed up. I can never bear parties for long.'

'Then you can take me home.' Her face was set and angry. 'The Petersons brought me. I can't ask them to leave yet. I've got a headache and I want to go home.'

'You'll have to excuse me. Fact is, I'm in a hurry.'

'A hurry! Where are you running off to in a hurry? Don't just stand there like a lump, Sebastian! Where are you going?'

'Oh, come on,' I said impatiently, 'if we're quick about it. I'll run you home.'

We were only a few yards from the car. This was a ramshackle pre-war Chevrolet unearthed for my use from the Government House stables. She exclaimed as we got in and at once began to wind down the windows.

'Tell your driver,' she said with a grimace, 'that it's time he had a bath.'

I switched on, started the engine.

'Well, Sebastian, you might say something.'

'What is there to say, Pat?'

'Oh, if that's the way you feel. . . .' She spoke carelessly and sat back, head turned, staring through the window. Suddenly, she twisted in the seat—we were already moving off down the hill—and said in a peremptory voice. 'Stop, Sebastian! Pull into the side and stop.'

I obeyed automatically and stalled the engine. 'What's the matter? Left something behind?'

'We've got to talk things over. I can't go on like this.'

'Talk things over? We haven't anything to talk over. I tell you Pat, I must get moving. We can talk another time.'

'Another time won't do,' she said. She spoke breathlessly. Her hands were clenched together in her lap. 'You've led me enough of a dance. I want to get things straight.'

'Look Pat, I'm serious. I can't stop now.'

'You can't stop! And half an hour ago you'd promised to come home with me.'

'No, that's not true. I never promised.'

'You can't have anything urgent to do. Can you, Sebastian? Just an excuse. You were dodging back to the Guest House, that's all. Giving me the slip.' The words came out uncertainly, in little rushes.

I tried to start the car again, but she knocked my hand from the dashboard and pulled out the ignition key.

'No you don't! Not until you answer me.'

'Give me back the key,' I said, trying to speak quietly.

Her eyes gleamed in the dim light. An untidy strand of hair lay across her forehead. I could hear her uneven breathing. I could hear the thumping of my own heart.

'When you look at me like that,' she said, 'I could dig

my nails into your face.' She curled her fingers round her bag. The words were half-strangled in her throat.

'Please give me the key.'

'No!'

I caught hold of her wrist. Quick as lightning, she had jerked my hand to her mouth, bitten my fingers. I swore and let her go.

'Pat, you little devil!'

'Have I hurt you? I hope that hurt! I've taken too much from you, Sebastian.'

'What a barbarian you are! I always knew it.'

'I've made you bleed.' She was staring at my hand, as if fascinated.

'Satisfied?'

'You must be careful not to get that infected. Cuts don't heal up well in Banda.'

'Thanks,' I said. 'You're very cheerful.'

'You mustn't dab it with a dirty handkerchief! Don't be an idiot, Sebastian. You're asking for tetanus! You can't take risks out here. I'll clean it up thoroughly when we get home.'

'Kind of you,' I said. 'You might have thought first before using your teeth.'

She took my hand in hers and pressed her mouth against my fingers and sucked. The warm, moist tip of her tongue tingled the torn skin. Bending sideways, her head was nearly in my lap. I felt her shoulders tremble. I realized then that she was crying. Her tears were wet on my wrist.

Reluctantly, I gave her my full attention.

'Pat,' I said. 'Pull yourself together. Stop it!' With my free hand I shook her, smoothed her hair. 'I thought you were tough!'

Her lips began to move over my fingers. She held fast as I tried to draw away. 'Oh God, Sebastian, I'm desperately unhappy. I love you. Don't you understand? I love you!'

148

She kissed my palm, my thumb, each finger in turn; still crying, still talking incoherently. 'I had to tell you. I couldn't go on.' She lifted her face. 'Since we came back from Hoyu, since that wretched quarrel, life's been absolute hell. I've had to prevent myself from 'phoning you a dozen times a day. Tell myself I had too much pride. . . . I knew you'd be at Captain Gardener's tonight. That's why I arrived so late. I was ready an hour too soon and I made myself wait. Made myself sit and watch the clock. . . . Then the Petersons saw my lights and stopped off. I'd given myself ten more minutes but I couldn't resist the offer of a lift. And the first thing I saw when I came into the room was Sebastian at the card table, the gloomy poke of your head. . . .' She was laughing now and crying at the same time. 'I was so happy just to be near you. To be in the same room with you again. You were pleased to see me, weren't you? But nothing stays as it should between us. And it isn't always my fault. Is it, Sebastian?'

'No,' I said. 'I never really believed this could happen. Never thought you'd like me enough.'

'I've loved one other man,' she said. 'And that was a hopeless business, too.'

I had extricated my hand from her grasp.

'You know what it is when you're abroad? Find you can do things you'd never think of doing at home. And because nothing's permanent, you sit lightly to the future.'

'Sit lightly to love?'

'That's what I'd meant us to do, Pat. You seemed, in a sort of way, inviolate. Secure within yourself. I still can't get it into my head that I've harmed you. Inconceivable, that you should be crying because of me.'

'Yes,' she said. 'I should have known better.'

'And I should never have touched you. Never come near you. But Pat, I'm still bewildered. How can you possibly love me like this when I stand for everything you despise?'

'That's no reason.' She was quiet for a moment. 'And if you felt differently about me, Sebastian, you'd know that it was no reason. You're so far from how I feel that I can't talk to you. Each time you open your mouth, you hurt.'

'I'm sorry. I'll not say anything more. I've made you unhappy enough.'

'So we go on as before?'

I moved her gently back on to her side of the seat.

'Be sensible. Do be sensible. Let me drive you home.'

She fitted the key into the switch and I started the car and drove off rapidly down the hill. The rush of air through the windows cooled the sweat on my face. Pat sat hunched and silent beside me. I drove mechanically, obeying her occasional directions. When, five minutes later, I stopped outside her house, she asked in a cold, precise voice if I wished her to attend to my hand. I thanked her and said no, I couldn't wait.

She gathered up her wrap and bag and we stood for a moment by the car. I saw her draw breath, take a grip of herself. Then, in the same unemotional, drained voice she said, 'So you're going to Government House, Sebastian.'

I did not answer at once. 'Good God!' I said, when I found words. 'Don't be such a *fool*!'

She turned and walked up the short path between hedges of hibiscus. I called after her but she did not answer. She did not look round. She let herself in and shut the door in my face.

I stood for a time in front of the house, undecided what to do. The road was very quiet. A clump of orange-red bougainvillea, hanging over the low garden wall, glowed in the light from the sidelamps. I would have liked to have gone in to her, but had sense enough to realize that there would be nothing gained if I did so. Already it was well past midnight and I had to find my way down to Mbonde

Avenue, to Martha Bifabishu's. Lucas—with an effort I remembered Lucas—was waiting my return.

In the end I started the car and followed my nose through the deserted residential streets until, more by luck than good judgment, I came out into the wide central square; the square that is flanked by government buildings and by the head office of the Bandaland Bank. Ahead, the palace hill showed up, high, dark, craggy; the palisades magnified by the night into an acropolis. A cat, belly to the ground, sneaked over the road. Nothing else moved. I turned left and drove over one of the rolling hills into the first of the African districts. I reached Mbonde Avenue; then discovered —too late to do anything about it—that I had mislaid the Commissioner's sketch map. I searched through my pockets. Switched on the dashboard light, scoured the car. The wretched piece of paper had disappeared.

I rattled the wire-gauze door and called her name again. '*Miss Bifabishu!*' Palm leaves scraped in a sudden stir of wind. The sky above me glittered with stars. There was not a light to be seen anywhere. In the distance, the dog I had disturbed was still barking; punctuating the darkness with short rasps of sound.

I heard the creak of a window along one side of the house. Martha's voice, when she spoke, was frightened. She told me to wait. A short while afterwards she opened the verandah door.

She led me into the small sitting-room and before switching on the light made sure that the curtains were carefully drawn across the window. We blinked, dazzled, the table between us.

'Why do you come as late as this?' She was standing with her arms hanging down, tall, unsmiling in a crimson housecoat. Her round cheeks shone like coal. 'They waited for you three hours. They could not wait longer.'

I explained that I had been out, at Captain Gardener's, and that I had not received her message until after eleven o'clock. I could see from the way she turned to glance apprehensively over her shoulder that she was still nervous. How could I be certain, she asked, that I had not been followed? I tried to reassure her. She begged me not to speak so loudly. She was, I decided, overwrought.

'Forgive my appearance, won't you, but as you must realize, I was asleep. . . . Now, sit down please. What can I offer you? I have no whisky, I am sorry.' She opened a box on the mantelpiece, said with a hopeless shrug. 'And they have smoked all my cigarettes!'

I asked who had been waiting to see me.

She hesitated, 'A few friends. Jacob and some others.'

'But the matter was urgent?'

She stared at me with her brown, wide-set eyes.

'Would I have written you such a letter if I had not wanted you to come at once?'

'And now I've arrived too late. They've gone—and you can't tell me anything?'

'Listen. I can tell you a little. Not all. I do not know all. For some time now I have been anxious. Not frightened, but anxious. It is not always easy to be a sister, Mr. Pole. My brother, you see, has never had cause to—to be afraid of me. He comes and goes freely, he meets, he talks in this house. He does not choose to confide, no, that is not Samueli's way. It is simply that he takes my trust for granted. I hear much that makes me unhappy. I hear the talk of foolish young men, the wild things they say. But my brother is no fool. I do not overhear talk that is dangerous. I have never, in my heart, believed that my brother meant even a quarter of what I heard him say. Now, today, I know otherwise. I know that he and his friends have only one clear goal in mind. And I have proof that they are prepared to use any and every means to attain this end. I cannot keep this secret. The burden is too great for me.'

She had taken a pace or two between the table and the wall. Now she turned, her arms held stiffly in front of her, hands clenched.

'You know, it is the same with the children. You wait, you watch, you listen to them—and then they go too far and you have to intervene. If you let them, they will break, thoughtlessly destroy. In their own interests you cannot allow them this measure of freedom. Violence, Mr. Pole, is bred from impatience, from lack of thought, lack of imagination. It is the quick way. The easy way. The children think so— and that is not bad. They need to be taught, to be controlled. But when men turn to violence, then they too need control and that is not always so simple. Who is there to say to them, not that way! You will make things worse, not better?

'Violence will never solve our problems or achieve our ends. I am not the only one to realize that. There are others, including those who were to have met you here tonight. But we are few, and we have little influence. We have tried counsel, persuasion, prayer. Nothing touches them. They have turned their backs on Christ. That is such a pity. They believe, in their foolishness, that because He was a European He has no message for them. *Love thy neighbour.* . . . Does He preach the colour bar, Mr. Pole?'

'Colour apart, none of us are good at taking these things literally,' I said. 'Never have been.'

She had nothing more to say and stood and stared at the floor. On the wall above her head hung Raphael's young mother, slightly smiling, pale, placidly confident. I looked from the painting to the heavy, hopeless black face beneath. Martha appeared to have abandoned the struggle.

'What do you wish me to do?'

153

She pulled out one of the upright chairs from the table and sat down very slowly, and slowly leant her arms along the polished top, folding her hands together.

'I do not know,' she said. 'You must act as you think best.'

'When do you anticipate trouble?'

'Tomorrow. That is why we sent for you. As I said, the matter is urgent.'

'Tomorrow?'

'I had forgotten the time. I mean, of course, today. In the Namzike. A demonstration is planned, rather than a disturbance. I know that Samueli—' She checked herself abruptly, glanced uneasily sideways, moistened her full, thick lips. 'I know that they wish to measure the strength of their support in the provinces. But precautions should be taken. In a few hours the Governor will be driving from Rua-rua to Mpulongwe, where he will go on board the lake steamer. The road should be well guarded. There are many bridges.'

'Miss Bifabishu, I'll be frank. I am going straight back to Mr. Lucas, the Commissioner of Police.'

'I am glad of that. He will understand. And you must warn him, please, that the men behind the disturbance are committed to violence. That they feel it is their duty to destroy in order to rebuild.'

'Who are these men?'

'The Commissioner will know them. There is no case yet to be proved against them and until they transgress the law, they are safe. The authorities will not touch them. They are careful. They are waiting their opportunity. They will not move openly until they have the full support of the people. The moment will come and then they will strike here in Banda, at the heart of the country. Mr. Lucas may already know this, but without the consent of the Governor he will be unable to act. The Governor, you see, is not afraid. He

154

has too little fear, too much faith—if that were possible. Mr. Pole, we are not yet deserving of such faith. . . .

'But you are in touch with the authorities. You can speak to Lady Mountclair, even to the Governor himself. And you must try to persuade them of the danger. These men need to be taken away from Banda for a year, for perhaps longer. They will lose their grip on the people. There will be no more trouble. But there is no time to lose! Go and persuade them, Mr. Pole, that in the interests of our country it is necessary to act *at once*!'

I drove up to Police Headquarters shortly before half-past two that morning. A sleepy African sergeant led me along a corridor and into the Commissioner's office. Lucas, seated behind a desk, was writing. He looked over the green-shaded lamp and told me, rather sharply, I thought, that he had expected me back sooner. Why had I kept him waiting for so long?

I sat down with a gasp of exhaustion.

'A variety of reasons. For a start, I mislaid that sketch map you'd drawn for me. Had a frantic time finding the place. Then I had trouble with a dog. Must have woken the neighbourhood.'

Lucas sat up even straighter.

'Your hand! No, the other one. Is that where the brute nipped you?' While I stared at the mark he whistled his anxiety. 'Mind you, we've practically wiped out hydrophobia, but you can't be too careful. There's a first aid kit in the office. Like to clean it up?'

I told him no, it wasn't the dog, and let it go at that. Lucas pushed across a tin of cigarettes and settled himself back into his chair while I gave him as accurate an account as I could of the interview.

'Namzike Province,' he said when I had finished. He

opened a drawer, pulled out a map. 'Finest trout fishing in central Africa. We've seen to that! Spectacular scenery. And tribesmen to match the mountains. Our live-wires from Banda work among 'em like yeast in a barrel of beer.'

I studied the map carefully. After listening to Martha, this was familiar ground. I followed the loops of the Tobi River as it curled through the hills to the north-east corner of Lake William. The road from Rua-rua to Mpulongwe ran beside the river all the way.

'Mind you, I've already taken a few precautions. Nothing elaborate. Sir Christopher doesn't hold with armed escorts and bodyguards. I can see his point. Better to do without them if you can. And in a way, it's simple enough for him. If he's careless, he only risks his neck. I've got to think about my reputation.'

Lucas leant back with a smile. He was a man playing a part; a part he had chosen for himself. The chair creaked as he stretched his shoulders.

'I've been unobtrusive—I hope. Muddled certain sections of the timetable for a start, so that the Governor doesn't necessarily run to schedule and arrives at places unexpectedly. Irritating for all concerned, I know, but Wakefield's a good sort and smoothes things over. Then I arranged with the Brigadier for an army exercise in the Namzike to coincide with the tour. Well, we haven't an army in the sense of the word. A few platoons of infantry. We had a cavalry division once—mules—until the tsetse did for them. Thought the Q.A.R. would stiffen my askari patrols—they're thin on the ground, up there. But Sir Christopher won't so much as catch a glimpse of a bayonet. Oh, I've given the matter attention, Pole. I'm not asleep on my feet and Rua-rua in particular has never had a reputation as a health resort. But Banda. . . . That's another matter. If I had the last word—well, the situation would look very different. Of course, I agree with the girl! Like nothing better than to do what she wants. Damned sensible suggestion. And as simple as A.B.C. I keep a tab on all the leaders. I've only to lift this 'phone, issue instructions and inside an hour we'd have 'em all exactly where we want 'em and where they should be—in the bag. *They* aren't worrying! *They* don't need to take precautions. The blasted fellows know very well that I can't touch them.' Lucas gave a sharp cough. 'Could have nipped this trouble in the bud, time back. But I need extraordinary powers. Nothing unconstitutional, damn it! Recognize a state of emergency and Bob's your uncle. But no, I'm to keep law and order in the country with my hands tied.'

'Samueli,' I said, 'has been deported before.'

'Bifabishu,' said the Commissioner, 'is growing older and wiser. He's tired of kicking his heels in the wilderness. *And*, what's more, he's keeping a firm hand on his followers. His discipline is impressive. None of them is prepared to give an inch away—until they're ready. I've smelt this coming for months. I don't reckon to spend my days at a desk. I'm out and about and I've felt the change; sensed that things were brewing up. And I'll tell you what's made me uneasy. In the old days the Bandala hopped this way, that way, like jumping crackers. There was no guessing which way they'd hop next. That's all changed. Something, somebody, in recent months, has given them a sense of direction. They've begun to know where they're going. And I don't like it. I don't like it.'

Lucas ground the stub of his cigarette into the ash tray.

'Their Press reflects the change. Instead of bicker-bicker among themselves, there's only one note now. Sustained anti-British propaganda. Whipping up hatred. They'll twist facts to suit their book—did you hear about Lobole's travesty of the Cotton Commission? We can't put a foot right. Jack Gardener's working himself to death, but he'll do no good. They don't *want* to believe in us, any more. No need to tell you why this has happened. Personally, I'm an authoritarian. I hold with discipline. In the long run discipline—not overdone, mind you, I'm no Prussian—works for happiness. Sir Christopher doesn't think so. He believes the fewer restraints the better. He's given the people too much freedom, too quickly. As a result they've become discontented, unruly, dangerous. You don't agree with me, do you? In theory, you're thinking, the Governor's right. But in practice. . . .

'There you are! What's the sense in talking? Time you got to bed—and I've work to catch up with. You can leave it to me, old chap. I'll do what I can. Can't do more. But what a sweat! What a damned unnecessary sweat!'

'I take it,' I said, 'you'll put the facts to the Governor?'

'And show him the red light?' Lucas frowned. 'He's a difficult customer. There's only one person who's likely to shift him when he's dug in his toes.' He shot me a quick glance. 'And that's his wife.'

'No,' he said, when I tried to protest, 'don't throw the ball back at me. I haven't much influence with Sir Christopher. I've none with Lady Mountclair.' He began to screw a piece of paper together in his fingers. 'I'm too outspoken. Haven't done myself much good in the long run. It was after she'd tripped up one of the most promising of my young officers. Haven't time for that sort of woman, myself, and besides'— he pitched the pellet of paper neatly into the wastepaper basket—'was bloody sore about Blackett. But, by all accounts, you're well in with her. Go ahead and convert her. Pave the way for me if you can.'

VII

I HAD rather less than three hours' sleep that night. The boy woke me with tea punctually at six o'clock. He took down the gauze screens from the window opening and the low sun, glinting up through the lacquered leaves of the banana palms in the garden, quivered across the ceiling in green waves of light. I lay and listened to the contented clucking of the hens that scratched among the huts in the servants' compound. The corner of sky I could see from my bed was, as usual, mistily blue.

I washed and shaved, breathing in the cool air. (In many respects this was the most pleasant hour of all the twenty-four. By the time I was ready for breakfast the sun, climbing vertically, had lifted over the palm tops and shadows were on the retreat.) The room boy pottered in and out, laying my clothes carefully over a chair, gathering up discarded socks, brushing, folding and hanging away my dinner jacket. I had long since accepted his presence; had given up doing things for myself. The climate was to blame. Every ounce of energy had to be conserved for the hot and humid stretch ahead.

The waiter at breakfast was as polite as always. His bare feet creaked on the polished tiles of the verandah, his heels an inch-thick slab of pink, seen from behind. Garden boys were watering the flower beds. Sprinklers were active on the lawn; whirling their lassos of rainbows steadily over the grass. The only other guest, a visiting geologist, made it a habit to bring a book with him to meals and we sat at either end of the long table, consuming paw-paw and fried eggs and bacon, drinking our coffee, in silence.

Everything that morning was exaggeratedly normal and undisturbed.

Elias reported for duty and, early as it still was, I decided to drive straight round to Government House. On the way we passed through a prosperous residential district. Here were the brick houses of the British traders and officials. The roads were edged with strips of shaven grass and planted with trees and flowering shrubs. Fat black nursemaids pushed perambulators along the pavements, walked hand in hand with their anaemic-looking charges. The parks had iron gates and gravel paths, seats, dark hedges and fantastic flowers.

On my arrival, I was told by the African butler that Lady Mountclair was not yet down. I asked him to send up a message; said I would wait. We were talking in the entrance hall, near the foot of the main staircase. The butler had padded away, I had taken a seat and had picked up a paper when my name was called loudly from one of the ground-floor rooms.

'That you, Pole?'

I opened the door of the small breakfast room opposite and looked inside. Douglas Cameron, in his shirt sleeves, was sitting at the table under a slowly revolving fan; in front of him a mammoth slice of pink-fleshed paw-paw.

'Thought I recognized your voice. On the ball early, aren't you? Have a cup of coffee?'

I controlled myself with an effort, said I would and drew up a chair. He pressed a bell on the wall behind him. A boy answered promptly, his ankle-length shirt speckless, his bright blue sash girdling a waist as slim as a young girl's. Cameron leaned back and harangued him jerkily in Swahili. The boy's face quickened with amusement. His eyes sparkled; he showed his brilliant teeth; he saluted and, with a whisk of his shirt, was gone.

'What was all that about?' I asked.

'Good bunch of servants they've got here,' said Cameron contentedly, spooning himself another mouthful of paw-paw. 'Hand-picked, of course. That laddie comes from the Hoyu district. I know his village. Probably met his father. They've a saying among 'em that if a man wants to fill his belly with meat, he's no business to lie in bed in the morning.'

'I thought you were ordering me some coffee?'

'So I was. I've discovered one thing about this country, Pole. You don't want to stand any nonsense from these fellows—if you're firm, they'll respect you. But for willing service—make 'em laugh!'

I glanced at him curiously. Africa seemed to have had a softening effect.

'Tell you how I tumbled to it, shall I? The driver I had, fellow's gone sick on me this week, malaria—take it you're dosing yourself with Paludrine, there's a lot of it about—when I first had him he was incorrigibly slack. Soon changed *that*, but I couldn't get to the bottom of the fellow, if you understand me. Sullen. Sheepish. Regular hang-dog expression. Had to drive most of one night, there was a hurry on. I was going into the Chief's *kraal* next morning and knew I'd be an hour or two, so I turned to the boy and told him to curl up in the back of the car and get some sleep. Impossible to make him understand! My phrase book was packed away and I couldn't be fished to dig it out, so I went like this.' Cameron put down his spoon, couched a cheek upon a hairy forearm, closed his eyes and gave a creditable imitation of a snore. 'The boy just doubled up and hooted with laughter. Never had any trouble with him since. Hundred-per-cent cheerful, efficient work.' And Cameron returned to his paw-paw with the air of one who has solved a tricky problem, once and for all.

'Very satisfactory,' I said. 'But schoolboy humour isn't

going to get you far with the educated African. And he's the man who really matters.'

'True enough. Moment you educate 'em, they lose their sense of fun. I've noticed that.'

The boy arrived with a pot of freshly-made coffee on a silver tray. As soon as he had gone, Cameron leant across the table and said, 'That's what comes of tampering with 'em. Better left alone. Rose won't have it so, but I tell her to wait.' He lowered his voice, hinted mysteriously. 'She'll discover soon enough who's right.'

I was on the alert at once, but found he had nothing definite in mind. He was affected by the general atmosphere; the prevalent feeling of malaise. To prick him, I told him that, the evening before, I had been dancing with Janet.

'Janet?' He looked at me suspiciously, with an instinctive tightening and thrusting forward of his jaw, as if he was preparing to bulldoze his way out through any impending awkwardness.

'Don't worry yourself,' I said, and laughed. 'She's put you behind her.'

He scraped his slice of paw-paw clean.

'You know, Pole,' he said at last, deliberately. 'You think you're too damn smart. Get you into trouble some day.'

I was given no time to retaliate. There were people speaking in the hall. I heard the gruff tones of the butler. Then the door of the breakfast room opened, the butler pressed himself as flat against the wall as his figure permitted, and Rose Mountclair stood on the threshold and stared in on us. She appeared surprised, a little disconcerted perhaps, to find us sitting at the table together.

'So *this* is where you are, Sebastian? I thought you'd given me up and gone.'

I had risen. Now Cameron appeared to remember his manners, for relucantly he elevated himself a few inches from the seat of his chair, stooping forwards. The butler withdrew, closing the door behind him, and she walked quickly round the table to put her hands on Cameron's shoulders and press him down.

'Have you everything you want?' She did not take away her hands and after a moment, a little uneasily, Cameron covered her left hand with his own.

'You've come very early,' she said. Her eyes accused me across the table. I make no concessions, she was saying. You must accept me as I am.

'I saw Martha Bifabishu last night. I need to speak to you.'

'You've been visiting Samueli again?'

'No, no, not Samueli. Martha,' I said. 'But it's about her brother and his friends.'

'Then we'll go into the garden. The day's not too hot yet. Douglas, you shall be left to finish your breakfast in peace.'

The gardens behind Government House are immaculately decorative, impeccably groomed. Twelve acres of smooth lawns, graceful trees, lakes, arbours, fountains, spectacular flowers. Surrounded by a high wall, in spite of their extent the grounds cannot be overlooked from any part of the town.

We followed the jacaranda avenue. The trees were in bloom. Fallen petals lay in drifts of violet on the grass, brighter than the bluebell mists of an English wood.

'When I first arrived here,' she said indignantly, 'the garden boys used to sweep them up every day. Think of it! Such a passion for tidiness! They went on sweeping them up, too, in spite of my orders. In the end, I had to have a showdown. Came out in a rage and made them put the whole lot back! They've left them alone since then.'

I knew I could not reach her. The barriers were up. She had detached herself; deliberately withdrawn.

'You were the first to warn me about Samueli Bifabishu,' I said. 'Please listen a moment. What I have to tell you may sound theatrical, unreal . . . not easy to talk of danger and

163

disturbances in a place as peaceful as this. But Martha sent for me last night. I've brought the letter along to show you. She's convinced me. I'm afraid it looks as if Samueli means business. Serious business.'

'Sebastian, you're talking like a detective novel. What precisely do you mean by serious business?'

I told her. An uprising. Riots. An attempt to seize power by force. She listened; shook her head.

'And Martha solemnly believes her brother capable of that? Samueli the leader of a successful *coup d'état*? But don't you see, any such attempt will be certain to fail from the start. Without popular support, he will get nowhere and whatever may be said to the contrary, the fact is that the great mass of our people are decent and law-abiding. As for the hooligans, the rabble, they're notoriously unreliable, impossible to organize. I'll grant you, Samueli can make a nuisance of himself if he chooses, but let's be sensible and view him in sober perspective.'

'I can only say that the Commissioner of Police isn't so sanguine.'

'Lucas?' She handed me back the letter, at which she had scarcely glanced. 'Remember, he is a professional. Soldiers behave in much the same way. You must have noticed how highly the successful army commander rates the skill of his opposite number, whom he has defeated in battle. It is in the Commissioner's interest to puff up Samueli's reputation, to deal with him not as a poor runt of an agitator but as a full-blown revolutionary leader.

'Another point. Give Lucas the shadow of an excuse and he will act repressively. That is the nature of the man. He means well but he's short-sighted and as limited in his outlook as an old-fashioned schoolmaster. His finest hour must inevitably coincide with an hour of national emergency. Because of this, he is pre-occupied with disaster. Then, at last, he will be granted the extraordinary powers he so

164

persistently demands. The prisons will be full; the hospital wards overflowing; machine guns will be mounted in the squares. And the people will be cowed, resentful, bitter—and the work of fifty years will be undone.'

We walked out from under the fragile, scented shade of the trees. The sun burned down on our shoulders; the grass crackled under our feet.

'And that hour, in your opinion, has not yet come?'

'No. And if we are careful, need never come.'

'Then you don't take a serious view of the situation?'

'On the scale you spoke of just now, no.'

'But you admit that Samueli could make trouble if he chose? And trouble of any kind would be likely to lead to broken heads and bloodshed?'

'In other words, why not round up all the suspects and put them neatly away before they can do any harm?'

'That makes very good sense to me.'

'And my answer to you, Sebastian, and I know that my husband's would be the same, is no, no, *no*! Not at any price. We will *not* be panicked into declaring a false state of emergency. I am confident that order can be maintained in Banda—in the future as in the past—by the normal police and security forces, without any recourse to special measures.'

'I sincerely hope you're right.'

'I take it Lucas knows the facts, as you learnt them from Martha? In that case there is really nothing more you can do. Sir Christopher returns tomorrow. If you wished, you could discuss the matter with him.'

'Yes, I would like to see the Governor.'

'Very well, then. You can leave it to me.'

We were walking by the edge of a lake. On the water floated vast round leaves with crinkled, upturned edges. Pale fish flickered in the depths. We stopped and watched them.

'You're not afraid, are you?' I said. 'Not many I've met share your confidence.'

165

'I put my trust in the Bandala. I know them. I know that they can be childish and irresponsible, easily swayed. But men like Bifabishu and Lobole touch their minds only and do not stir their hearts. I am not going to pretend to you that I'm satisfied. There may well be troubles ahead. Things may well get worse before they get better. But a spontaneous rising such as you suggest, the overthrow of our administration—that is out of the question. The newspapers do not reflect the true feeling of the country. We are not so unpopular. The work that Sir Christopher has already done here is recognized—and he has done a great deal. More, perhaps, than you realize. You still think I am over-confident?'

Her voice softened. She stood by my side, head bent, staring across the pond. 'But, Sebastian, the people love him.'

Back at the Guest House, I was intercepted by the head houseboy.

'Memsaab want to speak to you on telephone while you gone, Bwana. Leave no message.'

At once, and guiltily, I remembered Pat.

'This man just come.' He handed me a visiting card.

I read the name. *Jacob S. Mankele, M.A., Barrister-at-law.*

'Is he here? I'll see him at once.'

The boy swung open the double doors that led into the lounge.

Jacob was sitting in the far corner of the room, staring out through the windows. He was absorbed, lost in his own thoughts, and made no move, gave no sign that he had heard me enter.

'Good morning!' I said, and the words brought him to his feet with a visible start. He was dressed formally in a dark brown lounge suit. His shoes were brilliantly polished. With his blue shirt, yellow tie, handkerchief protruding from breast pocket, he looked every inch a prosperous, confident citizen of the new Africa. His bearing, however, contradicted his appearance. As he stood up, his hands fumbled over his pockets; his gaze roved the room. He gave me the impression that he was acutely nervous.

'I'm sorry to have missed you last night.'

'Mr. Pole,' he said, and took my hand as if he were clutching for support. 'She is dead. Martha has died in the hospital.'

The words were like a blow. For the moment I was stunned.

'Martha—*dead*? But I was with her—why, it was early this morning. A few hours ago.'

'I have seen her. They allowed me to see her.' He suddenly looked into my face—his eyes were painful to meet—and said, 'Her body was still warm. Such a small thing for the doctors, it seemed, to make her live, make her breathe again. She lay as if she were asleep. I had often watched her lying so, asleep. This time it did not seem very different.' His face was twisted. He was unable any longer to control his grief. 'Only there was no breath. No life.'

'But what happened? Was there an accident?'

'Very unfortunate,' he said. 'I am alone now. I have no future. But you are in no way to blame.' He added quietly, 'The house was watched. You were seen leaving.'

'I was seen leaving?'

'I do not yet know who passed on the information to Lobole.'

Everything was immediately, monstrously clear. I took a step forward, said, 'What happened to Martha after I had left?'

'They forced their way in. A group of our young men— those nearest to Samueli. No,' he said, lifting his hand, 'it is not as you might imagine. They had been misinformed.'

'How do you mean, misinformed?'

167

'I have already made enquiries. No one, not even Lobole himself, knows the reason for your visit. Martha—' unconsciously, he straightened his back '—would not betray us.'

'I don't understand. Why, then, was . . .'

'Listen, Mr. Pole. I will tell you. You are owed an explanation.' He glanced round, said half apologetically, 'Shall we sit down?'

'Of course!' I said. 'Your news—you must forgive me.'

'I had no wish,' he said, easing his trousers over his knees and sitting well forward in his chair, 'to involve you in our affairs. But the matter was delicate and we—that is to say, it would have been difficult—for us to approach the authorities. You will appreciate our position. There was much needless delay. In the end we sent for you at the last moment. I waited in the house with my companions until twelve o'clock. I did not expect you to arrive after that hour. Today, I woke late. Then I was told. The blow was severe for I was quite unprepared.'

He stared intently at the knife-edge crease of one of his trouser legs.

'Everything that I tell you I have learnt from one who was present. As I said, the motives of your visit were misunderstood. Martha told them again and again that she was innocent. They refused to believe her. They were impatient, angry. And what good reason could she give for admitting you? They demanded to know if she were still a virgin. She did not answer. Mr. Pole, she could not answer.' Jacob bent his head, crushed his hands between his knees. 'One of the men—I know him well, he is a medical student at the University—examined her. You see,' he said with an effort, 'Martha and I have lain together on various occasions. That was our secret. She would not leave her work with the children and on account of them was reluctant to consent to marriage. I was importunate. I should have been more patient. But for that she could have proved her innocence.

They would not have touched her. In a sense, her death is as much my crime as theirs.'

I distinctly heard a car drive down the road on the far side of the Guest House. The sweat was clammy under my shirt.

'The student found, at the same time, that physically Martha was not as most other Bandala women. I must explain that we have certain ceremonies in our country—ceremonies of initiation which mark stages in the development of our boys and girls. We believe, among other things, that a woman must have no pleasure in intercourse. Pleasure leads to temptation, temptation to misconduct—and indeed, this is the case. The missionaries do not understand these customs, use their influence against them, and when Martha grew to womanhood they persuaded the Chief, her father, to their view. She was never initiated. . . .

'But what took place this morning was a desecration.' Jacob's hands were knotted together. He was speaking deliberately in a quiet, mechanical voice. 'There in her house, without ritual, in the heat of anger, they performed the operation. In her brother's name, they revenged themselves on her body, for, Mr. Pole, it was nothing more than a revenge. Samueli, you must realize, is a proud man. He is the son of a chief, he has royal blood in his veins. He may profess to despise the Omuvomo, but in fact, on matters of custom, religion, tribal law, he is a fervent traditionalist. He has influenced these men. He has worked on their feelings. They are all anti-white. That Martha—as they had every reason to believe—had given herself to a European was a disgrace, a shaming of the blood. But it was a matter for the elders, for the council, for serious deliberation, not for individual action. We Bandala are sadly changed. The old bonds of tribal discipline are broken. They showed no restraint, no respect. They took the law into their own hands and although she was innocent, they killed her.'

169

He rubbed his face, his eyes, with his fingers, as if trying to free himself from an entangled dream.

'When our young girls are initiated, Mr. Pole, the operation forms the culminating point of an elaborate and beautiful ceremony. Every precaution is taken. In mind and in body, the girls are prepared. To minimize the pain, they stand for an hour waist-deep in the cold waters of a river. But Martha is no longer a young girl. She was unprepared. Afterwards the men came to their senses. They saw what they had done and were frightened and left her. A neighbour, roused by the noise, found her unconscious. Even so, I am amazed that she has died. I cannot yet believe it. At the hospital, they told me she was brought to them too late.'

I could not, at that moment, force myself to contemplate the catastrophe. I looked at Jacob, sitting opposite, and groped for a rational explanation.

'But who is to blame? Did Samueli give the order. . . .'

'Samueli gave no order. He knew nothing. It was Lobole who was informed. He lives in the same district. He has always disliked Martha, resented what little influence she exerted over her brother. No doubt he saw his chance to disgrace her and made the most of the opportunity.'

'Who could have known where I was going, last night? Only yourself and those with you. Who spread the rumour. . .?'

Jacob shrugged his shoulders. 'Possibly you were followed. I do not understand how it happened.' He added quietly, 'But it is of no consequence. The fault is mine. I should never have involved Martha in her brother's betrayal. That was my foolishness, Mr. Pole, and I have paid for it.'

'I'm sorry,' I said. 'I'm very sorry.' The words were inadequate. Jacob, staring again out of the window, did not hear them. After a while he roused himself, stood up, said he must go. I thanked him for coming and accompanied him to the door of the Guest House. He turned on the step leading down to the road, looking back.

'Things cannot stay as they are,' he said. His eyes were wide and apprehensive. Then he straightened his shoulders and I watched him walk out into the hazy sunlight, armoured in expensive suiting, a curly-brimmed homburg set at a defiant angle on his head.

I came back into the Guest House and at once telephoned the hospital. Put through to the women's casualty ward, I asked to speak to the Sister-in-charge. There was a considerable delay before a crisp voice with a slight Scottish accent sounded over the line.

Martha Bifabishu? Yes, the patient had been admitted at seven-thirty that morning. Condition critical. Suffering from shock and loss of blood. She had not responded to treatment and had died half an hour later without regaining consciousness. But Sister Crosbie had not caught my name. Was that Mr. Pole? Would I hold on a moment while she took the call from her own room? She had already tried to get in touch with me.

There was another period of silence and then she spoke again. The official, emotionless voice had relented. I was no longer talking to an automaton but to a bewildered and unhappy human being.

'Mr. Pole, this is a sorry affair. Mr. Lucas was here at the hospital a while ago, he asked me to let you know the facts. Now it's a case of manslaughter and no doubt they've all run for it. To think, we've often had that boy M'zimbwe in the wards!'

'M'zimbwe?' I said.

'One of the medical students. He was seen entering the house with the others. There can be no question that he carried out the operation. I call it an operation, but you realize, don't you, that the girl was the victim of a most brutal assault? Oh, these unspeakable rites! Are we never

171

to stamp them out? But it's no use. At heart they're still savages, you can't trust them. I've worked in Bandaland for fifteen years and today, when that girl was brought in, I was ashamed, yes, ashamed. What *use* is education? Where has M'zimbwe's medical training led him? As far and no further than mutilation with a kitchen knife! I can't talk about it, Mr. Pole, it's too horrifying. Here we are, for better, for worse, fighting disease, teaching them to lead healthy, decent lives, and then the devil in them is roused and pulls them down into darkness. In all my experience, and I should be hardened by this time, I can't remember a worse case. What are we to do with them? What are we to do with these people?'

After she had rung off I went into the lounge, called a boy and ordered a double whisky. I felt better, sitting down. In spite of the fans, the room was oppressively hot. I loosened my tie, opened the collar of my shirt. The boy returned and set the drink on the table beside me. I could not bring myself to look up into his face. The black hand encircling the glass caused me a momentary twinge of disgust.

But the boy seemed reluctant to leave and after shuffling his feet said in a voice of apparently genuine concern, 'Bwana not looking well. Bwana got fever?'

I said no, I was not ill, the whisky was all I wanted, and sent him away.

I sat in the empty lounge for perhaps an hour. I thought of Martha on the few occasions I had met her. Remembered her at the kindergarten; tall, intense, touching in her anxiety to convince. Heavy going, perhaps; a shade humourless, but estimable. Remembered her in more aggressive mood, playing the hostess, delivering business-like jabs aimed to puncture her brother's self-esteem.

Lobole had not been told that she intended to reveal Samueli's plans to the authorities. He had been informed that Martha was sharing her bed, that night, with a white

172

man. The denunciation, so far-fetched, so unreal; in its implied judgment so wildly off the mark, had an hysterical ring. Emotions in this country were crazy, incalculable. My mind leapt on—to Pat, standing only a few yards from these windows, taut, trembling, hatred in her voice as she shouted, 'You dare to paw me after touching that black ape! You're disgusting, Sebastian. All along you've made me feel cheap.'

Martha Bifabishu. Martha B. I saw again the name, abbreviated but recognizable, scribbled in pencil on paper. The name scribbled on the sketch map Lucas had drawn for me in Gardener's study, yesterday evening. The map I had held in my hand as I walked out of the bungalow and along the road to the car. The map that I had mislaid in the car and never found.

'Running away again, Sebastian? This is becoming a habit.'

And there was Patricia, after the scene that was best forgotten, gathering up her wrap, her bag from the seat between us. Patricia, convinced in her heart that I was going with another woman. Was it possible? I put down the glass and, to think more clearly, buried my face in my hands.

The small office sandwiched between Shell-Mex and the headquarters of the Equatorial Trading and Supply Company was closed. I rang the bell again, then gave it up, returned to the car and told Elias to drive me to her private address.

In the press of sweltering air, my body ran with sweat. Up in the residential area the streets were deserted. Banda lay shadowless, unprotected, exposed to the flattening glare of the noon sun. There was no escaping the white, impartial light. Perhaps it was not surprising that I did not recognize the road, nor, when we stopped, the house.

A boy opened the door and I asked him for Miss Jensen. 'Is she at home?' He looked at me with stupid eyes. I repeated the question. Somewhere inside the house a woman's voice, not Pat's, called, 'Who's that, Saraphino? Have you answered the door?'

'Is Pat there?' I said, speaking loudly.

Two things happened. Pat's friend, the girl with whom she shared the house, appeared at the end of the passage. And the door of the room on the left was jerked open by Terence.

'Oh Lord!' said Olive. Her hand went up to her mouth. 'It's you.'

She was clumsily-built, unattractive; a shorthand-typist at the Equatorian Legation. I had met her once before. She advanced a few steps up the passage and then stopped and stared at me. Her sharp, close-set eyes were not friendly.

'All right, Saraphino,' she said. 'You can go.'

'Where's Pat?' I looked from one to the other.

Terence drew in his breath sharply. 'Don't speak to him,' he said to Olive. 'He's no business to come here.'

'You deal with him, then. I'll make myself scarce.' But she lingered.

'I want an answer,' I said, growing impatient. 'If Patricia's not here, where is she?'

'Shall I call the boys, Terence?'

He silenced her with a gesture. 'Patricia's gone,' he said. 'You'll never see her again. That's all there is to it. Now get out—and stay out.'

'Gone? Where's she gone? I tell you I must see her.'

Olive still hovered in the passage.

'Terence!' she called, in a voice vibrant with malice. 'Terence! Tell him to go back to his native bitch.'

The words exploded in my head.

'So that's it! Then Pat *did* know!'

'She knew,' said Terence. 'She knew. And if she's put an

end to herself by this time, as she threatened . . .' He took a step towards me. He could scarcely speak. 'If she takes her own life, you'll have driven her to it. When I saw her this morning, she was at the end of her tether.'

'But it's all a misunderstanding. More than that—it's a crazy lie!' I gripped his shoulders, as if to shake sense into him. 'Talk to Lucas, talk to the Commissioner of Police. I was going about *his* business.'

'You're speaking the truth?'

'I'm not asking you to take my word for it. Lucas knows where I went, last night, and he knows *why* I went.'

Terence looked at me sharply; pushed my hands away.

'Come in here,' he said, stepping back into the room. Olive at once moved forward, as if to follow, but he shut the door in her face.

'Let's get things straight. You dropped Pat late last night and went on to this woman Martha's house. You don't deny that? And you never said a word where you were going or why?' He gestured hopelessly. 'You know how Patricia feels about these things. What's it matter whether you went to bed with the woman or not?'

'I'll tell you why it matters. Because others were told— and believed—that lie, Martha Bifabishu was tortured. She died a few hours ago, in hospital.'

'Died? That's pretty sudden, isn't it.'

I gave him the details as I knew them. 'And I want to know—I *must* know—who passed on the information.'

His eyes narrowed. He had been watching me keenly.

'I can see what you're after. You aim to pin this on Pat. Well, you're out of luck. You won't catch up with her now.' Terence glanced at his wrist watch. 'She's in Smithville.'

'In *Smithville*!'

'She 'phoned me early, wanted me to take her to the airport. She'd got a cancellation on the eight o'clock flight. I came round and found her in a fine state. I don't think

175

she'd slept. She was packing as much as she could take. I'm sending the rest of her stuff after her. I said I'd do that.'

I saw, for the first time, that the small sitting-room was in chaos. Trunks lay open on the floor, coats and dresses hung over the chairs, books were piled on the table.

'Tried to persuade her to stay, but it was no use. I know Pat. When she gets like that, it's a waste of time arguing. And I'd have given my right hand,' Terence said, in a voice that he could not prevent from shaking. 'I'd have given my right hand to have kept her here in Banda and made her happy. But I'm no use. That's the confounded part of it. You're the man she wanted.' He thrust his thin boy's face close to mine. 'And look what you've done to her!'

'Pat, Pat, Pat!' I shouted at him. 'Always Pat—and what I've done to her. Aren't you capable of facing what *she's* done to Martha. Because she's spoilt, uncontrolled, insanely jealous. . . .'

'Jealous? You fool, she loved you. You kicked her away. You're the type who'll break a girl when you're tired of her, she can go and hang herself for all you care. And because Patricia's passionate and single-hearted, you call her uncontrolled, insanely jealous. . . . D'you think I feel that—' he snapped his fingers, 'for any black prostitute when I know Pat's suffering. If the woman's dead, as you say she is, then she's the better off. And if Pat follows her, you'll be the cause of it all.'

There was no sense in prolonging the interview. Terence and I were no longer speaking the same language. Everything suddenly seemed pointless. I felt hot and exhausted and extraordinarily depressed.

I remember letting myself out into the noonday glare and walking down the path between the hibiscus hedges. Elias, watchful as always, sprang from the driver's seat and opened the car door with his accustomed flourish.

VIII

I DROVE to Police Headquarters. Lucas was out. I waited for a quarter of an hour in his office, sitting in a cane chair in the full draught of the fan. Then the Commissioner came in, mopping his face with a red bandanna. He took off his coat and hung it on a hook on the back of the door.

'Sticky,' he said. 'Confoundedly sticky.'

He did not look up until he had settled himself behind his desk, twisting the lid from a round tin of cigarettes and pushing them across. His eyes were slits in his cheeks.

'Sister ring you? Wretched business,' he said, striking a match.

'Have you caught the men?'

'No. Not yet. We shall, with any luck. I know five of the seven by name.' He stared at the blotting pad, frowning, the flame burning down the stick of the match until he flicked it out and dropped the stump into his ash tray. 'Doesn't add up,' he said at last. 'The Bandala are logical. Frankly, Pole, I don't get it. Why—what made them swing that way?'

I told him. I told him everything that Jacob Mankele had said to me, but I did not mention Patricia. Lucas sat with his unlighted cigarette in one hand, matches in the other, absolutely still, his face stone-hard.

'*Lobole*,' he said, half a minute after I had finished speaking. He suddenly jerked into forward gear, moving quickly, catching up with his long-delayed movements. He struck another match, lit my cigarette, then his, leant back in his chair and drew the smoke into his lungs with the satisfied air of a man who sees his next step ahead. 'Might be useful if you came. We'll drive round and pay him a visit.'

Before we left he spoke to one of his assistants over the telephone and a young police officer, an African, brought him in a small sheaf of messages, pinned together in the corner. Lucas flipped through the papers and handed them back without comment. Driving off in his car, he told me that the news from the Namzike was good. He had made the necessary arrests quietly and without trouble and had succeeded in by-passing the demonstration at Rua-rua. If everything continued to plan, the Governor would arrive at Mpulongwe later that afternoon, spend the night on board the lake steamer, sailing south, and arrive back in the capital, midday tomorrow.

Lucas broke off to instruct his driver. Soon afterwards the car stopped outside a row of rusting, corrugated iron stores; shops without windows and with cavernous, shadowy interiors. We joined the throng of Africans on the pavement (the shopping streets of Banda are always crowded) and he led the way down a side-alley. Native tailors crouched cross-legged in the shade of narrow balconies, turning the handles of old-fashioned sewing machines. Naked children played their mysterious games with pebbles in the dust.

Following him in through the shabby doorway into a cramped, dark office, I was temporarily blinded. Then I saw that the room was jammed with small tables and desks and that a dozen clerks in their shirt-sleeves were sitting there, shoulder to shoulder, with no space between them. Our entry caused a good deal of confusion. Some, who wished to stand, could not push back their chairs to do so until those behind them had moved. Files, account books, trays of letters, were heaped up in crazy piles. The air was stuffy and rank with the peculiar odour of African sweat.

178

'No, sir. Impossible to see Mr. Lobole just now. There is already someone with him. Did you have an appointment?' The clerk nearest the door was blandly insolent.

Lucas extracted a card from his wallet, handed it across.

'Will you take that up to Mr. Lobole.'

The clerk began to protest but several others (they may possibly have recognized the Commissioner) shouted him down. A child in a torn shirt and grubby pants was called in from the street. He took the card from the clerk and led us through the office into a small yard at the back. A rickety-looking outside staircase faced us, leading up to a door in the attic of the big building ahead. We could hear the clatter of printing machinery. The child scampered up the steps, knocked on the door. Looking up, we could see his woolly black head cocked sideways as he listened. He knocked again, harder than before, and then a third time. With a shrug of his thin shoulders he turned to come down, but Lucas was already climbing the flight of steps. I followed, hoping that the treads would bear.

Arriving on the small platform at the top, Lucas rapped smartly on the door and turned the handle. The door was locked.

While I waited, staring up, he held a brief confabulation with the boy. Then we returned to the office. No one appeared to know the name of Lobole's visitor—or when he had come. The clerks were suspicious. It was easy to see that they were lying.

We followed the boy out into the street and he led us through a maze of small lanes, bringing us out in front of the same tall building; the building filled with the rumble and clatter of machinery. Here the boy left us and we passed inside. The big newspaper press in the centre of the floor was silent; only the jobbing machines were at work. An African foreman in an overall came across. His manner was alert, deferential. At the far end of the room an iron staircase mounted to a green door—the other approach to Lobole's office—and up this staircase the foreman ran, to enact the same pantomime, knocking, listening (as best he could), shrugging his shoulders. Lucas followed hard on his heels. I followed Lucas. As there was no space at the top of the stairs we stood, perched uneasily, one below the other.

'I never saw Mr. Lobole leave, sir. I think he must go through the office. . . .'

'You said his visitor came down these stairs? When?'

'Mr. Mankele left half an hour ago. Perhaps a little more.'

'Mankele? You know the man, do you? And you're certain of the time?'

'I am certain, sir.'

'And he was alone. Not with Lobole?'

'No, sir. He was quite alone.'

'Is the door locked? I must see inside the office.'

The foreman hesitated, glancing round at Lucas for confirmation. Over the floor of the shop black faces gaped up, but the clickety-clatter of the machines never stopped.

'Go on,' Lucas said. 'You have my authority. Open the door.'

The handle was turned, the door pushed open and we crowded into an empty room. But the foreman, walking ahead, leapt back from the desk with a howl. He had trodden on one of Lobole's hands.

I remember that, of all things, I felt thwarted; angry with Jacob for his intervention, sickened by the killing. (We had pulled the editor out from between his chair and the desk, turned him over. His body was twisted, his expression grotesque. He had been stabbed many times.) But perhaps it was best, I told myself, that I should learn nothing more. Best that the chapter should be closed. I lay on my bed at the Guest House, wrapped in a towel, my body like a log, inert, through the heavy hours of the afternoon. Now and again I dozed and seemed to hear the racket of the small vertical presses; smell the pungent reek of printer's ink. The fan on the shelf behind the editor's chair whirred and turned its blind head slowly from side to side, and regularly, as the draught passed over the desk, papers, anchored with weights, fluttered and vibrated and were still again. A fitful breeze stirred spirals of fine sand, rustled the hot fine dust of the Nwambe. Lucas knelt on the floor. The foreman's mouth hung open; his eyes were wide and staring; as he stood he trembled, shook through the height of his big frame. Gerald Bulmers trod forward, his foot in the small of a bronze back, wrenching at the spear. The two killings had become super-imposed. Blood on the satin of an oiled skin. Blood on a white shirt and crumpled grey trousers. The wheel had come full circle and I was back where I had started. The one reality was violence. The one creed, an eye for an eye, a tooth for a tooth.

A houseboy came into my room at dusk to call me to the telephone. I went reluctantly—but it was Rose Mountclair. I was glad to hear her voice. She was, perhaps, the one person to whom I would have chosen to speak. She knew about Martha. She knew that Lobole had been killed. I did not have to tell her anything.

'Sebastian, this is not the moment to cry defeat! Don't you see that the others, that they'll need our faith, our understanding. We can't refuse them now. Forget, forgive? But don't be absurd! Has the African the prerogative of cruelty? Punish the offenders, certainly, but to despair of a race. . . . We must hold on to what we still have, hold on more tightly. We must believe in them. *Show* that we believe in them.'

She asked if I were coming to the rehearsal of the orchestra at the University in an hour's time. She reminded me that I had promised to attend. I did not want to leave the shelter of the Guest House but, when I protested, she insisted the more strongly that I should come.

Banda University stands on a hill north of the city; is approached along an avenue of tall gum trees. Their blotched and peeling trunks, vivid in the headlights, reminded me nostalgically of London planes. The main block is built in the cautious neo-Georgian style of the thirties and is flanked by newer and slightly daring experiments in glass and concrete. Elias drove through an arch into the main courtyard. Students were moving about under the lamps and I felt that the glances directed at the car were not, on the whole, friendly. Possibly this was my imagination, for when I got out and asked the way of one of the young men I was taken in charge at once and led, willingly, through a maze of corridors to the large hall where the rehearsal was to be held. I was early. A few students, holding instruments, turned to stare at me, then resumed their talk. Others were tuning, practising, and the hall was filled with odd, detached scraps of sound that fitted into no particular pattern. I took a seat at the back and waited, watching the entrance, for Rose Mountclair.

A student came up and sat apologetically, not on the chair next to mine but on the one beyond, and plunged into conversation. Was I interested in music? Did I know their conductor, the head of the faculty, Dr. Theodor Schütz? *The* Doctor Schütz! Hamburg, London, Chicago, Sydney— and now Bandaland!

The subject was a relief. I wondered, as I looked at him, how much he knew; what he had heard.

'And what do you play?' I asked. The boy was modest and confused. He bowed his head, his hands, with their long fingers, hanging between his knees. His voice was throaty and he mispronounced words.

182

'I am a violinist,' he said, 'but bad, bad.' He shied away from the personal to ask whether I lived in England. 'You are fortunate,' he sighed. 'We are so isolated here. I should like to visit Europe. Tell me,' he said, growing bolder, 'how large exactly is the Albert Hall?' He did not wait for my answer but rushed on. 'Is it true that in London white men drive the buses? Strange,' he said as I nodded again.

'Lady Mountclair tells me you've a fine 'cellist at the University.'

'That is true. You will hear him tonight in the Elgar Concerto. Perhaps one day he will play at the Albert Hall.' There was a pause. 'The Albert Hall, you would say, is one of the largest buildings in London?'

The conversation lapsing, I asked him about his national instruments—in particular, the xylophone made from hollow gourds.

'Yes, yes, they are played. Not here, in the University, but out in the country our people play them. They are toys, you understand. They are not for an orchestra.' A suspicion of arrogance tinged the throaty voice, the head lifted. 'But here is Dr. Schütz and Her Excellency with him. If you will excuse me, sir, I must go. Perhaps I will talk to you again, after the rehearsal.'

The players were assembling. There was a sprinkling of pink faces in the orchestra; professors and teachers, I assumed, on the University staff. Dr. Schütz, short, spherical, with a mop of up-brushed grey hair and a sunburnt tonsure, rapped on his desk and spattered them all with a guttural shower of advice and instruction. Then he nodded to the soloist, who settled himself in his chair and raised his bow. With a series of emphatic chords, the rehearsal started.

At the first pause I moved forward a few rows, the better to hear the conductor, whose words were worth listening to. Neither did the 'cellist disappoint. He was a gentle, wooden young man with a burly figure and broad shoulders. His wrists were finely boned, his fingers sensitive. Africans, I was beginning to conclude, should be judged less by their bodies and faces than by their hands.

At the end, I walked up to the platform. Rose Mountclair was talking to Theodor Schütz and I was introduced. Around us, students were putting instruments back into cases, gathering up their scores. The Europeans had drifted together into a loose group in one corner of the stage and towards this group I was eventually drawn, leaving the conductor besieged by a press of enthusiastic young musicians. A small, aggressive-looking man with a strong Lancashire accent promptly took me in charge. He had come from Preston, he told me, to teach mathematics to the Bandala.

'Aye, they're grand lads,' he said. 'We have 'em bright and we have 'em dull, same as anywhere else. But I tell you where they've got us beat. *Work!* Put us to shame! Taught in schools here before I came to University and, joking apart, if we were to come late to class, why the fellows would complain to the Head! I don't say they aren't sometimes misguided, but they've got the idea. Catch us up, that's what they've set their minds to do, and catch us up they will, if application's anything to do with it.'

He rattled cheerfully on. I did my best to appear intelligently interested and, at the same time, watched out for Lady Mountclair. After a while, I saw her on the floor of the hall. Four Africans were standing round her; one of them, the soloist.

Because I wished to speak to her, because my companion was no longer holding my attention, I was perhaps more alert than most to what was happening.

I saw that a group of students, who had left the hall carrying their instruments, had now returned and were shouting excitedly. Their excitement was infectious and spread from group to group. The atmosphere changed. I

184

had felt this change before, in Martha's room, on the day of the procession. The even hum of conversation rose sharply, as the note of a hive changes when the bees are disturbed, and at once the groups scattered about the hall were agitated and out of the flux a new pattern began to emerge.

The man from Preston had stopped talking. He stared over my shoulder, his eyes watchful and alert. The change was reflected in the faces of the other members of the University staff, standing on the platform. They were uneasy, anxious, doing their best not to show their anxiety, trying not to reveal by glance or movement that they were in any sense disturbed. By this time I saw that one group of students had made the Governor's wife their rallying point. Another cluster had gathered near the door and these—closely-knit, vocal—appeared to be chanting some sort of slogan. Then one man started to chase another between the rows of seats. A fight threatened. Several of the staff jumped down into the hall. Lady Mountclair, shepherded by students, reached the platform. The belligerent minority, followed at a distance by waverers, marched through the doorway, still shouting. Order was restored.

'I gather they're demonstrating in the courtyard.' (She had appeared by my side.) 'Nothing to be alarmed about, Sebastian—you know what students are. The porridge may have been burnt at breakfast.' I saw that she was talking for effect; others were listening. 'But here's the Principal. He'll tell us what is the matter.'

I knew the Principal by sight; had seen in the distance his stooping, grey-haired, diffident figure. He came rapidly up the steps on to the platform, followed by one of his African professors.

There was a certain amount of confusion in the courtyard and around the main entrance, he told us. Banda boat race night. . . . As he talked he made small deprecatory gestures, shrugged, smiled wryly, stabbed the air with his spectacles.

185

He had not succeeded in discovering, yet, what it was all about. None of the students involved was very definitive. All he could say at the moment was that they were making a great deal of *noise*. He regretted the inconvenience, but perhaps if Lady Mountclair would consent to follow the professor. . . .

The Principal turned to instruct his staff. One of the many students on the platform approached to apologize for the disturbance and to thank her for having attended the rehearsal. Then the professor, without further ado, seized the Amati and led the way into the wings. I hesitated, not certain whether I was meant to follow. She unceremoniously seized my hand and pulled me after her. The pressure of her warm, dry palm was reassuring.

I remember that we passed through empty corridors, across an open space between two buildings and found ourselves in a long, dimly-lit, institutional kitchen. Not a whisper reached us. The buildings were deserted. The professor strode rapidly forward, head bent, never once looking round. He carried the violin case awkwardly under one arm, supporting it with his other hand as if fearful that at any moment it might slip from his grasp. We came out at the back of the University and there, among crates and empty bottles and dustbins, our cars were waiting for us.

The overpowering bulk of the Governor's Daimler, the chromium corrugations of the splendid bonnet, glistened under the stars. But Elias and Lady Mountclair's driver were crooning mournfully over a star of chipped cellulose in the centre of one of the massive doors.

'That mark was made by a stone, sir,' said Elias aside to me, in a voice of shocked disapproval. 'They have no respect here. They dare to throw stones at Bwana Government's car.'

I drove back in her cushioned cavern, the driver sealed

186

away behind glass, the engine murmur distant as a dream. Elias followed in the Chevrolet.

'Listen, Sebastian,' she said. 'Three months after I first arrived in Bandaland, the boys at Karamoja burnt down their new school. The school they'd been crying out for, that they needed so badly. Their own school. An act of useless, senseless destruction that was like a physical hurt to me. Why? For no sensible reason under the sun. Don't think that they *want* to do these things. Their struggle is with the past. The old discipline was too rigorous. Abasement over the centuries doesn't help a people to develop. Sixty years ago, when a man approached the present Omuvomo's grandfather, he squirmed ten yards along the ground like a snake. No, don't talk to me about Martha. Not yet. Let me follow through with my thoughts.

'I told you when I telephoned, didn't I, that it was not a question of forgetting, forgiving? Who are we, to presume to forgive? I ask myself, sometimes, by what right are we here? I have my moments of doubt. The missionaries and the traders started it all. They had a certainty of purpose, a sense of direction, that few of us possess today. Their aims were simple, straightforward enough. The tribes to be shown the light. Markets to be tapped. Today, we are responsible, fairly and squarely responsible, for millions of Africans. This is a Protectorate. We are not concerned—at any rate should not be concerned—with our personal security. As I see it, our purpose is to help, assist, guide; *not* to preach, *not* to exploit; neither to take it upon ourselves to be shocked, outraged, angry, nor to place ourselves upon a pedestal. . . . We anticipate certain norms of behaviour that, quite possibly, we have no right to anticipate. Possibly, we are forcing them up too fast and too far. I don't know. But I tell you, Sebastian, in all seriousness, that we shall fail in our duty if we attempt to sit in judgment.'

'Surely we'll lose everything unless we act from strength?'

'Press them harder? Is that your solution?'

'I have no solution. I can't talk like this. How can I stay detached, how can I view things whole, when I'm involved. Directly involved.'

'So are we all, Sebastian.'

'Not the way I mean. Let me talk. I need to talk. Rose, do you know why Martha died?'

The demonstration at the University was described, in one short paragraph, in next day's edition of the Banda English newspaper; a four-page pamphlet called *The Beacon*. A few windows had been broken. A bonfire of chairs and trestles had been lit in the centre of the courtyard. The Principal had addressed the students and the rules covering the annual examinations were to be revised.

Lobole's murder made the headlines, overshadowing the discreetly-worded report that dealt with the death of Martha Bifabishu. No attempt was made to link these news items. The police, it was stated, were still searching for Jacob Mankele, who was believed to have left Banda. Six of the seven students who had forced an entry into Martha's house had now been arrested.

The city was quiet; the sky, as usual, hazy but cloudless; as usual, the sun wasted no time but swung up and hovered above the rolling hills.

I had arranged to lunch at the club with Gerald Bulmers. I got there early. My host had not yet arrived. Hunched on stools at the bar, talking earnestly, were Douglas Cameron and a man whose face I recognized, whose name I had forgotten. A man I could not, for the moment, place. Cameron nodded across. I ordered a drink and took a stool at the other end of the bar. The man had his back to me. Scraps of their conversation I could not help but overhear. As I knew Cameron, there were two subjects he was prepared to discuss at length. This morning, he was not talking women. He was talking cows.

I had not quite finished my first drink when, business apparently shelved for the time being, Cameron called loudly for another round.

'Pole, meet an old army pal of mine from Equatoria.'

'That's all right, Douglas. I know this bloke.'

'Why, of course,' I said as he turned. 'You're Peck. George Peck.' I picked up my glass, walked over, shook hands.

I asked him what he was doing in Bandaland.

He stared hard into my face. 'I've lost half my dairy herd. Some bug or other. Attacks them with a kind of cramp, a paralysis of the legs. Over they go, as if they'd been poleaxed. Once on the ground, you can't get them up again. Keep 'em moving, that's the only answer. Went to the Research Institute in Smithville—no change. Then I heard that Douglas was working in Banda. I reckoned he might know the answer. So I flew over with my blood samples.'

'I remember we came across to look at one of your cows,' I said.

'So you did. She was the first, as a matter of fact. I called in Hardcastle again, but he was out of his depth. Douglas tells me that the infection's carried by the native herds. Can't do anything about the cattle in the Reserve, but I've allowed my squatters to keep the odd cow—and that'll have to stop. By the way, Pole, your big friend's got it coming to him, just as I said he would.'

'How's that?'

'The drive's on now to clean up the country. Courts are chock-a-block with cases. Had a Government snooper around the farm, only last week. Kicked him out myself, don't hold with that sort of thing, but he'll get his information. The damn great fool's missed his chance. He should have pulled himself up years ago—or got out.'

'And if he's prosecuted, what's the punishment likely to be?'

'Stiff. No option either. Your friend'll go inside for a year or two and life won't be easy for him when he comes out. We don't stand for that sort of behaviour.'

'What behaviour?' Cameron asked, leaning forward to look round Peck.

'Consorting with natives,' said George crisply.

'Don't see the point of it. Why sleep with a black? Aren't there enough white women in Equatoria?'

I saw the Governor that evening. He looked brown and well, physically much fitter. As soon as we had seated ourselves, with an air of quiet triumph he handed me the copy of a cable signed by the Chairman of the Halliday Trust. The Board had considered my report and were prepared to finance the Nwambe Project.

I had not anticipated a favourable decision and the message took me by surprise. I could not, at once, grasp that my work in Bandaland was finished. Sir Christopher told me that I was to be congratulated on an impartial survey. Impartial? I thought of Rose striding angrily up and down her drawing-room, the pages of my typescript fluttering in her hand.

I sat and listened while he talked about the Project. The scheme that would soon take physical shape, emerge from the blue-print and the monograph, become a reality. The child of his mind, his imagination. The pointer to the future.

'Africa is big,' he said and his hands opened. 'She offers big problems. The Nwambe is one of her problems in microcosm. Before you, Mr. Pole, have reached my age, the whole question of race and colour will dominate the world, very much as the question of war and peace dominates the world today. This is a start, a step forward in the right direction. Possibly,' he said, with one of his sudden smiles, 'a first step that will be remembered.'

After a while, we spoke of Martha Bifabishu. The Governor's manner became remote, clinical, and confirmed what I had already suspected; that he was incapable of descending to personalities. The practice of clitoridectomy, he insisted, was on the decline, for the old cults had given way before the spread of Christian teaching. Initiation ceremonies were occasionally performed in remote villages and in outlying districts, but played little part in the life of the country as a whole. Recently, however, he agreed, there had been an attempt to resuscitate the old customs. These had been espoused, in the cause of nationalism, by the advance guard of intellectuals. The Governor, I noticed, shrugged this off as an inevitable teething pain.

We touched on the question of security measures. He listened, a little impatiently, to what I had to say. His reaction was instantaneous and complete.

'What an universal panacea it is,' he said, 'this "firm hand!" But why should I experiment with anything so foolhardy as a display of force? To do so might well precipitate the very troubles we wish to avoid. I have been aware for some time that our administrative harness has begun to chafe. The people are restless. I propose, therefore, not to tighten but to ease the restrictions which irk them. This, surely, is sound common sense.

'There is one law long overdue for revision. Many years ago, in a moment of panic, we put a ban on gatherings and processions. Now, laws in essence must be reasonable, and a measure such as this, which forbids more than twelve citizens to gather together in public, is an incitement to mass lawbreaking. Why encourage our people to defy us? Let them process, let them meet together. They will be far less likely to disturb the peace if they know they are acting within their rights.

'That is one example. The arrest or detention of suspects is another. Ask yourself, why are we here? To create a police state and to hold down a population by strength? But there is no need for me to labour the point.'

I knew enough to want to challenge him. I could have brought forward a dozen arguments. . . . But he had already spared me half an hour of his time and I could expect no more.

As I had hoped he would, Major Wakefield met me on the stairs on my way out. We greeted each other familiarly, like old acquaintances. The tour had been most agreeable. A welcome change of scene. And he had enjoyed some excellent fishing in the Namzike. Lady Mountclair had asked for me, he said, and we walked together to the door of the first floor drawing-room, where we parted. I hesitated a moment; then knocked and went in.

Rose was reading on the sofa. Two or three airmail editions of *The Times* were scattered untidily about. The thin paper rustled as she moved.

'You wanted to see me?'

'Why, of course, Sebastian. You weren't slipping away, were you? Isn't this goodbye?'

'I suppose it is. I'd not thought of it, like that.'

'I've heard the news and I'm deeply glad for my husband's sake. Don't you think he's looking well?'

I sat down in the chair opposite and picked up from the floor and began to piece together one of the papers. I had to do something with my hands.

'I shall fly back to England. Probably leave tomorrow,' I said, in answer to her question. 'Lucas will take a statement from me, he's made that clear. There was some talk of my staying on as witness. That's no longer necessary. But I shall go back through Smithville.'

Her interest quickened. I noticed the lift in her voice.

'Will you, Sebastian? Through Smithville. Why? To see Miss Jensen?'

'What would be the point? No, I've a friend who needs

192

assistance. A friend I want to help, if I can. One must do something.'

'Who is this friend of yours?' she said.

'A farmer. We were boys at school together. He's up against it, in concrete fact. I'm only working things out inside myself—but it's enough. It's a bond. I can't leave things as they are.' (Unconsciously, as I thought afterwards, I echoed Jacob Mankele's parting phrase.) 'Let me put it this way. Africa was once an outline in an atlas. Now I'm a part of it. One with the problems, the people, the intolerance. I can't just tear myself free by taking the next 'plane to Europe.'

'You can't tear yourself free. . . . How difficult,' she said. 'I think I can understand, up to a point. But you realize, don't you, that you're a misfit. You must admit that. You don't belong out here and you never will. If you'd like me to, I'll tell you why. I know you well enough by now.'

I looked across at her. One of her arms lay along the back of the sofa. Her big body was relaxed among the cushions. She was smiling.

'You're sensitive without being strong. You've a developed sense of responsibility without being responsible. It's altogether absurd for you to try to shoulder the shortcomings of a continent.'

'Absurd, I agree. But I'm entangled. Rose, how I envy the practical men. The men who tackle their problems one by one—and solve them. The men who lay one brick on top of the other. Who build—and satisfy themselves.'

We sat for a time in silence. I did not want to leave but had nothing more to say. At last she said, 'Sebastian, we've talked music often enough, but you know you've never yet tried my piano. This may be your last opportunity. Why not play for me?'

She prised off her shoes and put her feet up on the sofa. I rubbed my fingers on my handkerchief, sat at the piano and began to build, brick by brick, to my personal satisfaction, my own tower. From the stool I could see her framed in the angle of polished wood, beneath the slope of the raised top. She was lying back with her eyes closed. There, too, lay her shoes untidily upon the carpet. Rose was at ease; very much at home.

I built my tower and let my hands slip from the keys. The steady whisper of the fan took over. She stirred and opened her eyes.

There was only one more thing to be said; that I could say, now, before I left. (I could have spoken before, standing in the sun between the trees and the black water.) But who was I, to tell her that I loved her? That was my affair—not hers.

IX

I HAD wired Sneezer my intention. I had not expected him to meet the aircraft. But he was there. Soberly dressed in a town suit, possibly a little thinner than when I had last seen him, he dominated the group beyond the gate of the Customs enclosure. As I came out he walked across and worked my arm like a pump-handle, trying to speak, blinking, his round face flushed.

'Good of you,' he said. 'Good of you, Frump. Glad to see you. Let's have your bags.'

We drove the eight miles to Smithville smoothly in the coach along the wide, newly-surfaced, tarmac road. Far ahead, brilliant in the clear light, the buildings at the city centre glistened like cubes of sugar. The huts and shacks housing the overspill of the urban population—black— littered the plateau untidily on either side.

Sneezer did not say very much at first and when he began to talk, it was not about himself. He was concerned for his friend George Peck. George, he told me, was in trouble. I said, yes, I knew that his cattle were dying. I had met him in Banda. Sneezer grunted non-committally; gave me to understand that George had sunk a good deal more capital into his farm than he possessed and that his backer, a flash type, one of the get-rich-quick boys from Smithville, was stepping up his visits, ostensibly to keep an eye on his interests but in fact (so Sneezer asserted) seeing more than was good for either of them of Mrs. Peck.

'I'm sorry,' I said.

'So am I,' said Sneezer. 'George is a first-rate chap. He

was building up a nice place there. Had no labour problems. Was beginning to pull away when this hit him. Damned unfair.'

We drove into the city. The streets were crowded; traffic moved steadily between lines of parked cars that winked and glittered under the high sun. The tall buildings blocked away the breeze.

Sneezer had already fixed me a room at the Berkeley. We went straight to the hotel, walked through to the bar and drank beer. As midday approached, the press of people grew heavier, the noise of voices louder. We discussed nothing whatever of importance. I could not always hear what he was saying. We lunched in the dining room and when Sneezer talked, it was to grouse (unjustifiably) about the mediocre cooking. We drank our coffee, smoked a cigarette in the lounge, in silence. The lunch-time press had subsided; the room was quiet; only an African page boy passed from table to table, emptying the ash trays.

The big man filled to capacity the chair beside mine. The arms constricted his body, the mound of his paunch rose and fell, his head lolled unsupported, his legs sprawled across the floor, a menace to waiters and passers-by. He was drowsy. I looked at him and began to wonder what had made me come.

He roused himself, but it was to ask about my work, my future plans. I did not say much. I was not anxious to discuss my own affairs.

In the end, without preamble, I said, 'Sneezer, I gather things aren't going too well with you. Now listen, I'm serious. This is what I came for. Chuck it all in and fly back to England with me. I'll see you through.'

The chair creaked as he wrestled his great body round. A hand squeezed my arm. Cheeks suffused, mouth working, touched almost to tears, he appeared unable to find the necessary words.

196

'You're a good chap, Frump. You're a friend. Believe me, I'm grateful. Deeply grateful . . .'

I felt flattened by the sheer emotional weight of the man. Bottled-up with sentiment, he was overwhelmingly demonstrative. I tried to shake myself clear and approach the question along rational lines, but it was impossible to pin him down. He was vague to the point of irritation.

'Sneezer,' I said, 'if you can't lay your hands on the cash, for goodness sake say so and I'll buy you your ticket. You can pay me back when it's convenient.'

My arm was gripped again; the vast face approached; the emotional floodgates were opened. He'd come if he could, by God he'd come! He'd accept my assistance in the spirit with which it was offered. For the first time in years, yes, in years, a friendly hand had reached out to help him. But I must understand he was in a curious position. An embarrassing position. Not that he wished, in any circumstances, to trouble me with the details. He refused to discuss them. Sordid. Beneath contempt. A mess of a life. A wrecked career. He slid into a morass of self-pity out of which I had to haul him, huge, flabby and inert.

I levered the truth from him at last. I had arrived too late. Some days before, he had been summoned by the newly-appointed Court of Enquiry to stand before their Tribunal and answer charges relating to his way of life. This summons he had ignored. He had simply failed to appear.

'If they want me, they can bloody well fetch me,' he said with a sudden flash of spirit (the chair creaking again). 'But how can I leave the country, old fellow? I'm marking time, that's all I'm doing. Marking time till my arrest.'

We thrashed the matter out, there in the lounge of the Berkeley. And with no result. George Peck was quite correct in his assertion. Sneezer had it coming to him and there was absolutely nothing I could do to help.

The afternoon passed. Soon after five, we went along the

street for a sundowner at a bar Sneezer favoured, and from there we drifted into the Ritz. Seven o'clock saw us further along the same street at Hugo's. By eight we had reached the Rialto Club. Propelled forward on this interminable routine peregrination, we kept to ourselves and spoke to no one. As the hours went by, we grew gradually confidential. We sat over our glasses, our heads close together, and little by little eased ourselves of our burdens. We trod more lightly, laughed more easily at nine o'clock that evening than we had done at six. At ten o'clock the world had become manageable. At eleven, Sneezer suggested we might visit the *Eyrie* for a change of scene. We made our way to the building and ascended to the night club (too rapidly for comfort) in an automatic lift.

We found that we had arrived, awkwardly, during the floor show. The place was warm and smoky, crowded and very dark. The band was muttering to itself in a corner; a single spotlight moved with the dancer across the vacant floor. The girl out in the disc of light wore a narrow girdle and her nipples were spangled. The white, elastic globes of her breasts bounced as she danced. She took a few steps, then posturized, throwing back her hair, parting her lips sensually, staring at the audience with sleepily-lidded eyes. Sneezer was transfixed. I could not get him along at all.

We succeeded in reaching an empty table at the back. He collapsed with a sigh of pure satisfaction. 'Haven't had an evening like this since I was a kid in Paris!' The association of ideas was inevitable. The waiter came up and before I could stop him, the big fool had ordered champagne.

There was a good deal of noise. The band had ceased to play. The dancer had perched herself upon the lap of one of the guests seated next to the floor; was running her fingers through his hair. Sneezer's arm was around my shoulders; he was shaking with immense laughter. 'By God, Sebastian, I'll remember this!'

198

The dance continued. The champagne arrived. The cork popped, the wine frothed into the glasses. A man squeezed through the tables, came out on to the floor and advanced towards the girl, holding out his hand. The beam of the spotlight widened to include them both. Screwing up his eyes against the glare, pulling nervously at his tie, he handed her—an apple. Noise again, and Sneezer thumping the table. 'D'you see, Sebastian? That's rich. Oh, very rich! Aphro—Aphrodite. Why the devil didn't I think of that myself?'

The performance came to an end and the dancer turned her back upon us and walked between the red curtains at the side of the band. Art bowed to nature. Her exit, I felt, might have been better contrived.

'Good looking wench,' said Sneezer wistfully. 'Fine physique.' He insisted on clashing glasses for the third time. 'Makes one think, you know. Trouble is, never been much of a hand with women. Frankly, old fellow, white girls terrify me. Always have.'

The band crooned rhythmically, the floor was bathed in a crimson glow, couples began to leave their tables to join the shuffling, swaying circle, Sneezer spoke heavily, monotonously into my ear.

'Little girl in Paris. Met her in a dance hall. She brought me along to her place, afterwards. Nothing arranged, mind you. Nothing definite. Was opening the door when I panicked. Pressed some money into her hand and said goodnight and walked away. She called after me. I started to run. Heard her laugh. Heard her all the way down the street. Laughing.'

'Sneezer,' I said. 'Don't go on and on. You remind me what it's like to be young.'

'Never found it easy. Was never easy with a white woman. Nothing to say to them. Could have done with a wife, kept me out of this jam. . . . But I don't know. On the farms, it's difficult. They get disillusioned, bitter, and then they can be devils with the natives. By and large, you know, Sebastian, I'd say they were far worse than the men. Look at the Pecks. George never has any trouble with his boys. Mind you, they'll take the odd beating—and deserve it. Drunk out of turn, stealing, lazy, inefficient; God, they can drive you crazy! George is rough but he's fair, and at heart he likes 'em and shows it. Go into his house—that's another matter.

'I saw how it was when I first came out. Things are worse today. The truth is, they hate the blacks. Pathological. Mixed up with sex. The white women in this country are obsessed with sex. Marry a white girl and she'll poison your mind, slowly, over the years. She'll plant in you the seeds of her own hatred. I'm not exaggerating. I've seen it happen, and there's not a man who can stand up to it. It's the women, working below the surface, who are destroying any chance we have of happiness. I used to watch them twisting the screw on their servants, spreading mistrust, whipping up fears and prejudices. To hell with their bloody little narrow minds, I said. I'll have none of them! I was a rebel in those days, old fellow. So I took a native girl—and that was the start of it all.'

The drone of the big man's voice ended. The band shook gravel in hollow gourds. The couples jigged accompaniment; colours blinked as dresses shook and tossed. The crimson glow paled to amber, yellow; then progressed to green. The dancers writhed, gestured, span (an arabesque of entwined arms) gyrating in the gloom of an aquarium. The rhythm changed, green shifted to purple, and the dancers eased forward, rocking into the fluid pause and pace of a tango.

A fair head rested upon a broad shoulder. One couple in perhaps twenty, idly to follow round the crowded floor. One thread of the score weaving the pattern. And then I saw that the girl was Pat. . . .

I was suddenly angry—and lost all sense of discretion.

200

I should have left well alone. Instead, a thought came back and back to nag me. Watching Patricia, I thought it monstrous that she could act as she did and escape the consequences. True, she had been after a shaming, an exposure—not a killing. But unless Terence had written, she would know nothing, nothing of what had happened. And hers was the responsibility. Hers the weight to bear.

The dancing came to an end; the tight knot loosened; the couples began to drift from the floor. I touched Sneezer's arm and told him I'd be back. 'Just seen someone I know,' I said.

I twisted quickly through the tables. 'Pat!' I called. 'Pat!' She turned and saw me and I thought she would have fallen. I made a grab as she shrank back, face white, palms out to ward me off. All control left me. Too much to drink, perhaps. . . . But I think it was more the way she looked; the way she recoiled. I wanted to catch hold of her then and hurt her, hear her cry out. Make her see what she'd done. Force her to understand.

'Listen, Pat,' I said. 'You listen to me!' Her partner pushed between us, sent me staggering back a pace. I thrust him to one side, closed up to her, heard myself saying, 'You killed Martha. You and Lobole between you. Does that mean anything to you?' The man in the dark blue suit swore and swung his arm. As he turned, I looked straight into his face. Now I cannot be certain of this because the light was bad. Things were happening very quickly and I was breathless and confused. But in that moment I recognized —or thought I recognized—the policeman, the young lout who had assaulted Mr. Mero in the Mariatown Location. '*You!*' I said. He shoved me back a second time and I forgot about Pat and sprang at him. My anger focussed. I must have left myself wide open. His fist crashed into my cheek and I went down, bringing a table, bottles, glasses down with me.

The room was loud with voices. Women screamed. Above the tumult, Sneezer bellowed like a bull. 'With you, Frump! I'm with you!' Broken glass crunched; the sleeve of my coat was wet with wine. I picked myself up shakily and saw him coming, the man-mountain toppling, Sneezer berserk, his mouth open, foghorning through to the dance floor, a chair flailing the air above his head.

They threw us out—and I don't blame them. I'd taken my hiding, was prepared to go quietly, but Sneezer was violent to the last. Three men could not hold him. Hadn't they knocked me down? His friend! Dared touch his friend! Proprietor, bandsmen, waiters, guests, they ran us out of the club. It was pandemonium, with Sneezer struggling and roaring; an unwieldy, unmanageable, protesting, noisy mass of a man.

Beaten, dishevelled, we missed the entrance to the lifts and found ourselves on the stairs. Unsteadily, we began the long descent. Somewhere around the tenth or ninth floor, I vomited. Sneezer patted me consolingly on the back. 'We all get a little tight, now and again,' he said. 'Your turn tonight.' It was obvious that he considered himself stone cold sober. A few storeys lower, one of the light bulbs had failed and, as my knees were not too steady, I sat on the stairs in the centre of this patch of gloom, sweating and trembling. Sneezer sat beside me and dug out his cigarettes. After a while, in a matter-of-fact voice, his indignation cooled, he asked what had happened up at the *Eyrie*.

'Saw the girl I was going around with in Bandaland.' (I had already told him about Patricia.) 'Fellow she was with hit me.'

Sneezer grunted mournfully. 'Women. Always women. What did I say? Root of all our troubles.'

The side of my face throbbed. I leant back against the cool, smooth wall and in the darkness my heart ached for

Rose. I had achieved nothing. I was lonely and miserable. I needed her. It was as simple as that.

I have no idea how long we battled with that staircase. At one point I doubted if we would ever reach street level —and gave up caring whether we did or not. In the end, we did. There are bars in Smithville open for twenty-four hours out of the twenty-four. Sneezer knew one. We found it. 'Hair of the dog,' he said. 'A drop of whisky won't hurt you.'

The hours telescoped. The night came to an unexpected end. We had had a drink or two, it seemed, and there was the clear sky colourless overhead (black men in rubber boots rinsing the empty streets) and we were trying to find our way to the Berkeley in the half-light. As we came in through the lobby of the hotel, the night porter stepped quickly ahead of us and shook the small man curled up asleep in one of the row of cane chairs, opposite the reception desk.

'He's back,' we heard him say. 'Wake up! Your man's come back.'

The Agent had a thin, pinched, misanthropic face. He woke instantly, effortlessly; jumped to his feet, drew a sheet of paper from his pocket and glanced over the two of us with shrewd, unloving eyes.

'James Hardcastle?'

Sneezer's hand went dubiously to his chin. 'Time for a shave?'

'I should say not.' The little man smouldered malevolently. 'Hanging about for you all night. Want to see the warrant? You realize you're under detention? Failed to appear before the Tribunal.'

'My kit?' said Sneezer. He looked round, recognized the bag on the floor by the chair, pointed. 'That's mine.'

'All packed up. Clerk's waiting for you to settle the bill.' And the Agent yawned and turned away to collect his hat.

'This is it, Frump,' said Sneezer. I saw that, in spite of his efforts to appear calm, the big man was shaking. 'This is goodbye. Well, we've made a night of it. One hell of a night! They can't take that away.'

'Sneezer.' I said, 'You must write when you're through. You know my address. Care of the Halliday Trust, London —that'll do. I shall expect a letter.'

We shook hands on the pavement. He was reluctant to release his grip.

'You're all I've got to hold on to, now,' he said, while the Agent sucked his teeth and tapped with his toe, impatient to be gone.

I stood outside the Berkeley and watched them walk up the street together; the big man and the small. Their departure was farcical. Sneezer's steps were straying and the Agent zig-zagged with him erratically over the deserted pavement. The small man was leaning inwards at an angle, pushing, straining, physically unable to keep the large man on an even course.

At this moment of all cruel moments I had to struggle with laughter. Sneezer was no tragedian. Poor old fellow, I thought, he had always been one of the world's buffoons. . . .

I went to bed. I was not feeling too good. My head was muzzy and I wanted to sleep it out. I dozed for a time and then the noise of traffic in the street woke me. As soon as I was properly awake I remembered the scene in the night club. I turned over and pressed my forehead into the pillow and tried to escape. I did my best to escape, but my thoughts followed me and I lived it all again, detail by detail, and as I lived it I writhed and sweated with disgust.

After a while I gave up trying to sleep. I went over to the washbasin and rinsed out my mouth, put on my dressing-gown, 'phoned the dining-room and asked them to send up coffee. Nothing to eat. Just coffee.

The coffee came on a tray. Tucked under the pot was a

copy of the morning's *Echo*. The principal headline was staccato. The black letters leapt from the page.

RIOTS IN BANDA

I shouted aloud and pitched the paper into the furthest corner of the room.

Later that morning my telephone rang. I sat and listened and did nothing about it. On the table by my side, the coffee was cold in my cup. I felt I never wanted to move again. After a while the telephone left off ringing and the noise from the street took over.

Now that I was listening, I knew that the noise had taken on a shape, a pattern, that was curiously familiar. The confused murmur of traffic was stilled and at intervals a punctual, high-pitched whirr and rattle sounded along the road beneath. The mechanical clatter of tracked vehicles.

I sat in my chair and counted up to seventeen. After the tracks, the tyres. The hum of engines; the shrill whine of outsize tyres on tarmac. The pain across my head jabbed as I stood up and went to the window. I opened the bottom sash and leant out and looked down six floors on to the khaki canvas hoods of troop carriers. People were gathering on the pavements. Out to the right, the square at the end of the street had filled with a green-brown tide of military vehicles. I stayed where I was, at the window, and watched the army pass.

Despatch riders and a signals car brought up the rear of the procession. Then the clear blue sky began to vibrate with the hum of piston-engined aircraft. The 'planes swept low over the city and circled; the noise was deafening. In the lull between two waves, I realized that my telephone was ringing again.

The sky emptied; the throbbing grew distant as the 'planes dwindled. The 'phone shrilled. I pushed myself back from the window, went across to the bed, sat on the bed and lifted the receiver. Reception calling. Was that Mr. Pole? A Mr. Jensen was waiting at the desk and wished to speak to me. Olaf Jensen. Hold on please and they would put him through.

Olaf came to the 'phone and introduced himself. He spoke rapidly, now and again tripping up and sprawling over his words. Though he sounded nervous, I recognized that he was obstinate and determined. If I could not come to him, he would come to me. His sister, he said, had sent him. I tried to protest but he insisted. He must speak to me for her sake.

In the end I told him he had better come to my room. I did not want to see him. I did not want to discuss Patricia. But what else could I do?

There was a knock on the door. I had expected a fair-haired Scandinavian with a handsome, spiritual face. A short, dark, ugly man in a dusty suit and a dog collar walked into the bedroom. I could not believe that this was Patricia's brother.

'Jensen?' I said uncertainly.

'You must forgive me butting in like this,' he said. 'I believe you were once coming to the Mission.' His teeth were uneven, his smile pleasant. 'I'm sorry you never managed to arrive. Better luck next time. Meanwhile, whether you like it or not, you've become a myth in the location. Mr. Mero is a great talker.'

He sat down, refused a cigarette, asked how I was feeling.

'You don't look so good, if I may say so. That's a nasty bruise. Unwise of you to pick a fight with Colin Stein.'

'The policeman?'

'No. Colin's a lawyer. But he boxed for the University. Considered good in his class, I believe.'

'The man with Pat last night—was he never in the Police Force?'

Olaf smiled and shook his head.

'Now you mustn't think I'm eager to pry into your affairs,' he said. 'Pat's looked after herself for a good many years now. She's no longer a child. And we've never meant a great deal to each other, which was perhaps why I was surprised when she came in, this morning. But she's moved quickly, these last few days, has Patricia, and without consulting mother or myself. Flies back from Banda, throws up her job with the *Echo*, gets herself engaged to Colin Stein. Colin's an old friend, of course. Nothing so very startling about *that*. Two years ago, when she was working in Smithville, I seem to remember that she thought differently about him, but there you are, it's the prerogative of young ladies to change their minds.

'Now what is this story about an African girl? I had a most confused account from Patricia. I gather you said something at the club last night, which has upset her. She's determined to know the truth. She made me promise to come and see you. Apparently it's not possible for her to make the approach herself.'

'Look,' I said. 'I was drunk last night. How am I to know what I was doing, what I was saying? Tell Pat to forget it. Tell her not to give the matter a thought.'

Olaf stared at me, puzzled. 'Do you mean that?'

'Of course I do. I was crazy at the time.'

'I doubt if she'll be satisfied.'

'It was a mistake, a misunderstanding. What's the use of raking it all over? I spoke out of turn and I'm sorry I opened my mouth. She'll forget. I'm glad she's going to be married. That's good news.'

'You're not going to say anything more?'

'I'd much rather not.'

He shrugged his shoulders, looked disappointed. 'Well, I can't force you.'

He got up from his chair and crossed to the window.

Hands in his pockets, frowning, he stood and stared down into the street.

'What's happening out there?' I asked. 'A parade of some sort?'

Had I seen the day's papers? he said.

'Yes, I saw the *Echo*. Threw it somewhere, the headlines were enough for me. Riots, riots.'

'That's just it. Trouble across the border always excites our military men.'

'Are things as bad as that?'

'I hardly expect so. The Bandala do this sort of thing fairly regularly, don't they? But it's an excuse to put on a show.'

I joined him at the window. Vehicles were pouring out of the square. Light tanks, carriers, armoured cars. . . .

'How were things in the Protectorate when you left?'

'On the surface, fairly quiet,' I said. 'But the news this morning hardly came as a surprise.'

'Our turn next. I give Equatoria ten more years.'

'I can understand that. Seems logical. The issue over here is cut and dried. But I fail to understand why there should be these continual troubles in Bandaland.'

'Simple enough, really. Like changing gear in a truck. A question of matching tempos. If the people are trying to move faster than the administration—or vice versa—there's bound to be some grating of cogs.'

'That's the type of airy generalization,' I said, 'that I hardly expected from you. I've seen enough of Africa in these few weeks to realize just what it means in terms of human unhappiness and suffering, every time—as you say—the cogs grate.'

'You're right,' he said at once. He turned and looked at me. I realized, then, that he had the same pale blue eyes as Patricia. They lit his swarthy face. 'Forgive me. I've not yet come to grips with you. I do my best to handle our

208

overseas visitors tactfully—but you're in a different category, I think. You appear to have been exposed to the facts.'

I said nothing. He looked out of the window and then lifted his shoulders and laughed. 'I had a lady from England visit me a couple of weeks ago. Wanted to see the slums. I took her out to Five Springs, the latest of our shanty towns. I showed her men and women who are very slowly dying of starvation. I showed her children covered in sores, with warped and twisted bodies.' His shoulders shook again. 'All she said was, "Look at the poor donkeys!"'

'The cogs have always grated in Equatoria. Fifty years ago, when it was first a question of digging out the gold, the native had to be winkled from the reserves, forced to leave his lands and come to the town and work. He was happy where he was. The grass was tall, his children had milk, the corn could hide a man. But we needed his labour. Today, laws have had to be passed to prevent him flocking into Smithville, to earn the money to live.'

'What's the future of it all,' I said. 'Are you ever going to bring black and white together?'

'Not necessarily in our lifetime. But a lot can happen in a century. Take the attitude to the working class in your own country.'

'Can you compare class with race?'

'You can try. The parallels are very close. When Victoria came to the throne the illiterate labourer was only one degree removed from the animals he tended.'

'But he could be washed.'

'And reveal himself as soon as he opened his mouth?'

'He bred true,' I said. 'His future was in his children.'

'Black and white boys and girls will play together normally. Racial prejudice is inculcated.'

'But the children grow up. And then it's a matter of biology.'

'It is possible, I agree, that we're flying in the face of

nature. After all, there's no precedent. Our geographical situation is unique.'

'Dangerous talk,' I said.

He smiled and glanced at his wrist-watch and told me he must be going.

'Don't go yet.' (I needed to keep talking. I did not want to be alone again.) 'Olaf, tell me—is Pat going to be happy with this man?'

'With Colin? Why not?'

'Is she . . . would you say she was in love with him?'

'No. But then Patricia has never yet fallen honestly in love. I doubt if she ever will. Her nature is possessive rather than passionate.' He held up his hand; I was trying to speak. 'Yes, you want to tell me that she's in love with *you*. That you've broken her heart. Believe me, I know my sister. I was twelve years old when she was born and I have had ample opportunity to watch her development. She is her father's child. Father, as I remember him, was handsome, selfish, entirely inconsiderate, cruel. Cruel—not sadistic—only because he was unimaginative; incapable of appreciating any point of view but his own.'

'That's just it! What's the point of telling Pat the truth, when truth *as* truth is useless to her?'

Olaf looked at me steadily and said nothing.

'The girl died, but no one is fairly and squarely to blame for what happened. I'm to blame, in the first place, because I went around with Patricia—and then dropped her. Pat's to blame for jumping to conclusions and acting on them. The newspaper editor she informed—he's since been murdered—played his part and so did the gang of young roughs he brought in to investigate. The man the girl was engaged to—and had gone to bed with in the meantime—must take *his* share of the blame. So must the girl's brother, one of the leaders of opinion who are forging these young fanatics. On matters of tribal custom, the nationalist group over there are rabid. They circumcised the girl and she died, afterwards, in hospital. That's the story in a nutshell.'

Olaf still had nothing to say.

'On one side of the border, the black girl pays the penalty for suspected intercourse with a white man. On the other, the white man is sent to gaol for living with a native. This corner of the world is breeding intolerance. Miscegenation apart, I've seen enough to make me thankful I'm escaping. To wish I'd never come. . . .'

His silence began to annoy me. I wanted to taunt him; force him to answer.

'What does the Church do? Fight? Or sit back and watch? Take sides in the struggle—or try to perch on the fence? Is it possible to speak your mind as a Christian in this country and stay out of prison?'

Olaf began to pace up and down the room. When he spoke, his words were measured; his voice grave.

'A few of us fight,' he said. 'Certainly, we are becoming more vocal. But to aggravate the situation, to exploit grievances, to rock the boat in a precarious sea—that is not our mission. Unfortunately, the influence of the Church is waning. One cannot wonder at this. Sometimes, I agree, it is hard to accept the passive role. There are moments when I am tempted to use my small authority to encourage my people to resist. When I am tempted to rouse, to inflame.

'It is not easy to preach the virtues of tolerance and humility while many of those in authority set an example of brutishness and pride. Not easy to stand, helpless, in the face of laws, measures, regulations that make nonsense of our professed Christianity. My very position is anomalous. I move among my flock as the servant of a Church whose leaders in this country condone segregation and whose white congregations enforce the colour bar under God's roof.'

'Then you admit defeat? You have no answer, you're helpless? How can you go on?'

'God, in His wisdom, has chosen to place me here in Smithville. I do not, for one moment, question that He is right. I have my work. My people need me. I patch up their bodies. Mend their problems. Try to heal their lives. It is my duty to face today's storms. If I should fail to ride them, if I should fall, another will continue in my place. I am relatively unimportant. It is the challenge that counts. The challenge this continent offers to mankind.'

He was still pacing nervously up and down, up and down.

'Africa offers the supreme challenge of the century. The technological revolution is over. Man has emerged master of the machine. He has yet to master himself. But the brotherhood of man is on the way, the signs are everywhere about us. I don't doubt that, eventually, we shall resolve our feuds, master the art of human relationships. Nor do I doubt that this continent is to be the forcing house of the endeavour. The process will take time. These first years will be rough and painful. That is only to be expected. The first years of a revolution are necessarily painful. I pray God to give me the strength to continue.'

He stopped beside me, gripped the ledge, stared out of the window. His jaw had tightened. Suddenly, he swung round, his eyes on my face.

'I have my own personal fear,' he said. 'An unfortunate fear that makes nonsense of my faith. A fear that is always with me, that I am unable to escape. Sooner or later, my people will be driven desperate. They will rise and turn against the European and when that moment comes race alone will count, all else will be forgotten. They will forget the years I have lived among them. They will forget that they have learnt to love and trust me. They will see only that I am white and they will find me defenceless and they will kill me.'

He paused; then said in a quieter voice. 'I regret to say I am a physical coward.' He ran a finger round his neck, inside his collar. 'At night, in the location, I know what it is to be afraid.'

He went. After a while I roused myself, shaved, dressed, took the lift to the ground floor. The wireless was on in the lounge and people had gathered there and were listening to a communiqué from Banda. (The capital was still disturbed. Rioting had now spread to provincial centres. A District Commissioner had been murdered at Rua Rua.) There were troubled faces in the lounge and the talk was ugly.

I walked the short way up the street to the travel agents who were handling my flight back. I learnt that there had been a sudden rush of bookings. The 'planes were full for a week ahead.

'Always the same, as soon as trouble starts,' said the man at the airways counter. 'I'll try the other lines by all means, but you'll find they'll have nothing to offer. Mind you, if things should ease up over the border, I can promise you a cancellation on the dot.'

I left him my 'phone number and returned to the hotel. I had no plans. I did not feel able to cope with the emergency. Matters would have to take their course.

I sat in the lounge and thought of the men I knew in Bandaland. Gardener, Bulmers, Cameron, McDermott, Terence Hatch. Thought of the Governor. Began to worry about Rose.

Conversations went on round me. The uniformity of opinion was remarkable. If the British could not keep order in their own house, then the Republic had every right to step in and do the job for them. The talk of manœuvres was a bluff. The army meant business. The security of the Republic demanded prompt action. The natives over there were too damned uppish. Must be taught a lesson. Brought to heel.

213

I was surprised to find that it was already late afternoon. The day seemed to have got mislaid somewhere. I endured another communiqué, waiting always for the familiar name. Casualties were mounting. Three Europeans had been killed and twenty-eight injured in the day's riots. Tear gas had been used on two occasions. ('What the b——s want,' said my neighbour, 'is a dose of the old mustard.') I went out again and found the bar in which Sneezer and I had kicked off, the evening before. The barman remembered me. I had one small whisky and drank it slowly, making it last. The sun must have set. When I came out the twilight was thickening. Neon signs vibrated over doorways and across shop windows. I walked until it was dark and until I was tired out. I suddenly felt hungry; realized I had had nothing to eat all day.

I made my way back to the hotel. After a meal, to escape the loudspeaker and the people, the drinking and the talk, I went upstairs to my room. I sat and looked at my half-packed suitcases. Over the bend of the world, London seemed infinitely desirable, infinitely far away.

I sat and looked at my luggage and wondered if Olaf was right; wondered whether there was, after all, a future for the African continent. Any hope ahead for the divided land. And I looked for comfort, not to sweeping, far-reaching schemes and projects, but to small acts of kindness and generosity I had experienced—and already begun to forget. And as is inevitable, I thought my way back to where I had been happiest—in the lakeside bungalow below Hoyu. In the Garden before the Fall. . . .

I remembered the crowd outside Alastair's office; the crowd that gathered each day, squatting patiently on the verandah, overflowing on to the mown grass circle by the white flagpole; Africans in robes and in rags, old and young, men from cattle villages in the hills, from fishing villages on the shore of the lake, traders from Hoyu township; men who had come from near and from far to seek his help, to ask his advice, confident in the man they trusted, the representative of the Queen beyond the waters. And I remembered the mixed queue, men, women, children, waiting outside the door of Mary McDermott's small dispensary; Mary herself, brusque, bustling, the trained nurse in her element, bathing eyes, changing dressings, lancing boils. Sneezer, I thought, should have met Mary.

The telephone rang. A voice at the other end of the line said, 'That you, Pole? Got you at last! Cameron here. So you're at the Berkeley, are you? I'm coming right over.' He spoke with the breathless lift, the noisy emphasis, of a man who has been working fast—and enjoying it.

He would not say what he wanted. His voice hinted mystery. 'Just flown in, old boy. God, what a shambles! But the worst's over, I'm glad to report. Bit tricky while it lasted and we've said goodbye to some good chaps. But more when I'm off this damned buzzer. No business to spread alarm and confusion. Be seeing you.'

He did not keep me waiting long. He came into the bedroom dramatically. His gestures were over-life-sized. He shut the door; the door slammed. He took three quick steps across the carpet and the window rattled. He was keyed to an extraordinary pitch of excitement. I was astonished at the change in his face. His skin was grey, his cheeks sunken, his eyes brilliant. He did not look as if he had slept or fed for days.

'Well, Pole, he's gone. We're keeping it dark for as long as we can, but he's gone. Bit of a hero, the old man. The real stuff. Torn to pieces on his own doorstep. I've got Rose out, she's taken a packet one way and another. Saw it all happen.' He stood in front of me and deliberately, as if he were on a stage, brought out his cigarette case and flicked it open. 'This is where I hand over. She's asked for you.'

I could not, at first, grasp what he was saying.

'Rose—in Smithville? You mean, Sir Christopher's . . .'

'Had it. Killed this afternoon.'

'*Killed!* In the riots?' (Cameron nodded, tapping a cigarette on the side of the case.) 'That's bad, isn't it? That's a tragedy from every point of view. And Rose? How's she taking it?'

'Not too well. She was surprisingly bound up with the old boy, you know.'

'Surprisingly?' I said. Even at this moment, I could not choke down my distaste for the man.

'Damn it all, Pole, why beat about the bush? Theirs was a marriage of convenience.'

'I'll have to take your word for it,' I said. 'You appear to know more about her than I do.'

Cameron swore quietly and flicked his match towards the fireplace. 'Have you got such a thing as a drink?'

I had a hip-flask of brandy in my luggage and he helped himself to a tot in my tooth mug. The neck of the bottle vibrated on the rim of the glass. The man's nerves were taut as fiddle strings.

'Staff at Government House were 90 per cent loyal. So, thank God, were the police—to a man, I'd say. I hand it to those boys! Watched them sweep the streets, walking in with only their truncheons and wicker shields. There was to be no shooting—Governor's orders. What could they do? They were a few hundreds against thousands. I tell you, driving to the airport wasn't so funny.

'The police held the field. We had a 'plane waiting—but we had to get there. No traffic. Not a vehicle moving in the city, you understand. Road barricades everywhere and bands of local hotheads looting, burning, drinking themselves silly. At the time our position seemed desperate. The Governor killed, Government House surrounded, casualties mounting.

'Rose must be flown out. The 'plane was available. It was a chance—and we took it. But when it came to the point, I had a terrible scene with her. She refused to leave. Hysterical. Nerve gone. Had to fight her, force her into the car.'

He swigged off his brandy, rinsed the glass under the tap and put it back on the shelf above the washbasin.

'Thanks,' he said. 'I needed that.'

'But you got to the airport all right?'

'We got there.' He was retrieving his cigarette from the ash tray. 'Went out by a back entrance. Had the gates opened at the last moment. Then we just stood on everything, following the askari squad in the jeep. Took the crowd by surprise. They realized we meant business and scattered. I saw the sticks and stones coming and held Rose down on the floor between the seats. Had to charge 'em, there was no other way. To go slow would have been fatal. But you know how it is. Bad enough to run over a rabbit, with a woman in the car.'

'What happened to Sir Christopher?' I said.

'I'll tell you the story as I heard it from Wakefield. The crowd had broken through the entrance gates. They'd massed along the drive and over the steps. They were worked up, shouting anti-British slogans. The Governor tried to speak to them from the balcony, but he couldn't make himself heard. So he came down and with only half-a-dozen unarmed police to hold back the people, went right out under the portico.

'Brave? It was lunacy! Or call it an act of faith. And he might have succeeded—did succeed at first, Wakefield made that clear. Talked to them and they listened. The native is susceptible to eloquence, you've probably found that out. Great talkers, all of them. The old man let 'em have it hot and strong, and in the end they took it like lambs. Wakefield described it as mass hypnotism. There's no doubt he had an extraordinary way with him, the Governor. Felt it myself. And there's no doubt, too, that he was one of the best friends the Africans ever had, and in their hearts they knew it. Makes it all the more damnable that they should have killed him.'

'Been done before,' I said. 'Man tends to repeat himself.' Cameron shot me a half-startled glance.

'Trouble began yesterday afternoon. One of their newspaper chaps—fellow called Lobole—had been murdered and they'd staged a memorial service in the cathedral. When I say "they," in fact I mean the nationalist party. The political extremists. This Lobole was evidently something of a hero. I know he was a thorn in the flesh of the administration. Before the service they'd applied to the Governor and he'd granted them a dispensation from the Emergency Gatherings Act of '41. That mean anything to you?' (I nodded.) 'Result: hundreds marched up the cathedral hill in various processions. A thousand or two gathered afterwards in the City Square. The nationalist leaders had had a hasty whip round and organized a full-blown demonstration, right under the noses of the police.

'To make a success of the party, they had to polish up a grievance—and they didn't have far to seek. Your Nwambe Project, Pole, had been announced as going through. The Project no one really understood and no one liked the smell of. An agitator fellow with a name I can't remember made a violent speech and incited them to rise. Lucas did his best, but his men hadn't a chance. A couple of hours later the city was paralysed and rioting went on all night. As I said, the Governor clamped down on shooting and put Lucas in a spot. The old man was even reluctant to use tear gas. And in spite of everything, Rose still feels he was right. She can't forgive Lucas for turning the guns on them. I tell her, the Commissioner's a national hero. He's saved the Protectorate from the Republican army! Better his machine guns than Brens from over the border, but she won't see it that way. He went against her husband's orders. I reckon Lucas did a smart job of work myself. With Sir Christopher written off, someone had to take charge, show some initiative. Mind you, this all happened after we'd flown out.

'The Governor? That was bad luck. Cruel luck. The mob were eating out of his hand. He'd calmed them down, he'd reassured them. They were going away like good children to co-operate with *their*—accent on their—police; clean up *their* capital. Single-handed, he'd worked the miracle. Must have been the greatest moment of the old boy's life! And then, because some young fool of a photographer from Smithville—prepared to risk his neck (and an international incident) for the sensation-picture of the year—blunders in at the crucial moment, the whole thing topples. The whole edifice he'd built up collapses. Faith, trust, loyalty—blown to shreds like smoke. A reasonable crowd transformed into a pack of howling, raging lunatics. Not pretty. While the bloody fool was bumbling over with his camera, altitude eighty feet or so, grazing the roof, they came up the steps like a wave.

'What don't you understand? That a single light 'plane nosing in should be enough to touch 'em off? But don't you see, there was the green and yellow flag smack on the fuselage, clear as daylight. The flag they hate. They weren't going to stop, then, and reason things out. Type of 'plane meant nothing—it came from the Republic. And its appearance in the sky over Banda could mean only one thing. Betrayal. The Governor had betrayed them. They knew, we all knew, that advance brigades of Equatoria's army were sitting along the frontier. We had heard wireless reports of the parade here, this morning. Sooner or later, I suppose, if things hadn't mended, they *would* have come in. That's why, when the mob saw the flag on the 'plane, they took it for granted that their country was occupied. That the Governor had sold out. And they went mad. Tore him and his police guard to pieces.'

There was a short silence. Cameron had gravitated towards the washbasin.

'Mind if I have another?'

'Help yourself,' I said.

'But the troubles are over?' I said, while he poured another tot.

'Banda's quiet. I've not heard the latest from the provinces. You know, Pole, Lucas is a shrewd bird. Orders or no orders, he'd sited his guns, picked his gunners. When the showdown came, I gather he had the situation in his pocket inside half-an-hour.'

'At what cost?'

'Not more than a few hundred casualties, say the reports. They can spare them. Should be a lesson the Bandala won't forget in a hurry.'

I was walking again with Rose in the Government House garden. We had left the shade of the jacaranda avenue; the hot sun burned on our backs. I heard her voice. *'The prisons will be full; the hospital wards overflowing; machine guns will be mounted in the squares. And the people will be cowed, resentful, bitter —and the work of fifty years will be undone.'*

'I hope he's right.'

'Right!' Cameron stared at me over the rim of the tooth mug, shook his head. 'You should have been there, old boy. Had a close-up of their ugly black faces through the windows of a car.'

'And what's going to happen now?'

'Happen? Nothing dramatic. The Omuvomo will lose one or two of his Ministers. A handful of incorrigibles will cool their heels in the D.F.D. Whitehall will appoint a new Governor, big business rebuild its houses, and on we'll go. Regulations'll be tightened up, of course. Stricter control, more discipline. Which, in my humble opinion, is what the country needs.'

'And the Nwambe Project?'

'Entirely up to the next Governor. But I think it's probable that the scheme will be shelved. Tucked away in a pigeon-hole to collect the dust. Inexpedient. Put yourself in the new man's place. Would *you* shoulder that load at the start of your career? And if he has second thoughts and picks it up again in a year or two, he'll have learnt enough to put it back in the file and let it lie.'

'The Project was years ahead of its time,' I said. 'I should have had the guts to say so, openly, in my report.'

'Don't fret yourself. If you'd tipped off the Trustees and they'd put their big feet down, we should have still had riots in Banda.'

'You think so?'

'I'm sure of it. One excuse is as good as another if the mood's there. The mood's the thing.'

'I wonder. You know, Cameron, it was never my business to take sides. . . .'

'But Rose got hold of you? The devil she did! And that reminds me, what was the trouble with Blondie? Wouldn't she play?' The tooth mug clinked on his teeth as he smiled.

To change the subject, I asked him what were his plans.

'Mine? I'm going back to Bandaland. I've work to do.'

'And Rose?'

'No place for her, there. She'll be returning to England.'

'Where is she?' I said. I found it an effort to speak steadily.

'She's at the White Lodge. Guest of the President. The First Secretary's been round. We're not advertising her arrival—the less noise the better.'

Absently he helped himself again from my flask. I watched him. The room was quiet.

'You may not appreciate my advice,' he said, dashing in

221

a little water from the cold tap. 'But here's a tip, for what it's worth. Don't think I'm not bloody sorry for Rose. She's taken a packet. But as man to man, I'd go easy. Write her a note, say all the right things, and get to hell out of here. Hop off on the next 'plane home.'

'Leave her? Leave her at *this* moment. . . .'

'Listen to me, Pole. I'm trying to help you. Do you want the woman for life?'

'What exactly do you mean?' I said slowly. My heart was thumping, stifling me. I could not easily breathe.

'Just that. You're risking a great deal. Ask yourself the question before you knock at her door. I know Rose. Should do, by this time. Fascinating person, in many ways. A lovely woman. But take her over? Not on your life, old boy. Not in a hundred years.'

'If she wants me,' I said. 'If she needs me. . . .'

'You can't let her down?' Cameron took a step forward and slapped me on the shoulder. 'I know how you feel. Went through it myself. You're not the first to fall flat on your back, and you won't be the last. But remember this. She's demanding, masterful, a difficult woman—in every way. Once let her get her teeth into you and she'll drain you, suck you dry. You can say goodbye to freedom.

'You can see how it is with her. She worshipped the old man. Venerated his ideals. He was a little tin god to her— not a husband in the sense of the word. Good enough as far as it went. Certainly, he satisfied her *mind*. . . .

'Now she's lost Sir Christopher. That won't make things easier—don't kid yourself. He'll always be her ideal. You may be a nice, cultivated, musical chap, Pole, but are you setting yourself up in competition with a saint and martyr? You'll be a fool if you try.

'Yes, I know she likes you. She's said as much. *And* she knows how you feel. Of course, she needs your support. Needs sympathy and encouragement and all the help you

222

can give her. All right, it's different with you. I knew you'd say that!'

He threw back his head and laughed. The glass in his hand tilted and a thin stream of brandy poured on to the carpet.

'Go ahead, then. Give it to her. Give in to her! You will.'